MECHANICS·
MERCANTILE
LIBRARY.

Arthur F Mathews '06

THE UNCERTAIN HOUR

THE
UNCERTAIN
HOUR

A NOVEL

JESSE BROWNER

BLOOMSBURY

Published by Bloomsbury USA, New York
Distributed to the trade by Holtzbrinck Publishers

All papers used by Bloomsbury USA are natural, recyclable products made
from wood grown in well-managed forests. The manufacturing processes
conform to the environmental regulations of the country of origin.

LIBRARY OF CONGRESS CATALOGING-IN-PUBLICATION DATA

Browner, Jesse.
    The uncertain hour : a novel / Jesse Browner—1st U.S. ed.
    p. cm.
    ISBN-13: 978-1-59691-339-4
    ISBN-10: 1-59691-339-8
    1. Petronius Arbiter—Fiction.   2. Rome—History—Nero,
54–68—Fiction.   3. Suicide—Fiction.   I. Title.

PS3552.R774U53 2007
813'.54—dc22   2006030269

First U.S. Edition 2007

1 3 5 7 9 10 8 6 4 2

Typeset by Westchester Book Group
Printed in the United States of America by Quebecor World Fairfield

For Judy

> *"Death is plucking at your ear: 'Get on and live,' he says.*
> *'I'm coming.'"*
>
> —COPA, APPENDIX VIRGILIANA

H AVING DISPATCHED THE messengers and given his orders for supper, Petronius decided to go for a walk.

A low door led directly from his study to the kitchen garden. A boy was there, stooped over in the thin sunlight, cutting rosemary. A tiny brown puppy, tethered to the boy's ankle by a string around its neck, sat quietly at his side, sniffing at a weed in the pathway. Petronius could not see the boy's face; his hair was sandy, breeze-swept, flashing white and yellow as it caught the light. Unseen by the boy, a goldfinch alit on the path of crushed shells by his feet. It hopped onto the rim of his basket, looked within, cocked its head, and flew off into the orchard. The boy took up the basket and headed for the kitchen, leaning to the side to swipe a spray of mint as he passed. It was an elegant gesture, Petronius thought, and a wave of sadness swept through him and was gone, like the goldfinch. He stood in the shadow of the door frame and waited until the boy had returned indoors. Then he stepped into the thin sunlight.

He took one step, two steps, and stopped, stunned by a sudden, acute hypersensitivity. An ebbing breath of wind through the naked branches of the fruit trees; the varied calls of busy birds; the crunch of shells beneath his sandals; the crackle of a bonfire beyond the garden wall; the distant rumble of the surf and the nearer hiss of waves rising through the shale; the clatter of crockery and low murmuring from the kitchen. Smells— burning fennel, putrescent seaweed, thyme, brine, wood smoke, box resin. A million bright diamonds on the sea, a web of dancing shadows beneath the trees, one purple shard of nacre on the white path, a solitary dove on the spine of an outhouse roof. Momentarily overwhelmed, Petronius sternly took himself in hand. This would not do at all. He did not like to be angry with himself today, but he was perhaps a little disappointed by the banality of his body. Would it cling to the world today of all days, the hypocrite? Too little, too late. Now, of all times, was not the moment to give in to sentiment and nostalgia. A second-rate rhetorician in the marketplace was more imaginative than that. He stepped over a low border of samphire that separated the kitchen garden from the orchard.

In the springtime, the orchard was sewn with wildflowers— rock-rose, periwinkle, hyacinth, gillyflower—to provide early work for the bees, before the apple and pear blossomed. In the summer, the buzzing was all but loud enough to drown out the crash of the surf. Now the bees were asleep in their hives of woven fennel, and it was bare sand and the sighing of the wind. Petronius strolled abstractedly through the trees and stopped at the foot of the opobalsam, imported at great expense from Syria. Here, by the side of an ornamental canal, lined with smooth stones from the bed of the Savo and shaded by a pergola draped in oleander and viburnum, stood a small statue of Priapus, guardian of the orchard, carved of Megarian marble. The god held a willow sickle in one hand and his huge, erect penis in the other. He faced the back end of the orchard, where the baby Dionysus and his three nurses cavorted in an artificial grotto, above a cornucopia feeding water into the canal. Poor Priapus—condemned forever to observe, never to participate! Petronius gave his shoulder a sympathetic pat, then crossed over a miniature arched bridge and turned left, toward the sea.

The border of the orchard was guarded by a line of bearded herms overlooking a jujube hedge. Petronius passed through a gate in the hedge and emerged into the walled enclosure of the perfume garden, its beds trimmed back to the soil. Here, in warmer weather, his gardeners grew iris, cassia, fenugreek, marjoram, narcissus, spikenard, and styrax. None of it a patch on the balm of Gilead, as far as Petronius was concerned, but the homemade perfumes, bottled in crystal, made coveted gifts for his guests. In the opposite wall was another iron gate leading to a roofed colonnade, beyond which the cliff tumbled down to the beach. Here, Petronius paused. To his left, the colonnade led back to the house, where he had much business to attend to before dinner; to the right, it gave on to a small suite of rooms and a terrace overlooking the water, a place of jealously guarded solitude and contemplation. Petronius closed his eyes, sickened by his own weariness. Former consul, provincial governor, legion commander, he could not decide which way to turn.

A gardener was sweeping the walkway. "You. Salvius, is it?" The gardener stood to attention. "Tell Demetrius to meet me on the terrace." The gardener bowed and hurried off to the house, and Petronius turned right. He felt better already.

He followed the colonnade to a half-moon terrace where the cliff top dwindled to a finger of rock pointing due west. There he waited, staring out to sea. To the north, the strand swept unbroken to Liternum; to the south, it curved outward to the promontory at Misenum, with the Bay of Naples beyond and Pithecusa perched on the horizon. The pleasure boats of Baiae seldom ventured along this unsheltered stretch of coast, and the sea was all but empty at this time of the afternoon, the Cumae fishing fleet already beached for the day. A lone trireme far out at sea, on exercises no doubt, was making for the Bay of Puteoli. At this distance, it seemed motionless. Petronius leaned against the balustrade. He thought of the men on board, the slaves, the rats, the fleas. Each fully expecting to go to sleep that night, to wake up tomorrow morning. Nothing strange in that at all. No one, not even a slave or a flea, could ever go to sleep without that credulous trust in the dawn. He cocked an eye to the sky. The few clouds hugging the coast—they, too, seemed motionless, undecided, at the outset of their journey across the wine-dark sea to Africa, as to whether it was a journey worth rousing themselves for. Down below, Petronius's yacht lay moored against the wooden pier, the hollow clap of waves against its hull the loudest disturbance of a late autumn's afternoon. His mind spontaneously gravitated to the full store of provisions and fresh water in its hold, and he shook his head to dispel the vision. Even had he been tempted to set sail, to flee and sacrifice his honor, he wouldn't get very far. He was almost certainly being observed at this very moment. He closed his eyes again, breathed deeply, once, twice.

Underfoot, he felt a small pebble that had embedded itself in the leather sole of his sandal. He lifted his left foot and found not a pebble, but a square tile of black glass, no bigger than the nail of his little finger. It had evidently come loose from the mosaic border of intertwined vine leaves that encircled the terrace's marble inlay. But where did it belong? Petronius felt himself, knew himself to be pathetic as he went down on one knee to search for the tiny gap in the border. At that instant, a thousand thoughts raced through his mind, as fleeting and as piercing as the reflections off the sea, contradictory thoughts, admonitory thoughts, he could feel them arise and dissipate like waves without once being able to grasp their substance. He found himself pondering the nature of these thoughts even as they pursued their course, and it occurred to him that they were perhaps the infinitesimal fabric of consciousness, just as the fabric of the physical universe is said to be made up of invisible atoms which, in a moment of distraction, suddenly seem to come into focus, dancing before one's eyes. He wondered whether, if time were to slow to a fraction of its usual pace, one might examine these thoughts and find that each was a fully developed philosophy, sophisticated and coherent, on which an entire life might be structured. And if that were so, in an entire lifetime of such endlessly cascading thoughts, then the very one that he needed at this moment had already come to him, and he had carelessly discarded it. And so he continued to search for the minuscule hole in the mosaic into which this one tile would fit, though he knew he would not find it, even as footsteps sounded across the terrace.

"You sent for me, sir?" Demetrius stood at a respectful distance, tablets and stylus in hand. Petronius considered him a moment, opened his mouth to speak, then restrained himself.

"I want you to take a letter," he said at last. Demetrius immediately opened his wooden writing frame and poised the stylus above the wax. "Why don't you sit? This may take some time." Petronius gestured to a nearby granite bench, but the secretary shook his head deferentially. Petronius cleared his throat.

"'Titus Petronius Niger to Nero Claudius Caesar Augustus Germanicus. Greetings.'" He paused. The trireme, while never visibly progressing, had rounded the cape and altered its course toward the port. The minutes seemed to be playing a trick on him, concealing themselves, then rushing forward to a new hiding place. Petronius felt the blood rush to his cheeks and turned away from Demetrius, dictating now to the waves.

" 'Sire, time is growing short and I have much to say, I who once called myself your friend . . .' No; strike that, Demetrius. Let's start over." Petronius chided himself for starting this, of all letters, with a lie. Should he stand on his dignity? Was that the proper tone? After all, a copy of the letter might very well survive.

" 'Sire, the Senate and people of Rome . . .' No, stop. That's not it either." He kicked the base of the balustrade in frustration. The problem was, he didn't know what he wanted to say. He had been counting on inspiration, but he ought to have started drafting this letter years ago, he realized now. A man with his experience in warfare and civil administration should have been better prepared. What did he want to say? What could one hope to say? Oh, how could one think?

"Perhaps a bath, sir, to clear your mind?" Demetrius suggested demurely. Petronius stared at him, uncertain if he had been speaking aloud to himself or if the secretary had read his mind. Suddenly he grew hot.

"No, no, Demetrius," he snapped. "This is no time for baths. Are you out of your mind?" He turned back to the sea.

The sun had cleared the cape in the southwest and was now more than halfway through its arc from apex to horizon. The trireme had rounded the cape and disappeared. Down on the beach, the yacht's stern, barnacle-encrusted and glistening, had been grounded by the ebbing tide. How much longer until nightfall? It was impossible to tell how fast time was passing. All these journeys, measured by impossible, invisible increments. Where were the geometers, the clepsydras, the milestones when they were needed? Who can live this way? Who . . . ?

" 'Sire,' " he blurted, loud enough to startle a swallow from the eaves of the bathhouse. "'My life's journey is almost at its end, and I know not whereby it has brought me to this pass. A Roman understands his duty when he reaches this juncture, and you may rest assured I shall not fail in mine. Nonetheless, I will not descend into the valley without I turn for one last word with he whom . . .' Damn it! Damn it! Go away, Demetrius. I'll have my bath after all."

Demetrius, in no way offended, backed off and turned away.

"Wait a moment," Petronius said with the kind of abrupt modulation he had once used to inspire his troops on the morning of a battle. Demetrius stopped.

"I know tomorrow's a holiday, Demetrius," he said softly. "But I'd appreciate it if you would make yourself available throughout the night. I may need you late."

"Sir." Demetrius bowed and departed.

Now thoroughly irritated with himself, and in no mood to succumb to another fit of indecision, Petronius bounded briskly up the steps of his private suite and through a pair of bronze-paneled doors into the bedroom. It was here—or, in the heat of summer, on the lightly thatched porch outside—that he customarily took his afternoon nap, and it was here, at this citrus-wood desk, that he had sat writing several hours of every day for the past two years. The desk disgusted him now, a monument to misguided effort. A narrow vestibule led to the first of the bath chambers, from which there wafted a hint of lavender-scented steam. The slave Syrus, having stoked the boiler, stood in attendance at the doorway. At a nod from Petronius, he knelt at his master's feet, removed his sandals, pulled his tunic over his head, and loosened his loincloth.

"Is Surisca here?" Petronius asked over his shoulder.

"Yes, sir."

"I'll need you tonight, Syrus. Don't go into town until I call for you."

"Yes, sir."

"Come to think of it, tell the rest of the household staff . . . No, never mind. Ask Commagenus to come to me after my bath." Syrus bowed and padded off.

Petronius entered the bathing room, stepped down into the hot water. The granite tub, ledged with Parian marble, was large enough for four, but Petronius almost always bathed alone here. There was a larger suite of baths up at the house, including a sulfur tank and a heated swimming pool, that he used only with his guests. There, the walls and floors were adorned with elaborate murals and mosaics—blue dolphins in glass tile on the bottom of the swimming pool; ibises, alligators, and palm trees in the hot room; hunting scenes in the cold; sea monsters and mermaids in the sulfur; and amorous scenes from Greek mythology in the massage room. Petronius rather enjoyed the dolphins, which were remarkably lifelike and reflected the sunlight delightfully. The rest were a little vulgar for his taste, but they had come with the house and he'd never had the heart to paint over them. Besides, they were quite famous, the venue for notorious orgies under the former owner. The empress Messalina herself was said to have debauched an entire delegation of Cappadocian magistrates in the *frigidarium*. Having had Messalina once or twice in his youth, Petronius kept the artwork in part as a fond memorial to her appetites, which had been every bit as vigorous as the historians were already beginning to write.

Here, in the private baths, it was a different story. The walls and vaulted ceilings had crawled with the most lascivious vignettes imaginable, involving gods, goddesses, nymphs, satyrs, centaurs, Numidians, goats, and children. Petronius was not a religious man, but even he had been offended—at least, morbidly aroused, and he despised morbidity in himself as much as in any of his peers—by a scene of Cerberus being fellated by Venus, identifiable by her charming squint. Although it had all been whitewashed out some six years since, Petronius could still sometimes see, as though the image had been burned into his eye or was glowing through the paint, the dog's teeth dripping with gore and yellow saliva, and its black lips drawn back in an obscene rictus. Now, for the most part, his private baths were a place where a man could think, and dream, and consider his options. Here, the only concession to aesthetics was the ancient marble *kouros* he had brought back with him from Bithynia, a piece of special, personal significance, and even that—with its blind gaze and groping hands—Petronius thought of more as an object of meditation upon mortality and transience than as a work of art. He considered it a moment, shivered, then closed his eyes and lowered his head onto the cushion that had been left for him on the ledge.

෴෴෴෴෴෴

HE SAW HIMSELF pacing the streets of Prusa, a dismal provincial city nestled at the foot of Mysian Olympus, in Bithynia. He'd spent a long and unhappy week with the town fathers, poring over tax rolls and payrolls and debt-related documents. That afternoon, unable to tolerate another minute of their barefaced lies and dilatory tactics, he'd pushed away from the table and taken himself for a solitary stroll to clear his head and digest his ire.

He'd walked for some time, unaware of his surroundings, his head bowed in thought. The cobbled streets were slick under a light dusting of snow, but he heeded neither the temperature nor the curious stares that accompanied his forlorn musings. Yet another day wasted, his term of office already one quarter expended, and he had nothing to show for it but frustration and nervous exhaustion.

Gradually, he became aware of a drop in temperature, and of the inadequacy of his clothing against the coming storm. He

looked around; the streets were deserted, the upper reaches of
Olympus shrouded in icy mist and lowering cloud. A gray, viscous evening was at hand, and he did not know where he was.
He found himself on a small town square at the outskirts of the
city, in what had evidently once been a prosperous quarter but
had long since fallen on hard times. The plaza, ringed by squalid
tenements, was dominated on one side by the crumbling façade
of a decrepit townhouse stripped of all ornament, its weathered
door ajar and swinging on rusty hinges. From a half-dissolved
inscription above the doorway, he realized that he knew of this
house; indeed, it was one that the town fathers had discussed
at some length that very afternoon. It had once belonged to a
wealthy merchant, who had bequeathed it to the Emperor
Claudius some twelve years previously with the intention that
it be converted for use as a city office. The merchant had even
left an endowment for its conversion and maintenance, but that
had long since evaporated, leaving the lovely old house, like so
much property in Bithynia belonging to the imperial household, gradually to molder and decay. Now, to all appearances,
it was beyond salvation. Without really thinking, but perhaps
moved by some feeling of empathetic kinship with the sad ruin,
he pushed through the broken door and entered the dark, silent
confines of the house.

The interior was in a state of even worse dilapidation than
the exterior. Rugged vines covered the walls, their once-vibrant
murals faded and patched with damp blemishes. The flagstones
were cracked and tilted crazily, water pooling on the floor where
the heating pipes had ruptured. Some roof timbers had collapsed, allowing ugly stains of gray light to fall upon the degradation. No doubt, the house would have to be torn down, at
further expense to the town, which would borrow money for the
work that it had no intention of repaying, then borrow more to
begin a rebuilding that would never see completion. A sorrowful

wind whistled in the roof tiles, and Petronius had seen enough. But as he turned to leave, his eye was caught by a whitish glow emanating from the interior garden, partially visible through the vestibule. His first thought was that it must be a ghost, with its vaguely human form, and he stood rooted to the spot in apprehension, but it took only a moment to grasp that the figure was rigid and immobile.

It was a statue, of course, rising on a pedestal in the midst of a riot of plant life, a *rus in urbe*, a tiny wilderness dropped into the center of the city. Great blots of reddish thyme clung to the marble, enwrapping the figure's feet and ankles and threatening its shins. Grapevines strangled the columns and rafters of the peristyle that surrounded the garden on all four sides. Utter silence reigned, despite the wind rising without.

At the center, the life-size statue, a boy or young man, stood on a plain cube of marble, facing the atrium. It was what the Greeks called a *kouros*, a work from the dark centuries, the very last thing one expected to find in the private home of a respectable gentleman with middlebrow tastes. It was archaic in every sense, more Egyptian than Greek, with its stiff legs, its long symmetrical braids, fists loosely clenched at its sides, its stylized musculature, the ineffable, vaguely ironic curve of its eyebrows and curl of its lips. Even Petronius, with his limited repertoire, could plainly see that it represented an idea—the ideal of physical and moral beauty, united by nobility—rather than an individual. It was beautiful, to be sure, but disturbing, like a prayer or incantation uttered in a dead language. How such a piece could possibly have found its way to this house from the ancient temple or graveyard for which it had originally been intended was anybody's guess.

And yet, as he slowly circled it, Petronius found himself unexpectedly moved. The boy was talking to him, telling Petronius that the two of them had something in common; the boy was challenging Petronius to guess what it might be. Between the *kouros*'s era and his, a golden age had come and passed away, its glories forever faded, yet Petronius was the same as him: nothing had changed but the awareness of a hope irredeemably squandered. Now he saw the irony in the boy's expression resolve itself into mockery, just as a man is mocked by the memory of himself in his youth, when all of nature and society seemed to be an exudation of his own mind. Petronius saw that the boy was both himself as he had been in his own prime, exulting in his ignorance and infatuation with abstraction, and as he was now, a corpse pickled in its own brine and entombed in a distant land, an oblivion so complete that even his native tongue was no longer familiar to him. As unlikely as it might seem, Petronius felt something break painfully within him as he stood before that coldhearted boy and passively endured his withering scorn.

"Does he speak to you, too?" came a woman's voice from the shadows of the peristyle.

෴෴෴෴෴෴

PETRONIUS OPENED HIS eyes. Eight years later, looming over the bath, the *kouros* no longer spoke to him. He sighed in dismay. There was nothing for him in the hot water today, and where he waited to be wrapped in serenity he instead felt charged with enervating restlessness and anxiety, and consequently immensely exasperated with himself. He was fully aware of how fortunate he was—how few others in his position had been afforded the luxury of making plans, putting their affairs in order, making their peace—but this awareness gave him no satisfaction or rest. It was all wrong. Why were his feelings not lining up as he had trained them to do, like dutiful soldiers, snapping to attention at his command? This disquiet—it was not the Roman way, not the patrician way. Had the others gone like this, in disgraceful jitters, merely feigning their dignity and resolve? Had all their training failed them, too, at the last moment? Perhaps they had pulled it off somehow, reaching into a still inner core that seemed to be eluding him. Perhaps the problem was having too much time to prepare, rather than too little. Petronius ground his teeth in self-disgust. He had no fear of losing his composure, but he had always assumed—far too complacently, as it turned out—that, this moment come, everything would be perfect, including and especially the state of his soul. What else could possibly matter?

Petronius climbed from the bath and passed into the next chamber. Without pause, he leaped into the plunge pool, immersing himself entirely in the icy water. He opened his eyes. A spike of sunlight from the small window near the ceiling quivered before him, and he reached out for it. The light splashed onto his hands, and he cupped them as if he would drink it. This is the way, he thought to himself—you cannot drink it and you cannot hold it, but you can grasp it. If your hands and your tongue are frustrated, seek the sense that is equipped to grasp it, and you will be gratified. You are trying too hard—you know how to do this, you have trained for this your entire life, but your anger and your doubt are making you forget. It is the cold water, not the hot, that cleanses and dissolves the impurities. By the time he emerged to the surface, Petronius was laughing with pleasure at himself. But after only a few minutes of splashing and rubbing at his limbs, the skin gone taut and goose-pimpled, his mood had reasserted itself.

"What a load of crap," he muttered to himself as he padded into the massage room.

Surisca was waiting by the table, naked but for a cotton shawl wrapped around her legs and tied at the hip. Her hair had been elaborately braided and twisted into a bun at the nape, fastened with the silver brooch Petronius had given her at last year's Saturnalia. It was a fine bit of native craftsmanship, not made for a slave, but when his brother had sent it from Britain, Petronius had seen that it was not to Melissa's taste and had not even shown it to her. How Surisca had blushed when he'd presented it to her! Perhaps she had a boyfriend in town to impress, or make jealous.

"All ready for the holiday, I see," Petronius said, just to see that blush again. Surisca obliged, ducking her head as she warmed a dash of oil between her palms. Petronius took his place on the table, lying on his stomach with his arms at his side. Surisca began scraping his back.

The worst thing he could do, of course, was think this way: this is my last bath; this is my last massage; this is my last sunset; this is my last whatever. Hadn't he had more than his share of all these things, and been blessed with the ability never to take any pleasure for granted? It was gratitude he should be feeling; satiety, not regret; anticipation, not trepidation. Well, who in their right mind wants to die? That was beside the point—it was not a matter of whether, but of how. He believed as he had been taught, that all unhappiness is the product of unnatural desire; that all fear is ultimately the fear of death; that the banishment of desire should, in principle, vanquish the fear of death. What was it Epicurus had said? "Life has no terrors for him who has thoroughly understood that there are no terrors for him in ceasing to live." Petronius knew this in his heart to be true; he understood it. He was not afraid to die, yet here he was, clinging to the world as a ship clings to shore at an approaching storm, anchored in place by desire. It was not right. It was not proper. His thoughts should not be clouded at this moment.

Surisca was massaging his shoulders, her soft, brown belly so close to his face he could see the lovely down around her navel.

Her hands were soft, too, like a child's. How long would they stay so, after she'd lost her privileged position?

"Surisca," Petronius said. "What would you do if you were free?"

Her hands stopped momentarily, then continued to work.

"I don't know," she said after a while. A thrush flew in through the open door and perched on the windowsill. Then it swooped down and disappeared into the bathing rooms. It would surely break its neck trying to get out again.

"Would you go home?"

"My home was destroyed, and all my family is dead or sold."

"Oh? I thought you were from Tyre."

"I was raised in Tyre, but my people are from the Syrian desert. My village was burned by the Parthians."

She went on with her work in silence, moving down his body to his lower back, buttocks, and thighs. She stopped to drizzle more oil into her hands, then reached between Petronius's legs.

"How old are you, Surisca? Seventeen?"

"I think I'm fifteen, sir."

"You're very young. Surely there is something you would like to do?"

"I'm happy to serve you, Master. Will you roll over now?"

"But if you were free?"

She gave the matter some thought as she continued to administer to him. Her eyes were closed as her hands worked mechanically. She had kohl on her lower eyelids. Her thoughts, like his, were elsewhere. When she spoke, her voice was that of a thoughtless child caught up in a daydream.

"I suppose I would go to Rome and marry a baker." She giggled charmingly.

"You haven't been to Rome. It's noisy, smelly, dangerous. You'd live in a tiny room in a tumbledown tenement in a treacherous neighborhood. You'd pay an exorbitant rent and be kept up all night by the rattling carts. You'd better stay here."

"Still, I would. There's nothing in Cumae."

"Why a baker?"

"I have a friend who's a baker. He does well."

"And will he go to Rome?"

Surisca sighed impatiently. "This isn't working. Should I put it in my mouth?"

Petronius raised his head and looked down the length of his body. He had barely been aware of her hands on his penis, which was limp and shriveled like an old man's. That was a shame. He doubted that he would be in any condition that evening to make love with Melissa, which meant that this sad little interlude would probably be his last chance to take his pleasure with a woman, even though she was only his slave. He would like to feel it one last time, and Surisca certainly knew how he liked it, but ultimately what did it matter? Again, he felt himself overcome by weariness and uncertainty.

"Leave it," he said. "It's not important." Surisca immediately turned away to rinse her hands in the basin by the door. Petronius followed her with his eyes, his gaze lingering on the movements of her small buttocks through her shawl. When she stepped into the doorway and made her courtesy, the sunlight silhouetted her thighs. Petronius felt a lump of startling sadness rise in his throat and salty tears sting his eyes. This would not do at all, at all.

Petronius lay on his back for a while. He could hear the thrush, panicking in the next room. It would flutter and bang against the ceiling, and every minute or so pause to rest on an exposed rafter. Then it would resume its attempts to escape, always in the same way, never learning from its mistakes. And it would certainly die. That was his life now, panicking and desperate and doomed. It was banging against his ribcage, trying to get away to safety. But a man's life is not a wild beast; it is his property, a domesticated animal, and it ought to respond to its master's command. If he bids it to lie down quietly and await the sacrificial knife, it ought to do so obediently, with humility and trust. If a dog refuses to obey, whose is the fault? Why, the master's, of course, who has trained it inadequately. A man who cannot master his own dog can hardly be expected to master himself. Well, well, it was too late for a refresher course now—if he had to drag his own life kicking and snarling to the altar, so be it. There was nothing dignified in it, alas, nothing praiseworthy; but it would submit in the end, he would see to that.

There came a sharp crack, followed by a muffled thud, from the next room. The bird had found the window. Petronius sat up, eased himself off the table and returned to the bedroom, where a fresh tunic and his steward were waiting for him.

"Help me on with this, will you, Commagenus?"

Petronius grabbed the garment from the bed, then gave it a second look. "What is this yellow?"

"Baetic wool, sir. From Spain. Lilia found it in the market in Naples."

"It's very soft, isn't it?" Petronius held the tunic out for Commagenus, who gave it a brief appreciative rub between his thumbs before slipping it over his master's head. Petronius slid his feet into the sandals and the steward knelt to fasten them.

"Should Lilia put out your toga for this evening, sir?"

"No, I won't wear the toga tonight. This will do."

Petronius led the way through the curtained doorway into the adjoining dining room, designed with only two couches for intimate dinners, but rarely used. At the far end, a pair of doors gave onto the colonnade, facing the main house. Commagenus followed two steps behind Petronius. Here in the shade there was a slight chill, though the sunlight was still bright upon the orchard and the sea. Petronius stopped by a small altar to Apollo the Healer.

"What do you think? Will we be able to eat outdoors tonight?"

Commagenus stuck his nose in the air, like a hunting dog, and sniffed. "If the wind doesn't pick up, I should think. I'll have braziers set up by the dining couch, and some extra blankets handy."

"Do that." Petronius moved on. "Listen, Commagenus. I'll need the entire household on hand tonight. Tell everyone to stay put until you've heard from me."

"Tonight, sir? May I remind you, the festival . . ."

"I haven't forgotten. I'll release them all in good time, don't worry."

"Which companies, sir?"

"Every company."

"The field hands?"

"Every company. Send someone to the vineyards for Marsius and his boys. I want them all here tonight. Vellia can send them some bread and onions if they've missed their dinner."

"Yes, sir."

"Now, will you tell Vellia I'll be down to see her in a few minutes?"

"Yes, sir."

Petronius watched him hustle off along the colonnade. Then, glancing down, his eye was caught by the small golden Apollo at his feet, standing in a niche set into the half-wall. Petronius considered the god's bland, well-fed face, his elegantly pleated robe, his glimmering lyre. He was a local god, with his ancient oracle in a cove just over the hill, but neither he nor his Sibyl had ever been of the least assistance to Petronius. Suddenly, Petronius found himself flushed with anger. He strode into the bathhouse, found the dead thrush, and returned to throw it contemptuously at the idol's feet.

"There's your sacrifice," he muttered. "Heal that, you Greek pansy." He continued on toward the main house.

He had not gone ten strides when he saw Melissa emerge from the library, tall and straight as a statue of Athena. She wore a plain, sleeveless gown of undyed grayish wool, and her hair, the color of ripe flax, was gathered in a single long braid at the back, like a German's. She had not yet seen him, though plainly she was looking for him and he was directly in front of her. She seemed distracted, a little distraught, and she hugged her shoulders as if she were chilled. Petronius stood and watched her. He thought that, perhaps, if she turned away without catching sight of him, he would not call her back. Distraction did not become her, it revealed her age and made her seem fragile, which she was not. He could not bear to look at her. With dark shadows pooling beneath her high cheekbones and at the corners of her lips, she made him think of the tragic Niobe at the moment when she first notices that her children are missing.

But then she saw him, her eyes as gray and clean as pebbles on a beach, and he was overcome with remorse so that his own eyes grew wet when she smiled at him. And yet neither of them moved, and they stood like fools who are compelled to wade through their own ignorance at each new encounter. That felt especially true now, today, when, with the hours closing in, he had yet to find a way to unburden himself to her. Perhaps that was yet another duty in which he would prove himself derelict. The longer they stood, the greater the distance seemed to grow between them, until it might almost have been easier for each to go his own separate way. The smile wilted and died on Melissa's lips, then her breath caught and she brought one hand up to cover her mouth, as if she had seen something horrible rise up behind him, or had looked into his secret soul. Petronius felt as if he might never move from that place, but Melissa, ever the perfect Roman matron, instantly mastered herself and came to him, arms outstretched as if in reconciliation. Petronius envied her composure; in some ways, of course, her situation was far more difficult than his.

She took his hands in hers, and even at arm's length he could smell the strong, oniony scent of another man's sweat on her.

He pulled her to him and she rested her face on his chest.

"I've been to see the captain of the guard," she said with un-rehearsed detachment. Her hair smelled of iris; stray wisps of gray stood out at the temple, like cat's whiskers.

"Yes?"

"He's agreed to everything we've asked. Titus, I . . ."

"That's good. Then we'll get on with the preparations."

There was a silence, during which Petronius was again acutely, almost painfully sensitive to the world around him. The lengthening shadows stood out like knife blades on the path. He felt he could count every strand of hair on Melissa's head, every clattering stone on the beach below. Every point of contact between his body and Melissa's felt bruised and hot.

"It seems he served with you in Bithynia. He vouched for your honor."

"A centurion vouched for *my* honor? What was his name?"

"Oh, I don't know. Something or other."

"And?"

"And? Your guests will be permitted to come and go as they please. Isn't that what you wanted?"

"Of course."

"There will be pickets posted at the gate, at the front door, and on the beach."

"I'll have something sent out to them. It will be a long night."

"How thoughtful of you, Titus. I'll have my bath now."

"Thank you, Melissa Silia. For all this." Petronius kissed the top of her head and they parted, neither looking back.

It was strange, Petronius thought, that she had not more to say to him, nor he to her, on this of all days. Of course, he knew what she had done to win the centurion's cooperation, and it was only natural that the less they had to say about that, the better. Still, until she had arrived from Rome the previous week, bearing the news of his imminent arrest, they had not seen one another in six weeks, and even that visit had been overshadowed with foreboding and melancholy. Now, here at last was the golden opportunity, the moment of necessity for the two of them, and neither seemed inclined to broach the subject, or capable of doing so. When they'd first met in Prusa and become lovers—was it really only eight years ago?—she'd been disarmingly, even aggressively, direct; if she were cautious and circumspect now, he had only himself to blame. In a moment of despair and self-loathing, he had abandoned her without excuse or explanation—though an explanation had hardly been necessary. He had left her to sink or swim in the shark-infested waters of the imperial court, and she had acquitted herself admirably, against all odds. Now it was Petronius who was drowning, and she had come to him without summons, of her own free will, not only to warn him of the peril he faced, but to tend to him in his hour of need. Perhaps she imagined there was nothing left to say, but even at his most skeptical Petronius knew this to be wishful thinking. First of all, there is *always* more to say, to feel, to be confounded by. And then, even in the unlikely event that she had nothing more to say to him, she must feel that he had been groping toward a meaningful exchange of some kind, and she had offered him none of the encouragement she knew he would need. She had helped him put his affairs in order efficiently and affectionately; she had shared his bed; she had placed herself in some danger by consorting with him at this critical moment; she had submitted to a distasteful bargain to ensure the success of tonight's dinner; but she had yet to come to him and say: "Titus, if you have anything you need to tell me, now is the time to do it." And until she did, he could not. He could not.

She had already started for the bathhouse, and when she turned at his call and the hem of her tunic rose and rippled, it seemed to Petronius for one moment as if the cares of the years had fallen away, and that she was again as she had once been. But he saw at once that she had dropped her shoulders and allowed a kind of vapid languor to invade her gaze. She was the kind of person who yawned when she was afraid and stared with limpid intensity into the eyes of those who bored her most. To see her like this, sorely provoked by the day's unpleasant necessities, yet so serenely composed, with one hand on her hip like a waitress at a roadside tavern, was dazzling. He found himself staring at her in mute perplexity and desire.

"What is it you wanted to tell me, Titus?"

"I . . . nothing. I . . . it's difficult."

She cocked her head to one side, like a songbird, and smiled sympathetically, her eyes half-closed as if she would fall asleep right there on the path.

"I know it is," she said gently. "But you must bear up. It's almost over now."

Petronius watched her turn and disappear into the bathhouse. She was the most beautiful woman in the world, the only person he had ever wanted, and he had lost her as casually as one loses a ring removed before a swim and thoughtlessly knocked away. The important question was not why she had returned at the final hour to allow him one last chance to redeem himself, but why, after a week in her company, he had failed to do so. It was unlike her to allow him to idle in error for so long. What was she thinking?

He shook himself like a wet dog. He was thoroughly fed up with all this emotional turbulence and determined to be businesslike and efficient with the rest of his time until dinner, of which there was precious little left. True, it was not what he would have wished—dignity, pride, and Socratic condescension were more in order for a day like this—but it was what he was stuck with until he could find his balance and equanimity. Perhaps he would feel more himself when the guests arrived—after all, had he not been reared from birth and lived his entire life as a public man, a leader of men and patrician exemplar? Was it not natural for men like him to feel out of sorts in their own company? It was all the solitude of the past two years, all the introspection and writing, that had softened him.

He stretched his legs and strode purposefully into the house—through the library and the front atrium, past the interior fountain and pool, the mural of the seafront on the Bay of Naples, and down a long, narrow hallway to the service wing. He ducked his head to clear the low lintel of the main kitchen, and the dozen or so slaves ceased their chatter and stood to attention. Only Vellia, cracking urchins in a basket, saw fit to ignore him.

The vast oak table that occupied the center of the room was laden with goods recently arrived from the market—in fact, a cart was being unloaded just now in the rear courtyard—and Petronius contented himself with a stroll around its periphery while he waited for his housekeeper to finish her task. With a lazy flick of his hand, he ordered the slaves back to their work, which they resumed in silence, heads bowed.

On the near end of the table stood an assortment of large red earthenware bowls, filled with shellfish on ice—Lucrine oysters, mussels, cockles, Misenum urchins. They smelled strongly of the sea, whence they had been plucked only that morning, and when later they were opened and eaten, with perhaps just a dash of vinegar and olive oil, no more mystical communion could be hoped for with the depths and its creatures and the invisible roads that bind the empire to its own heart. The largest of the bowls, the size of a cartwheel, was filled with brine and held an enormous mottled lamprey, still very much alive. Beside it, a glistening sturgeon lay on a rush mat, its eye glassy and unclouded, alongside a smaller red mullet and a basketful of prawns. There were a number of open jars containing pickled Picene olives, olive relish dappled with coriander seeds, Sicilian honeycomb, Pontic pine kernels toasted oily and tan, Judaean pistachios shelled and roasted and pink as babies' toes. Beyond these, another mat was spread with a selection of the finest Italian cheeses. Among them, Petronius recognized a finely aged Luna from Etruria, stamped with a crescent moon; an oil-soaked Vestine from the Sabine hill country, wrapped in grape leaves yet still reeking of goat; and a divine, creamy Trebula, a local product worthy of the worship it inspired. But there were no beestings, he noted with disappointment. There were piles of fruit—Scythian sorb apples, golden Chian figs, Syrian damsons, and lumpy citrons from Medea—and of flat discs of fresh white bread. A slave was plucking little birds—guinea fowl? beccaficos?—and laying their naked, roseate pink carcasses in a neat line at the far end. Petronius grabbed an open urchin from Vellia's basket and a disc of bread, with which he absent-mindedly scooped the pungent roe from the shell as he pursued his tour of inspection.

Lucullo emerged from the oven room, his great fat face purple, dripping and beaming with pleasure. His tunic was filthy, bloodstained and spangled with translucent fish scales.

"Today's your day, Master," he said in his heavy, spit-flecked Sicilian accent. He wiped his sweaty palms down the length of his tunic and offered a perfunctory bow. "I've just got the boar in the oven."

"Umbrian?"

"You can smell the acorns in its flesh. I've stuffed it with Ebuso figs and chestnuts. We'll have the sweetbreads and black pudding grilled, with mulsum sauce."

"Excellent." Petronius felt his spirits lifting. "What's this?"

"That'll be your Lucanian sausage."

Petronius dipped his hand into the bowl and pinched off a sample of the raw mixture. "Not enough cumin, Lucullo."

The chef frowned. "The flavor strengthens with cooking."

"Still, not enough."

"You're wrong, Master, but I'll do it."

"What next?" The men stood side by side, Petronius a full head taller, and surveyed the room.

"Let's see." The chef rubbed his cheeks. "Besides the raw shellfish, you'll have roast sturgeon and mullet with pepper sauce, Baian casserole—Vellia found a bottle of brine imported from Byzantium, what a marvel—fried lamprey with vinegar sauce."

"Cost a small fortune, that lamprey," Vellia called out grudgingly from across the room, without looking up from her urchins. "Market's a madhouse, with the holidays. Emperor's in town, along with half of Rome. Not the good half."

"Put the sauce on the side. I like mine plain."

"I know. Then we'll have peahen stuffed with truffles and chestnuts . . ."

"That peahen was even more than the lamprey."

"Yes, all right, Vellia. By the way, where are the beestings I asked for?"

"Can't get beestings in December, Master, not even in Baiae. Woodcock from Phrygia, oh yes. Tunny from Chalcedon, why not? Black truffles from Aquitania, certainly. But no beestings."

"Go on, then."

"As I was saying, you have your stuffed peahen, some nice plump figpeckers in peppered egg yolk and Corycian saffron, turtle rumps, dormice in honey and poppy seeds, sow's vulva . . ."

"Honestly, Lucullo, you know I can't stand it."

"Yes, but your guests can't do without it, can they? Not the way I make it. Why else do you suppose they come? And we have fresh apricots and peaches for dessert, believe it or not, along with madam's favorite saffron honey cakes. Yes, and cheese and nuts and lupines and olives. And bread."

"Will it be enough?"

Lucullo squinted. "For nine? I dare say it'll do."

"And we're feeding the vineyard company tonight, in honor of the festival."

"The whole company?" Vellia looked up from her urchins for the first time, a frown of annoyance creasing her shrunken, leathery face. "Whatever should I feed 'em with?"

"You've got onions in the cellar, don't you? Just put on some extra loaves."

"Perfectly good onions," Vellia muttered, returning to her work.

Hermes, the herald slave, stuck his head through the kitchen door. Seeing Petronius, he stood to attention in his immaculate white tunic and made a low, formal obeisance.

"Marcus Valerius Martialis, sir."

"So soon? Very well, have him meet me in the library."

Hermes vanished, and Petronius turned back to Lucullo, who was shuffling his feet and sucking his fingernails, clearly anxious to be back at work.

"Lucullo, you've done yourself proud. I'd hug you if you weren't such a revolting specimen."

"Careful what you wish for. Saturnalia begins at midnight, and I'll be in my bath by eleven. Back to work." The chef waddled off into the larder. Petronius crossed the room and crouched down beside the housekeeper, whispering in her ear.

"Those guards by the gate, Vellia. You've seen them?"

"Yes, sir. The whole household's seen 'em."

"You're to feed them well tonight, you hear? Send them out whatever we don't finish. Plenty of wine, too. Not the Falernian; the Massic will do, but lots of it."

"Yes, sir. If I might . . . What are they doing here? Is the emperor dining with us tonight?"

"No, nothing like that. The fact is, Vellia, I'm under arrest."

"I see."

Petronius stood, hesitated a moment as if he might say something else, looked about the room, and left.

He found Martialis in the library, hunched over a game board of robbers and soldiers, a crystal cattle train in his hand, his wild black hair in his eyes. Incredibly, he was wearing a toga, of reddish Canusium wool, but it had been draped so inexpertly—stray lengths wrapped around the neck, lumps and folds in all the wrong places, both arms bare—that its effect was perfectly comical, like that of a mime on the stage. His shoes were spattered with mud and his cheeks streaked with some sort of scarlet paste.

"You look pathetic," Petronius said from the doorway.

Martialis looked up from the board and broke into a great yellow-toothed grin. "Good thing I wore it," he said, rising to his feet to clasp Petronius by the forearms. "Am I dining with the Great Artist tonight?"

"No. Did you walk all the way from Baiae?"

"I did, and I'm famished. I've been fucking all day. I found a fantastic tart down by the docks. She's got this great trick. She takes a stick of charcoal, see, and draws a ring around your cock, right down near the base. Then she puts on this bright red lipstick, and she says 'If I don't beat that mark, your blowjob's free.' And sure enough, when she's done, there's a red ring below the black one. It's fantastic. She could make a fortune in Rome."

"You stink, Marcus, you really do," Petronius said, pushing him toward the door. "Why don't you take that thing off and have a bath? The others will be here soon."

"Don't mind if I do. Can I have a snack first?"

"Go to the kitchen. Vellia will fix you up with something. I'll meet you in the baths."

Petronius sat on a bench while Martialis bathed, gnawing at a stump of bread. Petronius never ceased to marvel at the man's body—small yet somehow lanky, underfed yet somehow knotty with strength, and, only in his midtwenties, he was covered in twists of black hair from his neck to his toes. Petronius had never been to Spain, but he was told they were all like that—the young Lucan certainly had been, and not much older than Martialis. And they all seemed to have yellow teeth, too; it was no wonder that Spaniards were commonly believed to brush their teeth with their own urine. Petronius remembered the first time he had met Martialis, at a dinner that Lucan had thrown to welcome the boy to Rome and introduce him to society. Martialis was in need of a patron, some wealthy nitwit with literary pretensions looking for a brilliant, unsung poet to sponsor. Petronius had been making civil conversation with just such a prospect, a pompous old senator named Frugi, when Lucan had stepped in, Martialis in tow. Formal bows were exchanged all around, and Petronius had instantly sensed that the young Spaniard, freshly shaved and immaculate in a gleaming new toga, was ill at ease. (Petronius was later to learn that Martialis was always uncomfortable if he felt himself to be too clean, overdressed, or in polite company.) Almost immediately after the introductions, Frugi had turned to Martialis and asked him in all earnest whether it was true that Spaniards cleaned their teeth with their own urine. Martialis had fixed him with a gaze of infinite thoughtfulness, and paused before delivering his considered response in a tone of catholic benevolence. "Most of us do, senator," he'd said. "But I drink too much, and it makes my piss acidic, so I always try to use someone else's when I can." The senator had declined to sponsor him, but Petronius had taken an instant liking to him. He had set him up in a room at the Pear Tree Inn, provided him with a nominal salary, some hand-me-downs, and free meals whenever he saw fit to drop in on the Esquiline. That had been two years ago. They'd ended up in a most unconventional patron–client relationship, as Martialis had proven woefully inept at fawning, running confidential errands, and keeping appointments, while Petronius had left Rome under a shadow shortly after they'd met and was subsequently in no position to promote Martialis's social and literary careers. Instead, they'd done something very untoward—they'd become fast friends. They were as opposite as they could possibly be; sometimes, having taken the boy under his wing, Petronius felt as if he had adopted a very intelligent, very naughty monkey, not fully domesticated. And yet they loved one another, amused each other, argued bitterly about grammar, vintages, and Euripides. Martialis had spent a lot of time in Cumae—the gutters and whorehouses of nearby Puteoli were just filthy enough to suit him. Petronius could only be grateful that Martialis was not his real son, for if he had raised him from a child, he would have ruined him. For sure, he would have broken something inside him that seemed to be broken in most men he knew, but not in Martialis. He looked down fondly upon the boy in the bath. Petronius could not imagine how he was going to break the news to him. Clearly, Martialis suspected nothing as yet.

"It's a good thing you invited me tonight," he was saying, spraying half-chewed crumbs over the surface of the bathwater. "I don't have two coppers to rub together. Baiae is so damned expensive these days, you have to sell your soul for a taste of cheap sausage. I'd have had to go to Mucius's for my supper, but I'd almost rather starve than have to listen to any more of his so-called poetry. It's the only reason he entertains, you know, to corral an audience. And he serves the worst rotgut from Ravenna." He held his breath and dunked his head, reemerging with his face plastered with hair to the chin.

"You spend all your money on whores, it's no wonder you've got nothing to eat."

"That's the beauty of it. Chrestina didn't cost me a penny. I told her I'd act as her agent in Rome, introduce her to all the right people, and she did me for free."

"All the right people are right there under her nose in Baiae."

"Yes, but she's got a pimp in Baiae. And besides, Baiae's too small for someone like her. She's an artist, she needs a larger canvas to work on."

"But you don't know any of the right people in Rome. And look at you, Marcus. How did you ever convince her?"

Martialis stood and looked about for a towel. "I am a poet, Petronius, did you forget? A witty epigram, a seductive turn of phrase—it's always worth something in the marketplace, if you know how to sell it. Tomorrow, my verses will buy me fame, wealth, immortal glory. Today, they buy me pussy. As Catullus always said, 'the pot finds its own herbs.' Oh, hello."

Surisca stood in the doorway, towels in hand. She wore a full-length robe and the blank expression that she reserved for naked houseguests. This was hardly the first time she had attended to Martialis in the baths, and even Martialis knew better than to take advantage of a man's slaves in his own home, but he stood there, hands on hips, as unabashed, and with the same pretensions to irresistibility, as the swan before Leda.

"I prefer freeborn women to freedwomen, and freedwomen to slaves, but to me a slave as beautiful as Surisca is always a free woman," he purred.

Surisca placed the towels on a chair and began to back out of the room.

"Will you bring our guest a clean tunic and some nard for his hair?" Petronius called to her.

"Yes, sir."

To Martialis, who had climbed from the bath and was now

vigorously toweling himself dry, Petronius said: "Do you want to buy her?" Martialis paused and looked at him incuriously.

"Sure, why not? How much?"

"Twenty thousand."

"Lend it to me?"

"Never."

"Anyway, what would I do with her? Other than the obvious?"

"And you call yourself a poet? No imagination whatsoever. You may have a hairy body, but you've got a depilated mind."

"That's good—depilated mind. I'll have to steal that some-day."

"Meet me on the terrace when you're dressed. I've got something I need to talk to you about."

Petronius left the bathing room and made for the side terrace, which, facing south and overlooking a cove rather than the open sea, was protected from the prevailing winds and more suitable for entertaining. The kitchen slaves were busy preparing for supper, setting up braziers and screens, hanging wreaths and decorations, sweeping the flagstones.

Petronius leaned toward the sun, pulsing a few bare degrees above the horizon, low enough to reach beneath the bellies of the few lingering clouds and to caress them with fingertips of rose and lilac. Another few minutes and it would be gone, taking with it the last daylight Petronius would ever see. How had the afternoon passed so quickly? It seemed only a moment ago that the Praetorians had arrived with the arraignment, and yet it had been fully four hours since. And how had he frittered away those precious four hours? Worrying, fretting, chastising himself, when he might have been dancing, swimming, fucking like Martialis. Well, the guests would be here soon, and he had a sacred duty to them, too, one whose execution would surely help to restore him to a fitting state of soul. They'd all have heard the news by now—Baiae was a veritable cauldron of gossip—so he could dispense with lengthy explanations and condolences and get on with the business at hand. They wouldn't need to be told how to behave; only Martialis would have trouble grasping the Roman point of view on all this. He would not take it well, Petronius imagined. He would cry and moan hysterically, probably, and certainly he would urge Petronius to flee. You have a fully provisioned yacht at your disposal, he'd say. What would it take to bribe or overcome the sentry? With the freshening breeze you'd be halfway to Corsica before anyone even knew you were gone. You'll sail on to Spain, where my beloved uncle will welcome you into our mountain home. No one will ever find you there. You will never wear the toga again, or smell the acrid scent of purple dye. You will spend your days in the lovely woods of Boterdus, you will swim in our soft lakes of the Nymphs, and all you need for a fine and simple life will be provided for you. Sail away, Petronius, sail away! Will your precious honor preserve your rotting corpse in the grave, or stiffen your cock at the sight of some nubile lady mummy? We owe so little time to life, and all eternity to death, so let's pay off our small debts first, Petronius. Just look at that wine-dark sea out there, teeming with hidden life. The receding tide is beckoning to you, Petronius, with a million salty fingers. Plunge in, the sea is big enough to hide you, too, as you swim away to Bilbilis, and cold enough to wash away all these filthy notions of duty and dignity and glory. You will emerge cleansed and renewed on the shores of Spain, Rome but a dreary memory, the harmless shadow of an evaporated dream. Sail away, Petronius, sail away!

Yes, surely Martialis would be shameless and emotional. He would be a challenge and a trial to Petronius tonight.

With all the bustle of the preparations for the banquet going on behind him, Petronius did not hear Martialis approach; suddenly, he simply found him there, leaning into the balustrade and peering into the cove. He wore a fresh white tunic and braided sandals, his hair glistening and reeking of nard, which, unable to afford himself, he always overapplied when dipping into Petronius's personal stock.

"What secrets, Arbiter?" he whispered conspiratorially into Petronius's ear.

"The stink of an expensive whore is even more offensive than a cheap one."

"Getting stingy in our old age, are we?"

"Do you have any idea how much that bucketful of ointment in your hair cost me, Marcus?"

"Titus, let me tell you about the poor man who turned miser when he inherited a fortune. If he gets any richer, he's going to starve to death."

"Especially if he entertains parasites like you."

The two stood companionably side by side, staring in abstraction at the golden tide pools in the cove below, their surfaces blindingly opaque in the glancing sunlight. The slaves had finished their work and fallen silent; the surf had receded to the distant promontory, now barely audible as a wistful sigh; the larks were ascendant. The light failed abruptly, and a pair of crabs appeared as if by magic at the bottom of the nearest pool, fighting it out over a fish head. Petronius whirled around to face the open sea. The sunset was over, and he'd missed it.

"Damn it!" he barked. Martialis turned with him.

"What's happening, Titus?"

"Damn it, damn it, damn it!"

"What's the matter?"

Petronius spun away from Martialis and slapped his hands on the balustrade. He hung his head, as if in mourning or shame.

"I've had word from the emperor. I'll be dead by the morning, Marcus." Petronius had tried to say it flippantly, tenderly, even as he recognized what a stupid thing it was to say. But in fact, he had no idea how it came out, as he suddenly found himself light-headed, a buzzing in his ears, his knees giving way, and compelled to prop himself up against the balustrade. Nor did he catch Martialis's reply, if there was one. By the time he regained his balance and composure, the poet was weeping silently, his shoulders heaving. Petronius tried to place a comforting hand on his, but Martialis pulled it away.

Petronius began to talk. "Only to you, Marcus, could this possibly come as a surprise. What a fool you are. Have you been living in Scythia? Don't you know what's going on in Rome? They're using Piso's little conspiracy as a pretext to wipe out the entire political class. They tell me the streets of Rome are gridlocked with funeral processions these days. When Seneca and Lucan died, then Ostorius Scapula, then Annaeus Mela, then Rufrius Crispinus, didn't that give you some hint that I might be a marked man too? I knew them all, every single one. Frankly, it's a miracle I've lasted this long."

Petronius fell silent, exhausted and depressed, but at least Martialis had stopped crying. He stared out to sea, his eyes wild and unseeing. In his hands he held a small ball of amber that Petronius had given him once, long ago, on some forgotten occasion. He rolled it between his palms, which he then cupped over his nose, as Petronius had taught him to do in times of distress. After a while, it appeared to have its intended effect; or perhaps it was just hunger and the sea air. Martialis heaved several deep sighs.

"It's not that I'm surprised, Titus. I suppose I knew it would come to this eventually. But you might have found a gentler way to tell me."

"What could I do? I only found out about it a few hours ago."

"'Sit down, Marcus, I have something to tell you.' 'Marcus, you are like a son to me,' and so on. Not 'I'll be dead by morning.' I ask you, is that considerate?"

"Forgive me. I'm not myself this afternoon. You're right, it was very selfish of me."

"Selfish and cruel."

"You're right, son."

Martialis began to cry again. "And what am I supposed to say now? 'I'll miss you?' What would a *real* Roman say? Nothing about broken hearts, I imagine."

"Well, since you ask, I suppose a real Roman might try to make it a little easier on me, instead of wallowing in his own misery."

"You'd like that, wouldn't you? No scene, no mess, no recrimination. Well, forget it. You had your chance to adopt a dog, and you adopted me instead. This is what you get for giving in to your paternal instincts."

"Please don't be so bitter. It's not as if I'd chosen for this to happen."

"Oh no? Tell me you couldn't get out of this if you really wanted to. You have your yacht. You could escape."

"No."

"I don't know why I bother. Of course you won't. Anyway, if the warrant arrived this afternoon," Martialis, said almost as if to himself, "why are you still alive?"

"I've only been arraigned so far. My case, it seems, is being tried this evening at the emperor's villa in Baiae, so the death sentence won't get here until dawn. Look, Marcus. I'm luckier than most, with this grace period. When they came for Seneca, he had to do it then and there; they didn't give him enough time to alter his will. Vestinus wasn't even allowed to finish his supper. I'll have had eighteen hours. It's unheard of, luxurious. All the omens are good, I've got all my papers in order, I've said most of my good-byes, I'll have plenty of time to do right by the household slaves. A sky full of stars, a fragrant breeze, a very special supper. All told, a beautiful night ahead."

"And open veins at dawn," Martialis spat bitterly.

"I don't imagine I'll wait 'til dawn. You know, Nero always sends his 'doctors' along with a sentence, just to make sure it's carried out. I don't want any of them scurrying around while I'm at it, it would spoil the whole thing for me. I'd like it to be done before they get here."

"But can you be sure they'll wait until daybreak?"

"I've thought of that already. Come. The others will be here by now."

Martialis froze in horror. "Surely you're not going through with this dinner tonight?"

"Of course I'm going through with it. Why do you think you're here? Do you think I'd give you exclusive rights to my last words, so you can turn them into tawdry doggerel?"

Martialis's eyes instantly brimmed over like a little boy's, and his lips contorted and quivered. A Roman would have turned away directly to hide his shame, but Martialis stood fast, like Horatio at the bridge, as if he were defending something. Petronius felt the boy's dignity as a rebuke. He'd thought he was simply making a joke, but perhaps after all he'd wanted to see the poet cry just a little more. He hadn't meant to be cruel, but if it was good for a man to be mourned with tears, how rare and wonderful to be alive to see them! In a house full of Roman patricians, he could hardly hope to see anyone else crying in the course of the evening. He'd take the tears where he could get them, even if grudgingly offered. And besides, why should he, tonight of all nights, have to spend himself in tenderness for others' feelings? Surely there would be time enough to resent him after he was gone?

"Look, Marcus," he began in a tone he'd once used when compelled to demote a favored centurion. "I'm sorry, but you must try to understand. I have to take this seriously. The way a man dies is just as important as the way he lives. I'm very lucky, compared to many, to have this chance. I'll only have one opportunity to get it right. What should I do? Crawl under a rock? Wait for them to chop my head off like some wretched brick-maker?"

Martialis's tears continued to flow, drenching the front of his tunic, blinding him, slopping from his nostrils, splashing hotly off his upper lip. But he stood his ground, silent and accusing.

"Come on, now," Petronius said, reaching for Martialis's arm, which the boy jerked away sullenly. "I won't argue with you. You will just have to accept that I am to die. Is it really so hard? Can your life really mean so much to you?"

"I would run naked into a bog of pig shit to preserve it."

"Would you? I doubt it. Is that how you would have yourself remembered? You, of all people? You're the most ambitious nonentity I've ever met. You spend every waking moment trying to make people think well of you."

"Yes, but I'll die in bed, not like some pantomime Hector with one eye on posterity and the other on his voice coach."

"I have no doubt you'll die in bed, Marcus, biographer at your side. That's all I ask for myself: the chance to choreograph a fitting death. Do you know how rare that is, and how fortunate I am to have it? Isn't it what we all dream of—the chance to prove to ourselves once and for all that we are the person we'd always imagined ourselves to be? I'd be a fool not to jump at it. You know you'd do the same."

The first cool breeze reached them from the open water, and the peace of dusk descended. The surf was no more now than the easy breath of a man asleep and dreaming in a sling at the far end of the orchard. A fire crackled, unseen, beyond the garden wall. The last of the swallows dropped from the purpling sky and disappeared beneath the outhouse eaves; the first bat emerged, bobbed along the rim of an invisible vortex, and plunged into the treetops. First and last, last and first: of what possible interest or comfort could it be to Petronius that this was the most perfect evening since the dawn of time? We grasp at the world's beauty and draw it into ourselves, metabolize it, store it up against future famine and blight. Now that Petronius had a surfeit of it, he had no further use for it; it had been leaking and oozing from him all day, this attenuated concentrate, despite his every effort to contain it. It was dripping and splattering upon everything he touched and felt and thought, his every memory become a saturated, tacky thing, unrecognizable and clinging, unmanageable. This was what he could not convey to Martialis, or to Melissa—he felt himself in immediate danger of melting away entirely into a pool of liquid self, and must keep cool above all things. He was like an orgiast who has overindulged and must find a way to ease his path to sleep—either he can purge himself or he must walk it off, calmly and deliberately. On this of all nights, explosive purging was no option, howsoever convenient and tempting.

The lamps came to life in the dining hall behind them, flinging their muddled shadows across the cove to the far shore, and Petronius and Martialis turned arm in arm for the house. As they turned, the very last ray of sunshine was sliding off the sulfurous ridge of Mount Gaurus, and was gone.

"I'll tell you why I'm irritated, Titus, and then have done with it."

"Tell me, boy."

"You can't possibly be as calm and philosophical as you pretend. I hate it that you feel the need to act for my benefit. I can't bear it"—Martialis's voice cracked, and he coughed into his tunic for a moment or two before recovering—"I can't bear it that you are going to die and that I am never going to see you again and that this is how I must remember you."

"You've seen me drunk, Marcus. You've seen me naked. You've seen me beat my slaves. You've seen me put on a donkey's head and act out Apicius. Why must you remember me this way?"

"Because this is how you want me to remember you. Because, if they ever come, it is to me that the historians will come to find out how you died."

"I'm not acting, Marcus, if that makes you feel any better. I've had my moments today, it's true, but I've found myself again. I can promise you, however, that if I were acting, or if I should start to weaken later, it would be for my own benefit, not yours. After all, I still have to see in All Fools' Day."

Petronius and Martialis climbed a flight of shallow stairs and stood at the broad threshold of the reception room, its glass doors thrown open to the breeze. They paused there to allow their eyes to adjust to the bright light reflected from a hundred lamps off the gleaming floor of white marble.

"Stay close," Petronius said. "You'll see how they are with me. No wailing or gnashing of teeth from this lot."

Petronius was pleased to note that none of his guests had come in formal wear. Toward the center of the room, Melissa stood chatting in casual intimacy with Anicius, Lucilius, and Cornelia, goblets in hand. The slaves Nereus and Persis waited off to the side with a pitcher of mixed wine and a platter of pickled olives and smelts. Petronius had taught them to wait until summoned, contrary to modern custom, beyond earshot of his guests' conversations—so that, in this one house, at least, in all of Italy, they should not feel spied upon—and he was gratified to see that they had not forgotten their duty, even on this evening when they would be itching to prepare for the night's festivities.

In the far corner, their backs to the room, Caeso Fabius Arvina and his wife, Pollia, were admiring the bronze Diana, their shoulders bowed as if in supplication. It was the young couple's first time in Petronius's house, and Fabius had spoken more than once of his reverence for the Rhodian masters.

"Where's your friend Castricus, Marcus?" Petronius asked Martialis.

"I don't know. He knew we were invited tonight. I combed the streets for him, but he seems to have vanished into thin air. He doesn't like to miss a free meal any more than I do—he'll be here."

"Perhaps."

They entered the room, and Martialis immediately headed for the wine bowl, where he was intercepted by Nereus as he attempted to help himself to a ladleful of undiluted Surrentine. Nodding to Lucilius as he passed, Petronius joined Fabius and Pollia. As he approached, he saw that they were whispering to each other furiously, evidently in passionate confabulation over the bronze. The name Praxiteles was being bandied about.

"Do you approve, Fabius?" Petronius asked, interposing himself between man and wife.

"It's magnificent," Fabius said in sublime awe. Pollia merely nodded. "Is it really Hagesander, do you think, Petronius?"

"I believe it is. I found it abandoned, so we can never be certain."

"Mightn't it be a Praxiteles?" Pollia ventured shyly, blushing and ducking her head.

"I don't think so, my dear. Note the hairstyle, for one. No one wore their hair like that in Athens four hundred years ago. And then, see the patina? Smell it. Go ahead, put your nose right up to it. Very distinctive smell, that Rhodian bronze."

"What do you mean, you found it?"

"Found it. A few years ago, Melissa and I took a pleasure cruise up the coast. When we stopped at Spelunca for lunch, we asked the innkeeper if anyone knew where Tiberius's villa had stood. Turned out everyone in the village knew, and for a few bronze coins his sons took us on a guided tour of the ruins. It was all there on the shore, in plain sight. The villagers had stripped the whole place of every inch of lead piping, precious fittings, gold leaf, everything of value but the artwork. They had

no use for statues. I recognized this masterpiece immediately—
Hagesander, maybe Athenodorus. Those ropey muscles, just like
the Laocoön. For a few more coins, we hired some men to carry
it down to the boat for us, just like that."

"Did you really see the Laocoön?"

"Yes, it's still there, a little damaged but essentially intact. A
little big to cart away, though. Someone resourceful will get their
hands on it one day, I'm sure."

Pollia sighed. "How I should like to see that. Perhaps you can
take us with you on your next trip, Petronius?"

Petronius smiled ruefully down at her. "I should like nothing
better, my dear, but I believe that was my last cruise to Spelunca."

"Oh, Petronius!" Simultaneously, like actors in a stage com-
edy, Fabius and Pollia raised their hands to cover their mouths,
while all the color drained from their faces. Pollia looked as if
she were about to be sick, and she turned her face to the wall in
shame. Fabius made as if to get down on his knees.

"No, Fabius, no."

"Petronius, I'm so sorry."

"Stop now. Listen to me, Fabius. And you too, Pollia." He
pulled them into a tight circle about him, his arms draped across
their backs, hands clasped to the napes of their necks so that
they might not attempt to pull away. He spoke in a low, calm
whisper. "There is to be none of that here tonight. Tonight we
are here to celebrate, do you hear me? There are to be no tears,
no speeches, no farewells. We are here to eat, to laugh, to joke,
to hear poetry if necessary. It is what I wish, and you must respect my wishes. And we have my young Spaniard tonight; he
is your age, Fabius. Let us please show him what a Roman can
do when he puts his mind to it. Set an example, yes? Fabius?
Pollia?"

They both nodded submissively, abashed, eyes to the floor.
The back of Pollia's neck was hot, and Petronius could feel it

prickling with a sudden nervous sweat. It excited him momentarily, as if she were making a coded assignation with him, but
the feeling evaporated as soon as it announced itself. He'd been
strongly attracted to her when they'd first met, not long before,
at an entertainment put on by Lucilius, but it had come to nothing when she'd rebuffed him with exquisite subtlety and courtesy. She was far more interesting and thoughtful than her
rather conventional husband, but she was properly demure with
her elders, giving a false first impression of mousiness that would
certainly confound many a blustering senator when he tried to
bed her in the coming years. Petronius was certain that she
would scorn the louts and—when marital fidelity had exhausted
its first blush of sanctity and sanctimony—give herself only to
men like himself, men of the mind and the deed, if only he were
there to enjoy her. He gave her neck a quick squeeze, and that
of Fabius as well for good measure.

"Now tell me, young ones, do you know everyone here?"

"We know no one," Fabius said forlornly.

"You will find it very useful in your career to know a man before you meet him. You see that chubby, jolly old man with the
gray hair and pigeon toes? That is the senator Decimus Anicius
Pulcher, a very dear friend of my father's youth. You wouldn't
know it to look at him, but he is one of the bravest and most
honest men in Rome. During the persecutions under Tiberius,
my father fell afoul of Sejanus and it was only a matter of time
before his troubles caught up with him. In the midst of all this,
Anicius gets up in the senate—he was lean and athletic in those
days, with a booming voice—and defends my father at great
peril to his own career and health. He saved my father's life, no
doubt about it, and if Sejanus hadn't been brought down himself shortly afterward, there'd have been hell to pay for both of
them. My father died young, of fever, and Anicius took me under his wing, protected me, taught me everything I know about

being a man. He's rather given himself over to the pleasures of the flesh these days—he has a particular weakness for young boys—but I suppose he's earned it. Melissa worships him.

"The gaunt, ramrod fellow with the cropped hair is Gaius Lucilius Junior, the great Neapolitan lawyer. He came to Rome as a boy; that's where we met. We were inseparable, even as children. Studied Greek, rhetoric, and arms together, assumed the toga together, had our first whore together. He was the emperor's procurator in Sicily, and if you ask him very humbly he may read to you from the poem he's writing on the origins of volcanic activity. He's quiet, but don't let that fool you. Quite incredibly wealthy now, thanks to his marriage to Cornelia Felicia. That's her with the dyed hair and the bangles. Society lady, a little frivolous, no intellectual, but generous and compassionate and absolutely devoted to Lucilius.

"The other fellow, that scruffy boy with his face in the wine bowl, that's my client Marcus Valerius Martialis, a poet. Spanish."

Petronius, Fabius, and Pollia crossed the room. Melissa, Anicius, Lucilius, and Cornelia were laughing gaily over something as he approached. Cornelia was in blue with gold trimmings. She was dripping with pink sapphires and heliodor, and had dyed her hair mulberry red; it gleamed like unction in the lamplight. Martialis was with them, and joined in their laughter, but even from halfway across the room Petronius could see that his was forced, uneasy, as if he were trying to follow a joke in a foreign language. Petronius dearly hoped that poor Marcus would find his way into the spirit of things over the course of the evening, as it would be very tiresome if he were to require continuous cajoling. Petronius thought that Marcus, notwithstanding his provincial upbringing, had it in him to rise above his own emotional failings, but he couldn't be certain. After all, he hadn't even been certain of himself until an hour ago, so how could he possibly trust Marcus to behave?

At the same time, Marcus had been right about one thing: with all his literary connections, it was surely to him that the historians would come for a firsthand account of the death of Petronius. What if Marcus should speak out in anger and resentment? Although Petronius was confident of Marcus's love and loyalty, in one of his hot-blooded snits the boy was perfectly capable of doing lasting, even permanent damage to Petronius's reputation with a skewed account of the evening. A man's reputation is a delicate vase, vulnerable in equal measure to the malice of enemies, the prurience of strangers, and the clumsiness of friends. Petronius would be very sorry indeed if, for the sake of a well-turned phrase, Marcus in a fit of pique should throw a memorable epithet at him and it stuck, the way Tubero the Stoic had ensured that the courageous, honorable, and self-effacing Lucullus would be forever remembered as "Xerxes in a toga."

"There you are, Petronius," Lucilius said warmly, drawing him in with an arm about his shoulders. "We've just been laughing at you behind your back."

"Have you really? What have I done this time?"

"It's not you, actually," said Cornelia. "It's this funny little village you live in."

"What's wrong with Cumae?"

"It's so . . . Greek."

"Ah, you mean Greek like Homer and Plato? Or Greek like Euripides and Epicurus?"

"No, I mean the horrid sort of Greek. Greek fishermen. Greek vendettas. Do you know, as we were coming up from Bauli today, we ran into a nasty crowd on the main street. There was a poor woman on a mule, and they were taunting and tormenting her as they drove her through the village. They were all screaming at her."

"*Onobatis.*"

"Precisely—'donkey-mounted.' We were told she'd been taken in adultery. It was savage, backwards. You know, passing through those myrtle groves and sulfur pools from Baiae, it's as if one were stepping into another century. It's as if the Etruscans were never defeated."

"Vatia lived here quite happily. So did Cicero."

"Cicero hated it here, and you know it," Martialis said testily.

"In any case, Cornelia, if all those red-necked, Greek-speaking fishermen keep you vulgar rich out of Cumae, I'm all for them. The last thing I want to see is Cumae become another Baiae."

"No fear of that. There isn't even a decent dressmaker here."

"What's in the basket, Cornelia?"

"Oh, I'd quite forgotten. I've brought you some candles and figurines for the holiday."

"How thoughtful. I'll have Persis distribute them to the slaves." Petronius held the basket out at arm's length, and a slave stepped up from behind to seize and spirit it away.

With a sweep of his arm, Petronius gathered Fabius and Pollia into the circle. "Have you all met Fabius Arvina and Julia Pollia?"

"My congratulations on your election," Lucilius said, bowing. "We hear promising things of you in the courts, sir."

"Thank you, sir."

Petronius made the introductions. Martialis circled the group and surreptitiously sniffed at Pollia's hair behind her back. Petronius threw him a fierce, fleeting scowl, which Martialis returned with a cross-eyed grimace.

"Senator."

"Quaestor."

Commagenus appeared silently at Petronius's side.

"Vellia wishes to inform you that supper is served," he whispered. Petronius nodded.

"Have they all buggered off for the holiday?" Cornelia inquired.

Petronius looked at her in alarm. It was dangerous enough that her husband had been a close friend of Seneca's; far riskier, however, that she should still be affecting the coarse mannerisms of the emperor's late wife, Poppaea Sabina, almost two years after her death. In this day and age, such insensitivity to the shifting nuances of court fashion was more than enough to destroy a career, or worse. Petronius made a mental note to raise the issue with Lucilius before the evening was out.

"Yes," he said, touching her lightly below the elbow to turn and guide her toward the door. "They've buggered off for the revels and left us to fend for ourselves. I do hope you won't mind carving the boar."

"I'd gut him with my bare teeth for a taste of Lucullo's sow's vulva."

"That's the only reason you're here, isn't it? You people disgust me, you really do. Still, I think you'll be pleased."

Petronius and Cornelia glided toward the door, and the others followed, making a cheerful noise. But at the top of the stairs, they paused and gasped collectively. Even Petronius himself, who had given the orders, could not help but be impressed.

At the center of the terrace, the great pergola of Lebanese cedar had been hung with garlands of fragrant melilot entwined with roses, drooping between the crossbars and spiraling down the posts. Chains of silver bore crystal lamps like sparkling fruit, twinkling and winking among the viburnum, shrouded in the smoke rising from censors of myrrh and filtering through the leafy canopy, twisting off into braids that climbed and vanished on a steady, gentle breeze into the cloudless night. A sliver of yellow moon quivered over Pithecusa. The air was laced with thyme, incense, and burning fennel.

Beneath the pergola, the great semicircular dining couch had been prepared for nine, overlaid with mattresses, cushions, and a single vast counterpane of purple silk embroidered with gold and silver thread, which glowed and pulsed in the crystalline lamplight. The couch was sheltered from the wind on two sides by a great hinged scrim of Nile reeds, painted and lacquered in gleaming scarlet with Egyptian motifs, that Petronius's great-grandfather was said to have procured from the household of Cleopatra during his prefecture of Egypt. The surface of the water table, an ornamental pool at the axis of the couch, was afloat with small ceramic dishes and lamps in the form of pleasure craft and waterfowl; the dishes, nudged toward the diners' side by a plashing fountain, held mounds of olives, nuts, and relish. Larger bronze platters rested on the basin's edge, heaped with cold steamed fish, raw oysters and vinegar on beds of crushed ice, the roast eggs of songbirds, and figpeckers baked in peppered egg yolk. Nine slaves, one per diner, stood at the ready around the couch to help the guests with their sandals and provide them with napkins and goblets.

Melissa was at his side, resting gently against him. He put his arm around her waist and spoke to her in a whisper.

"Are we not to have any time to talk in private?"

"Are you sure that's what you want, Titus?" she replied. "You've had me to yourself all week and done nothing about it."

"I need . . . I've needed to find the right words to say to you."

"I'll be here when you've found them." And she moved on down to where Lucilius awaited her with outstretched arm. Petronius followed her with his eyes. Was it that she'd changed so much since that day, eight years earlier, when they'd met in the ruined merchant's house, or that she'd changed not at all?

ᘘᘘᘘᘘᘘᘘ

PETRONIUS SQUINTED INTO the dark shadows of the peristyle, and was just able to discern the silhouette of a cloaked woman. She stepped into the courtyard, but the light was failing there, too, and he could make out no distinguishing features of her face.

"Who are you?" he demanded sharply.

"An art lover, like you," she said somberly.

"What are you doing here?"

"What are *you* doing here, Governor?"

"You know me?"

"Everybody in Prusa knows everybody else. You're the only man in Prusa I don't know, so you must be the governor."

She was an Italian, with a powerful Cisalpine accent, perhaps from Mutina or Verona. Petronius thought she might be a whore, especially given her impudent way of answering questions with questions. Perhaps he had interrupted an assignation—this dismal relic would certainly offer a discreet trysting spot in a town where privacy was at a premium—and her client was lying low somewhere nearby, waiting for an opportune moment to make his escape. And yet it seemed unlikely that an Italian whore should have found her way to this dreary provincial city. That she was of the lower classes, in any case, was perfectly clear. Petronius took her for a soldier's wife.

"I ask you again: What are you doing here?"

"There are few enough places in this city where a woman can go to be alone with her thoughts. Now there's one less."

"Why should a respectable woman need to be alone with her thoughts?"

"Why should the ruler of a great Roman province spend his afternoons dreaming among the ruins?"

"I'll escort you to the barracks."

"Thank you, Governor."

They walked through the darkened streets, instinctively choosing the smaller and less frequented ways, neither of them wishing to be recognized, either individually or in each other's company, though it would have made little difference in any case, as the town was as vacant and silent as if it had been evacuated before an oncoming army. Every so often, they passed beneath a torch or lamp placed at important intersections, and as they did he would turn to get a better look at her. She kept her head down and held the hood of her cloak tightly beneath her chin, so he had to be content with fleeting glimpses. She was not young, perhaps in her late twenties, but her posture was upright and strong, her gait confident in the incongruous fur boots she wore—swag, no doubt, from one of her husband's campaigns in the north. Her hair appeared to be the lightest brown, almost blond, and her full lips, though somewhat dry and cracked, betrayed a kind of erotic or sensual disdain. Her nose was small and sloped, a legacy of the Gallic invasions of centuries past.

Her name was Melissa Silia. Her husband was Aulus Junius, a centurion of the local cohort, attached to the Fourth Scythian. Petronius knew it by reputation, a legion despised by the high command for its laxity and want of fighting spirit. Aulus had seen some action in Illyria and Pannonia, and had risen through the ranks on the basis of plodding, brutal competence, but since then had been posted from one dismal backwater to the next. He and his wife had lived in Prusa for the past three years; it would probably be his last posting, as he was to retire within eighteen months. He had not yet decided whether to settle on his allotment on the River Savus in Illyria, there to raise beans and cabbage, or to sell the allotment and return to his family cooperage in Cremona. The couple had no children.

All this she told Petronius with detached candor, as if providing the biographical background of a stranger at a judicial inquiry. It came pouring out of her unbidden, and yet, for all her frankness, there was something hard about her, something that had been damaged long ago and poorly reset. She didn't need to tell him how miserable her life was—that came through eloquently just in the cold facts—or that she held her husband in haughty disdain. It would have been improbable, Petronius imagined, to endure a life one hated for so long and not to develop calluses. He sensed that he was not the first stranger to whom she had related this story. It came out of her almost as if by rote, the way a refugee might tell the tale of her lost family to every passer-by, in the forlorn hope of hitting on that one in a million who had relevant information. It was also as if she didn't fully grasp the significance of the accumulated facts—as if, were she to explain them patiently enough to all who would listen, someone out there would finally be able to tell her what they meant. That was it—she seemed to be in shock, unable to absorb the enormity of the disaster that had befallen her. Petronius had seen civilians behave that way in warfare, following the destruction of their community and family.

She told him that she was the daughter of a Cremona cooper who had married her off to the son of his rival in the hope of consolidating their businesses and monopolizing the local trade. Her new husband, ambitious but stupid, had instead joined the military shortly thereafter, with forlorn dreams of glory. In his absence, she had gone to live with her in-laws, who had treated her with bullying contempt, more like a slave than a daughter. She had been lively and flighty then, and had begged her own father to take her back, to no avail. Ultimately, and against all odds, her husband had been promoted again and again, having been consigned to the ninth cohort of his legion, the weakest and therefore the one from which the ablest soldiers were transferred elsewhere. When he was promoted to centurion, he sent for her, and she had lived in military barracks ever since. He had seen no action in many years, and thus had had no opportunity to enrich himself on booty, his dreams of glory faded to dull anticipation of a comfortable retirement.

All who are born poor believe they were born for something better, that some mistake has been made. She never once suggested that she was more sensitive, more artistic, or more recep-tive than her peers, but it seemed obvious that she must have been. What kind of soldier's wife moons about in ruined court-yards over ancient statuary? Either she was incubating her dreams, or she was mourning them.

She did not say what had become of those dreams; she didn't need to. She had no education to speak of, and was somewhat vulgar of speech, but a ferocious intellect blazed in every word she uttered. Having been raised with no great expectations above her sex and station had not prevented her from being bitterly disappointed in life. She was bright enough to recog-nize that her misery, having failed to devolve into resignation or blindered complacency, remained her saving grace. Miracu-lously, after all these years, she still seemed to cling to some desperate scrap of hope that something might yet be salvaged from the debacle, and as a result she was afraid of nothing. Why else would she be walking through the dark streets with a total stranger?

They walked in silence for some time, Petronius awed and en-chanted by her body language and tone of voice, to which he paid the closest attention. She seemed to be telling him all this not in any attempt to elicit his sympathy, but rather simply because he was there, a convenient sounding board for private thoughts that had outgrown their confinement. It was unlikely that she had anyone in her personal life in whom to confide them, but then again, how unusual it would be to find someone, anyone, of her Stoic thoughtfulness in a provincial military outpost.

"You've given this a great deal of thought," he said finally.

She shook her head and dropped her shoulders. "I have a great deal of time on my hands."

"And how have you determined to resolve your dilemma?"

Again she shook her head. "I don't understand your question, Governor."

"What are you going to do about it, Melissa Silia?"

She laughed, and a spark of lamplight glanced off a white tooth. "I'm not stupid, Governor. I know what you asked me; I just don't know how you could ask it. What would you expect me to do, a thousand miles from home, a woman with nothing but her good name to protect her? Should I seek a divorce, do you mean, and somehow find my way back to Cremona, where no one wants me?"

Petronius thought he knew what she might do, but her questions had been purely rhetorical.

She went on coolly, unruffled. "As it happens, I have already resolved my dilemma. I resolve it anew every day, by taking refuge in my own thoughts and milking the consolations of philosophy."

"Is that why you are speaking so brazenly to me?"

She stopped in her tracks and looked up at him, but still he could make little of her face in the dark.

"Am I brazen? I suppose I am. You seem like a nice man."

Now it was Petronius's turn to laugh. "If that's all it takes," but he held back when he sensed that he had offended her. "Forgive me."

"That's all right. It doesn't change anything."

They went on again in silence, and by the time they began to slow their pace as they neared the barracks, Petronius was smitten. He would offer himself as her lover and give her a new life, a new future. Not now, but soon; she should not think him impetuous, or profligate in his gifts, or lightly enamored. Let her know that he was not the same as other men, that he was more than "nice," that he had come to save her. How sweet would her gratitude be; how well he would reward it!

They stopped some few blocks from the camp gates; she would go the rest of the way by herself. There came the faintest glow from a kitchen hearth through the chink in a curtain; he positioned her so that it fell on her face. It was not much, but it was the best sense of her features he had yet had. She seemed to him to be very beautiful, her cheeks rosy from the cold, her eyes glistening. She lifted her face to his and he knew that she would let him kiss her if he wanted to, fuck her right there in the doorway, as she'd surely done before with other strangers generous enough to listen to her story. Instead, he bowed, wished her well, and walked away.

ℜℜℜℜℜℜ

AS HE SHEPHERDED his guests down the steps and across the terrace, Petronius was pleased above all that the weather had held so nicely, allowing them to eat outdoors in mid-December. The formalities of indoor dining would have made it so much harder to establish the kind of relaxed intimacy he sought for the evening, and that came so much more naturally to Asian than to Italian gatherings. A dinner party is like a river, Petronius thought; it must be allowed to flow, to reconfigure itself, to rise and fall within the shifting banks of conversation and conviviality. Sometimes it may be slow and lazy; at other times it may rush headlong and reckless through treacherous shoals, perhaps even claiming a victim or two. But to contain it within the rigid conventions of a formal Roman dining room and its hierarchical seating assignments is to tame that river, to make it a soulless canal. There are occasions when that becomes necessary, but this night was not one of them. On the outdoor dining couch, a broad and open sigma, none was higher than any other—all heads pointed toward the center, the axis, all congeniality focused, all sense of status erased. Decorum was Hermes, not Zeus. After a few drinks, they would all be children again, lying together on a communal bed, careless and conspiratorial on a mattress shaped like the new moon—the moon of the Saturnalia, All Fools' Moon.

Petronius could sense a great feeling of happiness, radiating like a low-burning fire. Privilege; satiety; gratified expectations of elegance, poetry, and justice; incuriosity rewarded—these were the components of what his peers called happiness. It was what they were feeling now—the weather and the sea and Mercury, the Cumaean god of commerce, were cooperative, equal participants in the evening's pleasures, nothing more and nothing less than expected. This was Petronius's knowledge of happiness, too. And if, for the merest moment, he allowed that it was lazy, or false, or impious to entertain the imposture, it was a self-correcting imbalance, like a water clock, that never allowed movement to overtake it. The thought was there, and it was gone; even when it lingered, as it lingered now, long enough to register, it registered only as a shadow of itself, as we note the bird flying above us by its shadow underfoot, and when we look up it has gone. Petronius's guests were happy; more importantly, if asked, they would have identified themselves as happy; and therefore Petronius was happy.

"Shall we?" With one arm lightly encircling the waist of Cornelia, the ranking matron, he led them down the stairs. At the bottom, Martialis was waiting in his borrowed tunic with a worried look on his face. He had evidently gone on ahead to fret and pace in the darkness. He hardly bothered to lower his voice as he waylaid the party.

"When are you going to tell them? They have a right to know."

"Tell us what, Petronius?" Cornelia perked up.

"The menu, my dear." And to Martialis: "They already know, Marcus. Please don't bring it up again. Now come with me." Petronius hooked him with his free arm and led him, mute and unresisting, to the dining couch. There, the group dissolved, some moving to the left, others to the right as they flowed around the couch and sought their natural places. As each sat on the edge of the mattress, assigned slaves deftly removed and stowed his or her sandals. The guests draped themselves across the couch so that, in a moment, each reclined on his or her left elbow, facing the center, in positions that corresponded precisely to those they would have assumed in the dining room: Martialis and Melissa to the left, in the family places, with the third position left open for Petronius; Anicius, Cornelia, and Lucilius in the places of honor; then Fabius and Pollia on the right, in the places of lesser prestige, leaving the seventh position empty for the missing guest.

Petronius muttered a rote invocation of the gods, and the dinner was officially under way.

"Who is our absent ninth, Petronius?" Lucilius inquired, spitting an olive stone into his fist and dropping it onto the marble ledge of the water table. Petronius remained standing, like a chorus master, at the opposite side of the basin.

"It was to have been Martialis's bosom companion, Lucius Castricus, but the rumors sweeping through Baiae seem to have swept him right off the coast. He is not to be found. I believe he intends to leave us in the lurch."

"For shame."

"Poor form."

"What have you done, Petronius?" Martialis barked, glaring into his goblet. "Have you mixed perfectly good Surrentine with Vatican rotgut? You may have no respect for your guests, but surely so precious a vintage did not deserve to be slaughtered?"

The remark drew a general chuckle that very nearly masked the discomfort of Martialis's palpable anger and embarrassment over his absconded friend. Castricus had clearly been scared off by the threat that hung over the evening. Petronius could hardly blame him. He smiled indulgently, aware that, with the evening now officially launched, posterity was watching and potentially recording his every move. He was also acutely conscious of the irony of having a biographer who mocked him and theatrically indulged his own grievances. He smiled, but he worried: he couldn't very well remind Martialis explicitly of his duty to pay attention, could he, or compel him to be of better cheer?

"Before you malign the wine, Marcus," he said, "you may be interested to know that it was laid up in the consulship of Lucius Apronius Caesianus, and is therefore a year older and considerably more mature than you. Mellower, too, one hopes. Also, it is not Surrentine, but Falernian, from vineyards that belong to this very estate."

Martialis smiled bitterly. "Is it Petronius we dine with this evening, or is it Lucullus?" He was not, apparently, in a forgiving mood, and Petronius decided to ignore him for a while and see what that might do to improve it. He took an oyster and a slice of citron from a passing tray, and watched the creature shrink from the spray of acidic juice. Then he slipped it from its shell and held it on his tongue, allowing his mouth to fill with the vapors of brine and live flesh. He was pleased to find that the intense pleasure of raw shellfish, a tiny package of squirming life unadulterated by the ubiquitous putridity of garum and asafoetida, was one he was still able to enjoy.

He stepped back, out of the coronet of light, to observe the gathering of those with whom he had chosen to spend his final hours. They were being swarmed over now by slaves bearing trays of food, wine, and shaved ice, but they were alone among themselves, as Romans were everywhere and at all times. They leaned into each other, as if connected by invisible filaments, not of love, but of hunger, the way baby birds strain open-mouthed toward their mother. Were they friends? Petronius was reminded of another dinner—had it only been eight years since? In Tigranocerta, in Armenia, during a brief lull in the fighting, General Corbulo had entertained a delegation of Parthian noblemen, and invited Petronius to attend. He had been fighting the Parthians for some time now, and had killed any number of them, but had never seen them up close in a relaxed social setting. The men held hands when they walked. They rarely spoke to each other without touching, at the elbow, at the waist, at the shoulder. They would often reach out, grasp their companion's head, and pull him in so as to whisper intimately in his ear, as if they were lovers. Petronius had never seen Romans behave that way. Lucilius had been Seneca's intimate for many years, the recipient of many confidences, but Petronius had never seen them touch. Here were seven Romans lying on a couch together, all with much in common despite differences in age. If one were to ask them about the nature of friendship, they would be able to quote the appropriate Greeks with easy familiarity; if one were to ask them who their friends were, they would answer without hesitation. If one were to invite them to play a game, in which they were required to name those they would invite to attend to them as they lay dying, they would thrill at the challenge and clamor for the first try. Petronius himself, a week earlier, would probably have named precisely these people here before him tonight, confident that each would be in Baiae for the season. And here they were, as if by magic, so how was it that he suddenly felt a longing for the company of his steward and his chef? What were Commagenus and Lucullo doing at this very moment? The thought of Commagenus reminded Petronius of the task he must attend to before he could join the party in earnest. He slipped away and found his steward waiting for him in a small guest bedroom at the end of a quiet hallway.

At the bedside table, a single lamp was lit. Its golden orb of wavering light left the corners of the room in darkness, but shone upon a set of items on the tabletop: a brass wine krater, embossed with Olympic scenes; a thick wad of Egyptian cotton, combed free of seeds; a roll of linen bandages; the golden-hilted dagger which Corbulo had presented to Petronius in personal recognition of his contribution to the destruction of Volandum. Petronius had never yet drawn blood with the gift. He picked it up and bounced it in his palm, assessing its weight and balance, and sat at the edge of the bed. The hilt glowed like a living thing in the lamplight, all coiled energy like a panther crouching to strike. He closed his fingers around it, dousing the glow.

"Let's try not to be too messy about this, Commagenus. There's still a long evening ahead," he said. The steward bowed and stood at hand, a towel draped across his forearm.

Petronius held his left wrist over the krater, tilted at a slight angle, and the dagger at the artery. It would have been far more efficient, he knew, to open the vessel at the elbow, but that would not have served his plans for the evening. He also had to take care not to sever the artery entirely, but merely to slice into it, and to that purpose he had tested the blade earlier against a leather strop and found it good. This action he was about to undertake, he had seen it done countless times by friends, fellow soldiers, and enemy captives; in his mind's eye, like any Roman aristocrat, he had so often rehearsed his own turn at it that it now seemed perfectly natural, part of a daily routine, like shaving. He nodded at Commagenus, who moved forward to drape the towel across his lap. He pushed the blade into the skin and pulled back smartly—again, as he had done countless times at the throats of his enemies. There was no pain worth noting. The blood began to flow in controlled spurts into the krater. There was some minor spattering at first off the bottom of the bowl, but the towel spared his tunic.

This was not bad. There was no fear, only detachment at the

sight of his own life's blood filling the bowl. That was how he knew it would be, that there could be no failure of resolve. But his spirit was still troubled, his mind hot and restless—the serenity and acceptance he had sought all day were still missing, and that was not how it should be. He ought by now to have been able to let it all go, the doubts, the questioning, the clinging to unresolved desires and ideas. What a man of his age and accomplishments had yet to answer for, he could not imagine; and still his mind was behaving as if it had further work to do. Physically, he had long since been prepared; the spiritual did not interest him, as he did not believe in the immortality of the soul; but emotionally, he had been surprised and disappointed to learn that day, he was as unripe for this departure as if he'd never picked up a philosophy book in his entire life. His thoughts were muddled, fervid, tumbling over one another like water in a cataract, when they ought to be gentle and softly flowing now like a broad river emptying itself into the sea after the long journey from its source. "He who understands the limits of life knows that it is easy to obtain that which removes the pain of want and makes the whole of life complete and perfect. Thus he has no longer any need of things which involve struggle," Epicurus had said. Petronius had expected that the distraction of hosting the dinner would lift him from this mire of confusion, but he'd been wrong. Fortunately, there was time left to remedy the situation.

Petronius knew from experience and experiment that a soldier on the battlefield generally dies if he loses more than three or four pints of blood from a gushing wound. By that calculation, he figured that he could afford to drain about one pint every two hours over the course of the evening before he became seriously incapacitated and was forced to take leave of his guests. Having tested the krater earlier, he'd found that one pint of liquid reached to the javelin held horizontally at the shoulder of an Olympic athlete embossed on the side. His blood had reached that level now, and he nodded to Commagenus, who waited with the cotton and bandage. The steward knelt at Petronius's feet and pressed a thick wad of cotton to his wound. It bloomed bright red even in the few moments it took to wrap the bandage around his wrist and bind it tightly. They both stared intently at the dressing; neither knew what would happen next. If it failed, Petronius would be dead within minutes and the dinner would have to be interrupted, the loved ones summoned for a hasty, unsatisfactory good-bye. If it held as planned, the festivities could go on all night, if need be, with no farewells necessary at all. They waited, Commagenus every bit as focused on the binding as if it had been his own wrist. After a minute or so, when it became clear that the flow of blood had been successfully stanched, Commagenus exhaled an almost inaudible snort of relief through his nostrils.

"Good," Petronius said. "Now I want you to fetch Syrus, Demetrius, Hermes, Lilia, Vellia, and Lucullo in here. Be quick about it. I have guests waiting for me." Commagenus bowed and fled.

As a soldier, Petronius was gratified when a well-laid plan was executed efficiently and effectively. This one, to all appearances, was proceeding as foreseen. He had long known—long before the date of his death had been fixed—that he should die at the table, as it were, and not on the dais, as so many with intellectual pretensions had done and would continue to do. Far better to die with saffron than with rhetoric on one's lips. Lucan had botched his own suicide entirely, ridiculously reciting from his own mediocre epic poetry, making a fool of himself for all eternity. Seneca had done little better—it was still hard to believe that he'd actually had the gall to bequeath to his friends "my sole but fairest possession: the image of my life"—but he'd been lucky enough to have an excellent and loyal wife to doctor the account for posterity. Still, in all fairness, they had stayed in character: lived as orators, died as orators. And Petronius, known throughout Italy as a purveyor of exquisitely elegant entertainments, felt that at the very least a similar conformity was required of him. If one had a reputation, however unfair, as a debauchee, people would be puzzled and skeptical if one were said to have died as a Stoic. Ultimately, they might doubt or reject the account given of one's death, and then one's name would die with one's body. In a culture of fame and imagery, there can be no ambiguity—the people's expectations must be met—if posterity is to pay any attention whatsoever. Glory is most often said to be won, but Petronius suspected that it was generally the outcome of negotiation and compromise.

Petronius sat at the edge of the bed, staring into the half-full krater. How easy it must be to give a speech and then fall on one's sword, and yet how often it is botched. His own was, by far, the harder option: to entertain one's friends, to ensure their happiness and satisfaction throughout the evening in accordance with the sacred duties of hospitality, to see to every detail as if it were an ordinary Saturnalia banquet, and simultaneously to stage-manage one's own suicide. Had it ever been done before? And should he pull it off, would posterity recognize the astounding feat for what it was? True, it would have been far easier to wait until his guests had retired for the evening before opening his veins, but that would not have been the public death befitting a man of his stature. And, should Nero prove too impatient to wait until morning, and send his cutthroats to interrupt the entertainment, as he'd done to poor Vestinus, the entire effect would be spoiled. But if they should arrive and find the suicide already in progress, they would be more likely to leave him and his guests in peace to see it through with dignity

and decorum. Even the emperor and his thugs were able to recognize the public relations value in that.

A cough at the door alerted him to the slaves' arrival, and
Petronius found that he had been slumped over like a drunk,
staring at the floor between his knees. He resumed military posture, back straight, chest out, palms on thighs.

"Come," he said.

The slaves shuffled in and stood in a line by the door. The
room was small and dark, but meeting them in here allowed
Petronius to keep his voice low, out of earshot of the rest of the
household. Several of the slaves stared at the bandage, yet by now
they must surely all have known precisely what was going on and
why they had been summoned. It was a difficult position for
them, Petronius understood—these, his most senior slaves, might
reasonably expect to be granted their freedom tonight, the sole
shining ambition of their lives achieved, and at the same time
would feel obliged to make a show of sorrow at their master's
death. He looked at each in turn. Would any of them actually feel
any grief? Petronius found it extremely hard to imagine that,
in their position, he should be feeling anything but elation and
impatience. He decided to make it brief and to the point; why
force them into a dumb show that neither performer nor audience would appreciate? The burdens of freedom and self-reliance
would assert themselves soon enough, a whole new wardrobe of
sorrows for a new life. He cleared his throat. When he spoke, he
was surprised to find his voice piping, his breath forced.

"Each of you is granted his freedom upon my death, which
will certainly come before dawn. Until then, you remain on
duty. In the strongbox in my study there is a sealed scroll and a
purse for each of you. The scroll contains your articles of freedom, the purse your five percent manumission tax. When I am
dead, the lawyer Gaius Lucilius will inform each of you in turn
of your inheritance. Some receive property, others cash. Please

do not importune him in any way until the reading of the will. Now you may return to your work."

Petronius slid his right hand down his thigh to his knee. One by one, the slaves stepped forward, knelt before him, and kissed his signet ring. They had all shared their moments of ostensible intimacy with him, exchanges in which an outside observer might be uncertain about the nature of the relationship that bound them, but master and slave understood that no exchange of improper intimacies was required here. Even Vellia, who had served in his father's pantry and known Petronius since the day he was born, as she struggled to her knees offered nothing more personal than a fleeting, kindly smile and a kiss prolonged and emphasized just briefly beyond the strictly formal. Only when it came to the turn of the scribe Demetrius, who made his obeisance with water on his eyes, did Petronius fear that the decorum of the moment was in danger of being compromised. Perhaps this was only natural. Demetrius had, after all, been privy to Petronius's most private thoughts. Demetrius might be justified in believing that his master was a man, with all a man's feelings and regrets, who might be worth a moment's mourning. Despite himself, Petronius was touched. He leaned forward to whisper into the slave's ear as he kissed his ring.

"Did you have something you wanted to say to me, Demetrius?"

But as Demetrius pulled back and rose to his feet, Petronius saw only fear in his pale green eyes. It was the fear of a man who has crossed an ancient, swaying footbridge over a yawning chasm, only to stumble on the final step. The slave had misunderstood the question, taking it as the prelude to a rebuke that might somehow jeopardize his manumission and inheritance. Petronius saw that, had Demetrius been feeling even the least portion of compassion, such a misunderstanding would have been impossible. There was never any danger that Petronius would be mourned by the freedman Demetrius.

"Never mind, never mind," Petronius muttered, immediately turning toward the approaching Lucullo in order to give Demetrius a chance to slip away, no doubt to his great relief.

A minute later, Petronius found himself alone again. It was time to return to the dinner. It was not his way to play absentee host, and they would be wondering what had become of him. First, he needed to assess his physical condition before standing. His wrist was throbbing, but certainly no worse than the myriad minor wounds he had sustained in battle over the years. His left hand was slightly numb from the pressure of the dressing, but that would have to be tolerated. His mouth was dry and his head ached; that could soon be remedied with a glass of wine sweetened with honey. There seemed to be plenty of strength left in his limbs, enough at any rate to return under his own power to the terrace and his guests. He suspected that, once he'd found his place on the dining couch, he'd be fully capable of assuming all his functions with his customary vigor and charm. He stood slowly, found that he was not as light-headed as he'd feared, and doused the lamp.

He paused a moment at the top of the steps leading down to the terrace. The dining couch faced away from the house and toward the sea; the guests were unaware of his presence behind them. Gentle tides of quiet, sophisticated conversation and muted laughter lapped up against the steps, interrupted here and there by an eruption of hilarity. Slaves were clearing away the first course of light dishes in preparation for the meat course, setting replenished dishes of relish and white bread afloat on the water table, trimming lamp wicks, and wiping clean the basin's edge with sprigs of green mint. At this distance, there was no distinguishing the scene from any other small dinner he had given over the course of the years. This was how he had wanted it; in his hastily scrawled invitations, he had explicitly enjoined his guests to behave as if this were an ordinary event, to avoid morbid sentiment and to remain light of heart; above all, no tears or farewells. Confident that these were all people who would take his instructions to heart, he had been concerned only that the atmosphere might be tainted by forced gaiety and hollow mirth, but now he saw that he need not have worried. They were genuinely enjoying themselves, going about the business of being Roman nobles with their customary ease and self-possession. Petronius smiled weakly and told himself that he was well pleased. He descended to join the diners.

There was a brief lull as Petronius took his place at the rear of the dining couch while Commagenus removed his sandals and Nereus poured a flagon of cold water over his hands. Persis stood by with a goblet of honey-sweetened Gaulish retsina strained through a colander of snow; he waited until his master had reclined between Melissa and Anicius before handing it to him. Leaning upon his left elbow, Petronius sought to obscure the sight of the dressing on his wrist, but without a toga it was impossible to hide entirely. He caught several of his friends glancing at it momentarily before looking away, as if it were a shameful infirmity. Melissa subtly rearranged her shawl so that it fell across Petronius's bandaged arm.

"That's a lovely tunic you're wearing, Petronius," Cornelia said gaily. "And what a delightful color."

"It's new on the market in Naples. Baetic wool."

"From my part of the world," Martialis said dully.

"I expect everyone in Baiae and Puteoli will be wearing them soon. You know how they are."

"Yes, I know," Petronius said. "But please, don't let me interrupt the conversation. What were you saying just now when I arrived?"

There was a hesitant, almost guilty pause, as if they were schoolchildren who had been caught in slander, and yet Petronius was quite certain that they had merely been engaged in the usual vapid gossip about politics, writers, or real estate. He popped a dormouse into his mouth and ground its tiny bones between his molars. An unction of warm honey and lightly toasted poppy seeds coated his palate, entirely obliterating whatever little taste the dormouse itself brought to the combination. He had been eating these crunchy little treats his entire life, yet had never been able to fathom their popularity, other than the coarse, visceral pleasure of eating anything fried crispy. He silently vowed never to eat another.

"We were discussing the problem of finding a decent house at a decent price in Baiae," Anicius Pulcher said sheepishly.

"Ah, yes."

"No, it's true," said Fabius. "There's nothing to be had on the bay for less than two million anymore. Unless you're willing to settle for a fisherman's hut or a tenement brothel."

"It's getting so you'll have to look in Pompeii for something affordable."

"Without a water view."

"Or Cumae."

"God forbid."

"I'll ask again," Petronius broke in. "What do you people have against Cumae? It's a picturesque, old-fashioned seaside village—the kind everybody claims to be looking for."

"It is not, Petronius," Anicius said. "It's a dark, forbidding, superstitious place, with its tunnels and its sybil and its tumble-down necropolis. You can't find an oyster in the marketplace for love or money. The stench of sulfur in the air and water makes you think you've relocated to the underworld. Plus, with only one road in and one road out, the traffic is always backed up at the gates, especially during the season. Of course, *your* place is charming, Petronius, so long as one stays on the grounds."

"And tell me again, Anicius, what it is you love so much about Baiae? Is it the drunken beach parties every night? Is it the ridiculously high prices fetched in the market for all your imported delicacies? Is it the crush of yachts so thick you can barely reach your mooring? Is it the unholy groveling before the season's celebrity caterer? Or is it the fact that, with prices so high, none of the locals can afford to live there, so the cost of services is double what it is anywhere else in Campania?"

"I'll tell you what it is, Petronius. It's the light. There's something special and unique about the light on the bay. It's like nowhere else in the world."

Petronius eyed the older man warily. In his prime, as a voice of conscience in the senate, Anicius would never have allowed himself to recycle such a dismal platitude. Had it really become such an effort for him to engage his mind, so that he found himself constantly having to borrow from the trash heap of clichés, like a perpetual guest who must rely on his hosts for a change of clothes? Petronius could not believe that Anicius was content simply to be the harmless, amiable old pederast, that he had given up the struggle altogether. He loved him still, of course, but it was painful to watch. Even in old age, even on the very brink of death, a man ought to be able to recognize himself in the broad light of day. If he could not, how could he possibly hope to find his way in the dark?

Petronius's musing was interrupted by the arrival of a phalanx of slaves, who swarmed the terrace bearing platters of meat and clean implements. The Umbrian boar had not yet been carved; it was presented to the master with its belly slashed, plump figs and glistening chestnuts tumbling like viscera from the cavity. Steam rose from its interior, coiled around the ankles of the slaves and condensed on the cool marble ledge of the water table. Lamplight played on the boar's scorched, lacquered back, got stuck in the beaded amber of its juices, and slid unctuously downward toward the perfumed anus. The moist aroma of roast flesh reached his nostrils. Petronius looked away from his favorite dish and down the beach toward Misenum. The lamps were glowing on every terrace along the coast between his and Vatia's place, and across the water on the island of Pithecusa. Beyond the promontory too, no doubt, the carcasses of boars and sows and piglets and lambs and songbirds were gleaming on their bronze and silver and gold platters, offering up their laden steam to the sallow, hungry gods in heaven. Petronius's gaze idled upward to where the crescent moon was now entangled in the melilot woven through the pergola. The sweetened wine had cured his headache, he noticed, but his head now felt as empty as a drum, and he had a fleeting vision of it as it might be twelve hours hence, roasted and stuffed with Chian figs and chestnuts. When he lowered his gaze, he found himself staring at a platter of sausages, delicately selected and arranged by Melissa Silia, who reclined beside him with an expectant smile.

"You must eat," she whispered.

"I seem to have lost my appetite," Petronius said dully.

"Please try." She held a dainty white Faliscan sausage to his lips, and Petronius noticed for the first time that her nails were painted a pale shade of lilac, and that she had perfumed her hands with lavender oil. When had she done this? Very suddenly, a great lump of emotion swelled in his throat, and he ducked his head to conceal the tears that had risen to his eyes. That she had taken such pains, such private moments, to make herself beautiful tonight—down to the scent of her hands, which no one but she and he would ever know—seemed to him to be the most moving token of her grace and tact, a secret message that he might so easily have overlooked. He raised his head to accept her offering, and in the fleeting instant that their eyes met, and she registered the tears in his, her own grew moist, and her lip trembled infinitesimally, but her composure did not crack. The sausage tasted like nothing but rancid gristle to him, and he felt each warm globule of warm fat compress and burst repellently against the roof of his mouth, yet he smiled as he forced it down.

"It will do you good," Melissa said warmly.

"What good could it possibly do me?"

"It pleases me."

"Are you growing maternal in your old age, Melissa?" he joked, but it was the wrong thing to say. In apology, he brushed her fingertips with his lips and deposited his last tear in the palm of her hand.

He turned to Anicius on his left, who was twisting a section of sow's vulva between his fists, seeking the right angle of attack. Petronius noticed something he had never noticed before: that Anicius's scalp, where it was revealed beneath his thinning weave of gray hair, was flaked and peeling, as were the pink inner shells of his ears. "Have you tried the Lucanian?" he asked.

"First things first," Anicius said, nodding at his hands.

Petronius took in each guest on the couch to his left. None had touched the boar or the sausage. Suddenly, it seemed very important that someone, anyone, should bear witness to the sausage. The sow's vulva was an easy touch, and Lucullo was justly famous for it, but it was on the deceptive simplicity of the sausage, its emblematic qualities, that the success of the evening rested. Petronius suddenly felt this with an urgency verging on panic. An entire life's work might be vested in a sausage, rightly seasoned, yet why would no one try the Lucanian? Was there, perhaps, something wrong with it, or had they all agreed to conspire against it, or against him? His head spun with the possibilities. After all, not every plot was a fabrication; this was just the sort of thing Nero and Tigellinus excelled at. He turned to his right, and found himself looking directly into Martialis's eyes, of precisely the same saturated yellow-green as Petronius's prized myrrhine ladle. Martialis was studying him calmly, gnawing on a length of Lucanian sausage.

"How is the sausage?" Petronius whispered. Martialis cocked an eyebrow quizzically.

"Why don't you try some?"

"I think I will." Without breaking eye contact, Petronius accepted a length of sausage from his guest and nibbled at it. Suddenly, he found himself panting, sweating, his eyes welling with tears of relief.

"Too much cumin," he laughed.

Martialis leaned forward until their foreheads were almost touching, and Petronius could see every hair follicle on his cheek. "Never complain, never explain," he said, and the world resolved itself into its old, familiar configuration.

"A poem, I think," Melissa said, clapping her hands commandingly. "Who will give us one?"

Fabius leapt to his feet. "Fetch me a harp!"

"Best leave off the harp, Fabius," Pollia suggested gently. "And the singing."

"No harp, then. Here we go." He recited in Greek, in an accent that would have been the delight of his boyhood tutor but made him a laughingstock in the streets of Nicomedia.

But when the artichoke flowers, and the chirping grasshopper sits in a tree and pours down his shrill song continually from under his wings in the season of wearisome heat, then goats are plumpest and wine sweetest; women are most wanton, but men are feeblest, because Sirius parches head and knees and the skin is dry through heat. But at that time let me have a shady rock and wine of Biblis, a clot of curds and milk of drained goats with the flesh of an heifer fed in the woods, that has never calved, and of firstling kids; then also let me drink bright wine, sitting in the shade, when my heart is satisfied with food, and so, turning

my head to face the fresh Zephyr, from the overflowing spring
which pours down unfouled thrice pour an offering of water, but
make a fourth libation of wine.

Fabius bowed modestly to the smattering of polite applause.
"That was lovely, lovely," Cornelia said, speaking out of the side
of a mouth bulging with masticated figs.

Fabius's choice of poem had not been a felicitous one, and all
but he were duly aware of the gaffe. The mood of the evening
did not call for ancient Greek devotionals, but for something
more modern, raucous, risqué even. It was typical of Fabius that
his selection was so conventional, and Petronius watched Pollia's expression as she struggled to reconcile her loyalty and her
embarrassment. He wondered if she ever regretted having married Fabius. Petronius liked to imagine that Pollia would be
much happier with a man like himself, yet he had to admit
that he'd been very much like Fabius at his age—high-minded,
detached, ambitious, a typical product of the empire. A very
conventional young man, to whom happiness had been a con-
vention, too. Glory had been everything—glory and service.
Without that, he was nothing, homeless, pointless, so what use
was it to seek personal fulfillment? No, that's not right—glory
and service *were* personal fulfillment. So long as he excelled and
furthered the purposes of Rome, he had had no use for any
other kind of happiness. He had been happy, in his manner, in
the manner of conservative young men who find a way to live
without having to think very hard about anything. Fabius was
just like that. Certainly, he had a glorious career ahead of him,
providing he managed to shed some of his youthful idealism and
prudishness, but what kind of a life was it going to be for a
woman who outshone her husband at every level? She was spir-
ited and willful enough to carve something out for her herself,
Petronius supposed, but she was going to have a hard time of it

in the face of Fabius's limited imagination and correct expectations. Petronius suspected that she'd have been happier with someone of less ambition and more soul.

He bit into a delicately carved slice of boar haunch, and had immediately to raise his hand to his mouth as a warm, smoky rill of drippings escaped his lips and ran down his chin. Lucullo had been right—the meat, tender as a young cheese, was suffused with the aromatic quiddity of the Umbrian oak forests in which the boar had lived and died. For the briefest interlude, Petronius felt a startling, intimate connection to the creature, as he had earlier to the oyster, and wondered if this heightened sensibility were some sort of premonitory accommodation to his own oblivion.

The conversation was pursuing its own course.

"Now I know that few of you will credit it," Anicius was saying, "but I was a boy in the reign of Augustus, and back then vast stretches of that beach were deserted."

"What, between Nesis and Puteoli?" Fabius asked incredulously.

"Certainly. Nothing but rabbits. Those rabbits are all gone now. When I was a boy, you could walk half a league without seeing a house. Just fishermen, hawking their catch. You paid in drachmas, shekels, whatever. You barely heard a word of Latin around here back then, nothing but Greek."

"Not a patch on Cumae, then."

"You know," Petronius said, "I think I've had about enough of all this slander. Cumae was good enough for Aeneas, wasn't it? The father of Rome landed not five minutes' walk from here. It was good enough for Varro, for Pompey, for Cicero, for Sulla, for Vatia, for Philippus. It's good enough for me."

"And you know what they all had in common, don't you?" Cornelia brayed thoughtlessly. "They all *retired* here. They went to Baiae for fun, but came to Cumae to die."

Like a flickering flame, the conversation died just as a fresh, salt-laden wind swept across the gardens, rustling the trees in the orchard and causing the lamps beneath the pergola to swing gently. The guests, protected by screens and braziers, experienced its passage largely as an auditory phenomenon—a sequence of subtle variations on the theme of polite shushing. The miniature flotilla in the water table had been set in motion by the breeze, and they watched in detached distress as their supper floated away, beyond reach at the very moment when they sought its distraction. Mortified beyond expression, Cornelia rubbed her eyes with her fists. With barely a sound, a battalion of slaves emerged from the shadows and descended upon the dishes, plucking them from the water before even one had reached the far edge of the basin. The remains of the last course were offered round one last time, while new platters—bearing fried meatballs, black pudding, boiled hare, kidneys and sweetbreads bathing in a pungent yellow sauce—emerged from the kitchen. The guests followed their approach with a show of interest that ill concealed their discomfort. How sincerely concerned they were for Petronius's comfort! How awkward and sweet of them!

"Could that be silphium in the sauce?" Anicius inquired incredulously. "It's been so long since I've seen it, I've quite forgotten what it tastes like."

"Alas, I've not seen silphium on the market these past twenty years or more," Petronius said. "They tell me it's all but extinct, even in Cyrenaica. This is asafoetida, from India. It's a reasonable substitute, I suppose, but I'll never get over the disappearance of silphium. I feel genuinely sad for those of you who were too young to have tried it."

Martialis snorted derisively into his goblet.

"You do not care for silphium, Valerius Martialis?" Cornelia asked with studied naïveté.

"I've never tasted it, Cornelia Felicia," Martialis said. "But from everything I've heard, it was more a status symbol than a condiment. An entire island was enslaved so that a handful of senators might sprinkle stinking grass on their fish and impress their friends. Now that it's gone, let Cyrenaica sink back into the sea; it's of no further use to anyone."

"I am not a patrician, Martialis," Lucilius chided gently, "yet I was able to appreciate silphium very much for its own exquisite, unique perfume. Despite its price, not because of it."

Martialis was preparing a retort, but was cut off before he could deliver it.

"Who is Vatia?" Fabius put in. A roar of mirth arose from the elder members of the company.

"Servilius Vatia! What a man!"

"What a legend!"

"Sit up a minute, Fabius," Anicius said, pointing southward across the parapet and inlet. "You know that big villa on the water down the beach? The one with the two grottoes, between the lake and the cape? You can just see, there are four torches flaming on the terrace there? That's Vatia's house."

"When I first bought this place six years ago, Fabius," Petronius said, "I thought the sailors were rioting in Misenum every night. It turned out it was just Vatia's orgies. You could hear them clear as day all along the beach."

"His fishponds grew the finest bearded mullet in the land, but he became so attached to them, he'd have to send to market for his supper. If one of those mullet failed to eat from his hand, he'd lose an entire night's sleep worrying over its health."

"One year he cornered the entire market in *garum* from New Carthage, and if you didn't want to eat vinegar on your fish that year, you had to come pay homage to him and leave gifts of gold for the holy chickens in the temple of Apollo."

"Most men would have been crushed by the burden of leisure he bore so effortlessly. He was a hero to many."

"The caterer's guild of Naples named a dish after him. It was called 'Vatia's Standard.' It was a duck, stuffed with truffles, then stuffed inside a goose that was stuffed inside a peacock that was stuffed inside a heron that was stuffed inside a swan that was baked and gilded with egg yolk and gold leaf and carried in at the end of a long pike by a company of chefs dressed as legionaries and haruspices."

"He was fabulously wealthy—he'd been commander of the Praetorians at one point—but he acted like a vulgar freedman, boasting and counting his money at the dinner table and farting ostentatiously and being familiar with his slaves. Still, everybody loved him, you couldn't help it—he never apologized for anything. He was happy to be exactly who he was, and no one could tell him any different."

"It's true," Petronius added. "When I first came to Cumae, the very first day I moved in, along comes this slave boy, trotting down the beach with a heavy platter. On the platter was a whole roast piglet, and in the piglet's mouth was an apple, and in the apple was a dart, and when I removed the dart the apple fell neatly into two pieces, and sandwiched between them was a silver medallion that was stamped with an invitation to dinner that very night. It was so tasteless and common, I had to laugh out loud. But from then on, I knew exactly whom to turn to whenever I needed cheering up. He was never depressed, never had any self-doubt. I rather envied him, that lack of self-consciousness. You could never tell if he was unaware that people laughed at him behind his back, or if he knew and just didn't care. He used to say: 'Pretend I'm dead. Say something nice about me.' He was one of a kind, and when he died of liver poisoning I remember thinking that the world would never see his like again. And then I met Martialis here."

"And I confirmed the suspicion."

"The only person I ever knew who didn't like Vatia was Seneca. He couldn't bear him."

Lucilius groaned and buried his face in his palms. "Oh please, don't get me started on Seneca."

"Why, what's the matter with Seneca?" Martialis asked with a feeble affectation of nonchalance.

Lucilius sighed. "You know, those last two years of his, he was not at all happy. After his downfall, he traveled up and down southern Italy trying to 'forget politics,' but he couldn't get over not having a handy audience for his sermons. He was never in one place long enough to really buttonhole his host and give him the full treatment. He started writing me these long, moralizing letters. Me! Now you know, Seneca and I were friends for a long, long time, but I never had much patience for his ethical pretensions, considering the way he lived his own life. Socrates he was not, no, nor Diogenes neither. I started receiving these haranguing letters, streams of them, exhorting me to live better this way, think better that way, analyzing my problems, as if he knew anything about my problems! There are some people, you know, they just can't help themselves, they always think they know what's best for a person. How Nero put up with him all those years, I cannot tell. They were a match, all right—salt and pepper. And do you know, I feel sure he was making copies of those letters with an eye to future publication. In fact, he told me once that I would be famous because of those letters. How fortunate I am to know you, I wrote back.

"Anyway, in one of his letters, he reminded me how he and I had once walked along this very beach, and when we passed Vatia's place he had said 'There lies Vatia.' And I'd asked him what he meant, Vatia wasn't dead, and he'd said that he might as well be because living the way he did wasn't living at all, it was hiding from life. Leisure was noble if spent improving oneself, but idleness was a kind of death in life, et cetera, et cetera. And do you know, he was so pleased with himself for coming up with this pearl of wisdom that he could never pass by Vatia's place after that without shaking his head and sighing 'There lies Vatia.' A hundred times I must have heard him say it, 'There lies Vatia,' and each time as if it were a fresh insight. He was devastated when Vatia died, because they buried him somewhere else. The funny thing is, I'm not sure he ever even met Vatia."

Petronius felt Martialis shifting uncomfortably at his shoulder. It was only natural that the boy should be uneasy. Growing up in his little Spanish mountain village, he'd been weaned on stories of his famous countryman Seneca, a distant cousin from Cordoba who'd gone off to Rome and become an illustrious playwright, a renowned philosopher, tutor to the emperor! When Martialis first arrived in Rome, a wide-eyed provincial with ringlets in his hair, he'd been deeply impressed by Seneca, who was still playing the elder statesman and sage mentor, even though he was in his final decline and could barely show himself in the streets in the daylight hours. How warmly Seneca had welcomed him! Martialis was the last man in Italy who still thought Seneca a great and powerful politician, and believed the promises he'd made about introductions, shamelessly, in front of people who knew only too well the sad truth of his reduced circumstances. No one who had come to love Martialis had had the heart to disabuse him, so that again he was probably the only man in Italy to be shocked and dismayed by Seneca's arrest and suicide six months later, lumped in like a common criminal with Piso's conspirators. And even afterward, when Seneca's widow Paulina survived her own suicide attempt and began spreading the unlikely tale of her husband's heroic, Socratic last moments, only Martialis was taken in. So now it can't have been pleasant to hear those who knew his cousin far better than he discuss Seneca's foibles so casually, barely a year after his death. Petronius felt a feeble wave of sympathy pulse through him, but it was not strong enough to move him to a word of compassion. After all, he had already seen a vision of Martialis's future—the one in which, after a dignified pause for mourning, he found a new patron with better political prospects, composed appropriately flattering verses for future emperors, and achieved the fame and notoriety he'd dreamed of since boyhood—and it did not involve any sacrifices to the memory of dead, disgraced mentors.

The moon had finally disentangled itself from the pergola and, its jaundice purged by the high winds, hung silver in an empty sky the color of raw sinew. Petronius judged by the echoes from the cove that the tide had turned and was advancing. It would soon overtake and lift the bow of the stranded yacht down on the beach. In another hour, the boat would be free to sail, if there were anyone needing to sail her. Petronius considered the unpleasant irony that, in his final hours, all of nature had been transformed into an exquisitely accurate timepiece.

The night had grown colder, the warmth of the braziers intermittent and barely adequate, the breeze steady against the screens, bowing them like sails. Petronius realized with a mild start that some of the guests had been issued blankets of reddish Canusium wool. When had this happened? Had he fallen asleep? It would not be long before he would need to return for another round of bloodletting, and he feared that it would affect him more severely than anticipated, perhaps incapacitate or render him unconscious, and thus put a premature end to the dinner and inconvenience his guests. He resolved to keep his wits sharp while he still had them. He leaned into the water table abruptly and stuck his head beneath the frigid water. He opened his eyes, and the shadows cast on the granite floor of the basin by the wavering lamplight across the floating platters looked like the shadows of clouds migrating across the face of a mountain. He thought of Mysian Olympus, above Prusa, on a crisp day in early May, before the saffron had been planted and the slopes were still a chalky gray.

ฃฃฃฃฃฃ

PETRONIUS HAD BEEN determined to pursue his acquaintance with the centurion's wife, though official duties kept him in Nicomedia longer than he would have wished. Ultimately, it took him almost two full months to redeem his promise to himself. Once there, he made a halfhearted pretense of furthering his investigation into the city finances, but in fact spent much of his time wandering the streets in search of the woman. He sought her several times in the ruined house where they had met, varying the time of day in the hope that she kept a regular appointment there, but to no avail. Now, the *kouros* seemed to mock him even more cruelly for his obtuse fantasies—a grown man, with the full power of the empire behind him, skulking through the byways of an obscure provincial town for a woman he barely knew—but he had a purpose that counterbalanced his frustration and shame. Naturally, he could not seek her out in the barracks, the one place he could be sure of finding her, and his face was too well known by now for him to spend much time in any one place where he would attract unwanted attention. The town fathers resented him venomously; the merest whiff of scandal would be enough to prompt a letter of complaint to the Senate that would immeasurably complicate his life and pursuit. Even so, he grew desperate enough to throw caution to the wind, and found himself, but poorly disguised in a Canusian cloak, loitering for hours by the gates of the barracks. It took almost two days of waiting until she finally emerged, wearing a long-sleeved tunic and rough woolen shawl and carrying an empty reed basket on her arm. Having had only the most cursory glimpse of her face at their first meeting, he could not even be perfectly certain that it was her until he studied her gait, the way she walked like a senior magistrate in measured strides, shoulders thrown back. The plaza was almost deserted; he could not follow her directly without drawing the scrutiny of the picket at the gate. Waiting until she rounded the corner, he turned up a parallel alleyway and made for the marketplace, where he found her dawdling among the stalls, halfheartedly picking over the meager selection of fruit and vegetables. It was there, ridiculously posing as a fellow shopper, that he closed on her.

He stood at her side, not knowing how to reintroduce himself. It was not that he was afraid of scaring her off—there was nothing of the skittish or the shy about her—but that he wanted to make a powerful impression upon her and had little experience of such matters. As nothing came to mind, and as he was anxious not to squander the opportunity, he simply leaned to his right and bumped shoulders with her. When she looked up in irritation, all he could do was smile foolishly back at her, at a loss for words. She was very beautiful, more beautiful even than he had thought she would be, and her beauty was enhanced rather than mitigated by a suggestion of hardness, or perhaps it was sadness, around her eyes. Her eyebrows were thick and darker than her hair, and there was a hint of silky down above her upper lip. Her lower lip was somewhat swollen, pouty, as if she had spent her entire lifetime drinking milk from the spout of a pitcher. Her skin was pale and matte. Her hair was indeed light brown, the color of ripe wheat, straight and fine, pulled back in a simple braid that ended between her shoulder blades.

It took a moment or two for her to place him, and when she did her expression changed in only the subtlest of ways, registering neither shock nor triumph nor delight, but simply acknowledgment of his presence, the way one might look at a pair of scissors that one had misplaced and found again. It was an extremely gratifying way to be looked at, at least for Petronius, and it was all he could do to keep from blushing.

"Well," she said at last. "Have you come for me?"

He nodded stupidly and followed her, not altogether discreetly, as she led the way from the market, up the steep cobbled streets, and out the eastern gate of the city that opened onto the lower slopes of Mount Olympus, planted with flowering cherry trees in walled orchards and, higher still, with dark groves of filbert, heavy with pale yellow catkins. Beyond were the saffron slopes, fallow until the summer planting. At last she stopped where the path took a sharp turn to the north, and turned to him, her hands folded demurely in front of her.

"Here I am, Governor," she said. "What is it that you want with me?"

He did not know what to do, or what to say to her, so he had her right there, in the shadow of an overgrown embankment. With her left hand she stroked the hair at the back of his head, smiling indulgently as one might at a child who had just said something clever and poignant, while with her right she pushed at his shoulder, preventing him from kissing her. Although he gave no thought to anything but his own pleasure, or to prolonging the encounter beyond his own satisfaction, she maneuvered herself beneath him with practiced self-interest, as if she were alone with her hand, and climaxed before he did, shuddering throughout her entire body yet exhaling the very barest whimper, and maintaining an enigmatic smile throughout. That smile, tender and superior at the same time, as though she were gratifying the whim of a sensitive boy, was both shocking and intensely, almost painfully, arousing.

Afterward, he watched her as she lay on a bed of moss absorbing the sun, deep in thought. He was captivated beyond words, and, despite his earlier promise to himself, he struggled to find something to say about his nascent feelings that would not sound trite or precipitous.

"What it is that you're about to tell me," she said without turning her head, "I urge you not to say it."

"I wasn't going to say anything."

"I've been married since I was sixteen, Governor, and my husband still tells me he loves me. It doesn't help."

"You don't believe in love?"

"I don't believe in talking about it. Whenever I hear a man say the word 'love,' I check my ankles for leg irons."

"This isn't the first time you've done this, then?"

"No."

"And you suppose all men are the same, do you, Melissa?"

"Oh, I'll admit you have more money and power than Junius. You're better looking, more educated, and infinitely more sophisticated than he is. You are certainly more intelligent, and you do make love better than he does. Perhaps you're even a little more subtle. But in everything that's truly important, I dare say you are just the same."

"And yet you gave yourself to me."

"And yet I gave myself to you. Just please don't talk to me about love."

He remained in Prusa for another week, delaying his return to the capital and his official duties on the feeblest of pretexts. They met every day, sometimes for an hour, sometimes for an entire afternoon, always in the same deserted spot below the saffron fields. It was she who made the appointments, she who determined the amount of time they spent together, she who wordlessly dictated every variation in their lovemaking. Identified from the very outset as a supplicant, he had no say in the matter, instantly relinquished all his authority, so that when she continued to address him as "Governor," the title assumed an aura of gentle, ironic contempt that he relished. When he had exhausted every possible excuse to the town fathers, whom he nominally continued to consult as his reason for remaining in Prusa, he simply stopped attending their meetings altogether. It must have aroused their suspicions; they could easily have had him followed, but he didn't care. He would have met her in the central forum, had her straddle him on the steps of the temple of Isis if she had asked him to. Who knew what she told her husband? Petronius never gave it a thought; from the moment he was with her, he was nothing, he disappeared, he was a crumb at the corner of her mouth, thoughtlessly licked away by her indifferent tongue. He was in thrall to her benevolent disdain.

Was it improbable that he should have succumbed to her so thoroughly, so suddenly? It was not sudden at all—Petronius came to believe that he had been waiting for her all his forty years. As for the intensity of his passion, he had never believed in romantic love, had had no interest in its vocabulary or conventions. Now, wary of exploring the nature of his feelings for his lover, all he knew and all he cared to know was that he was consumed by desire that, in the consummation, made him feel consummately known by the consumer, in a way that he had not even suspected he wished to be known by anyone. He felt like a piece of fruit, a most delicious apple whose sole reason for existing is to be eaten, and that some miracle allowed him to be reborn each time he was devoured, only to be devoured again and again. If this was love, he thought that perhaps it was indeed best that he say nothing to her about it.

Despite his age, his travels, and his accomplishments, Petronius was strangely inexperienced in the ways of love. Like many men of his class—like Nero himself—he had been debauched by an older woman sent to him by his mother. She had been perfectly competent, and not unattractive, but he had been only fourteen years old and had found the whole thing unpleasant and unnerving, especially when she'd screwed up her face as though she were in pain and howled like a stuck cat in an orgasm that he saw, in retrospect, was surely faked. After that, his experience of physical relations with women had been essentially limited to assignations of convenience with patrician wives either bored with or ambitious for their husbands, and prostitutes of the high and low kind alike—all of whom had every motivation to be pliable and obliging. It was not that he had not had ample opportunity, should he have sought to exploit it, or that women did not find him attractive, which was a matter of indifference to him. It was simply that he had no interest in procreation, no inclination toward marriage (despite its evident benefits for his political career), and no particular talent for emotional intimacy. Other men, he gathered, used sex as an instrument of power, revenge, violence, communication, perversion, or the stroking of their tender egos. For Petronius, it was an instrument of release, and nothing more. He had found it to be extremely useful when trying to unwind after a day on the Senate floor or the battlefield, and at its very best the act might perhaps evoke certain transient feelings of invincibility or belonging, but not for long and certainly not for keeps.

But all that changed irrevocably in Prusa. It was *her* he needed, not just anybody. It was *her* body, and her body alone, that he craved. In her arms, he soon found it almost inconceivable that he had ever managed to perform sexually in anybody else's. Every detail of her body seemed to have emerged fully formed from the workshop of his imagination. More than anything else, it was her smile, the mere thought of which, in the sleepless hours before the dawn of a new day would find him pacing the floor in anticipation of their next meeting, would bring him to tumescence. Like the Christians, who were said to confess their sins to their priest in return for absolution in their god's name, their lovemaking felt like a form of confession, and he emerged from it each time in the serene confidence that his priestess had peered into his soul and found evidence of his every weakness, his every act of dishonesty and deceit, his every unwholesome impulse. Far from absolving him, however, she delighted in each discovery of his degradation, she was charmed and flattered by it, because each was a tribute and a prayer to her power and beauty.

She was always there at the saffron fields when he arrived, because she knew how arousing he found it to be observed upon his approach. Still fifty paces away, he found himself stiffening, and he often took her where she stood, leaning against the embankment, without so much as a word passing between them. Indeed, it was not until their third day together that he even saw her naked body, and when he did it reinforced everything he thought he already knew about her. Hers was not like any female form he had ever seen. Far from the Roman ideal of plump, rounded curves and soft, yielding surfeit, she was all angles and hard surfaces. With almost no fat to cushion them, the tight muscles of her abdomen and buttocks crowded and throbbed against her skin. Her breasts were small, hard, and pointed, her nipples like tiny, rough-edged pebbles, her hip bones jutting scimitars. Her pubic mound was a clenched fist. She seemed to him like the demon goddess of some arcane Eastern cult, ever ready to demand the sacrifice of flesh from her worshipers.

When their time together was limited—and she never bothered to explain the circumstances that dictated her timetable— they would make love twice, the first time at his furious, incontinent pace, the second at hers, far slower and more deliberate. If they had an entire afternoon together, they went at it three, four times, he glorying in his gathering exhaustion, she unchanging and inexhaustible, as if even his most titanic effort—even had he been able to move mountains or summon earthquakes on her behalf—were a matter of mere mortal busy-work, perceived in all its self-importance from the heights of

Olympus. She climaxed as often as he did—she made very certain of that—but it was never accompanied by loud frenzy or followed by languor. Instead, while he lay still prone and panting, she would stretch out on her back, cradling her head in the palms of her hands, and direct her gaze skyward, her eyes darting back and forth, like a philosopher pondering an issue of great moment. At such times, he learned better than to interrupt her thoughts. Once, when he had sought awkwardly to express the emotion that was pressing painfully against his ribcage, she had turned upon him the most chastening of scowls.

"Words are for speaking the truth, Governor," she'd said coolly. "If you insist on loving me, you are far more likely to express it honestly in your silence."

He never learned more about her personal history than he had on their first walk together, nor did she ask him any but the most superficial questions about himself, his history, his ambitions. He could not say whether her cool detachment was a form of self-defense or a proclamation of invulnerability. He knew that he was at fault in this—that a more experienced man would not require such things to be explained to him—and his lack of insight made him feel blundering and stupid in her company, but she still made no concession to his confessional urges. That she was unhappy in her marriage, or at least infinitely bored, was a given; that she despised barracks and provincial existence was equally evident; but concerning what she might reasonably expect from the rest of her life, or what she would change if she could, she never spoke at all. Was her marriage childless by choice, accident, or nature? Who were her other lovers, her friends? If asked, she pretended not to hear, or changed the subject, or responded with some irrelevancy. And as for her expectations of him, or of any potential advantage a centurion's wife might derive from her liaison with the most powerful man in the province, she was as silent on that score as if he were merely a figment of her imagination, as he sometimes felt himself, with perverse, submissive gratitude, to be.

So it came as some surprise, not long before he was due at last to return to Nicomedia, that she arrived bearing a gift wrapped in muslin.

"What's this?" he asked as he unwrapped it.

"Keepsake," she shrugged.

It was a ladle, some eighteen inches in length, of the most translucent, transcendent myrrhine, yellow-green with veins of purple and white. As he slowly turned it in his hands, the purple veins grew fiery in the sunlight, the white alternately milky and tinged with bloody red. The craftsmanship was flawless, the crystal polished to an icelike sheen. Although Petronius had no expertise in such matters, he knew immediately that it was a priceless artifact of some ancient Eastern campaign, for nothing so beautiful had ever been made by Roman or even Greek artisans.

"Where did you get this?" he asked incredulously.

"Aulus picked it up years ago at a bazaar in Arrabona. He thought it was pretty, and he passed it on to me to serve wine at drinking parties."

"It's worth a fortune. Did you know that?"

She shrugged again. "I've already given it to you. I can't ask you to buy it from me now."

"Won't he miss it?"

"He misses everything, but he won't miss that."

As he cradled it gingerly in his hands, Petronius considered what a perfect, typical gift it actually was, coming from her. It was of immense value—undoubtedly worth enough to change her life forever, had she chosen to sell it—and yet she had given it to him so casually, as if, for foolish, sentimental reasons, he were overestimating its significance. It was the way she gave Petronius everything. It meant nothing to her; whether or not she grasped how much it meant to him—and he was never quite sure that she did, despite the fact that he made no effort to conceal his dependence on her charity—his avidity for every crumb she threw him was a source of endless, titillated amusement to her. That, needless to say, only made him more greedy of her.

What did she feel for him? Petronius told himself that he did not care, so long as they were together, but it was a lie so transparent that he could not maintain it even to one so beguiled as himself. He must know, but she was consummately evasive. Perhaps, despite her protestations, she was really waiting for him to declare himself first? That he must not do, though his enslavement must have been so perfectly evident that such a declaration would surely have been redundant. In her presence, scanning her face for any sign of weakness and parsing her words for a confession of any sort, he felt like a small child among adults who do not wish their conversation to be understood; he felt that she must be saying *something*, or concealing *something*. At times, he felt that she was merely interested in his power and wealth, and would continue to seduce him with her opacity until she had obtained what she wanted; at others, it seemed equally plausible that she needed him as much as he had come to need her, but that, as someone whose entire existence theretofore had depended upon the whims of selfish men, she could not bring herself to throw herself upon his mercy, lest it prove no more merciful than the others'. He could not know, and he began to wonder how he could attach her to him. He was prepared, of course, to make the wildest promises, and to keep every one of them, but he could not do so until she asked for them.

As the day of his unavoidable return to Nicomedia approached, however, his resolve began to crumble. He could not leave without some token of commitment from her. And finally, on the eve of his departure, as they lay together in the gorse, he abandoned the last tattered shreds of his scruples.

She stared into his eyes and stroked his cheek with her knuckles, a quizzical smile playing on her lips, as she considered her response. The air was faintly laced with lavender and cherry blossom, and the bees busied themselves loudly in the fruit trees. At last, she said: "Is it really so important for you to hear me say it?"

"It is."

"Why?"

"I live in fear of losing you."

"So if I say I love you, that means we are bound together forever? Is that what you believe, Governor?"

"Doesn't it?"

"You'll have to wait, then. You need a clearer head than that to love me."

The very day after his return to Nicomedia, word came from the west that every province of Anatolia was to contribute a cohort to reinforcing the eastern frontier, where the war in Armenia was threatening to resume. Without hesitation, and despite its patent unfitness for combat, Petronius volunteered the ninth cohort of the Fourth Scythian legion, and within days her husband had been marched off to muster at Caesarea Mazaca.

೫೫೫೫೫೫

NEREUS WAS AT his side with a towel the moment Petronius lifted his head from the water table.

The plunge had not helped; if anything, his head seemed even tighter and emptier than before, and for a brief moment he felt wholly inadequate to the task before him. He had felt the pull of these memories growing stronger every moment as the evening progressed. Was it, he wondered, the loss of blood that made him so vulnerable to them, or the imminence of their extinction? He knew it to be quite true from his experience on the battlefield that men see their entire lives unfold before them in the moments before death, yet it was not by any means his entire life that he was reliving in these transitory visions. He had scarcely had a thought to spare this evening for his parents, his childhood, his lost friends or the men he had killed in battle. No, these memories were more like the coded dreams of a man troubled by an unresolved problem. They conveyed a simple message, a sibylline instruction not at all difficult to decode, if only—as she had suggested all those years ago—he could manage to clear his head. Just then, sensitive as always to his mood, Melissa rested her cool hand against the small of his back beneath the blanket, and his confusion resolved itself into something lesser, something more familiar, like Proteus subdued by Menelaus.

"You appear to harbor a special bitterness against Seneca, Lucilius," Anicius was saying. He had dropped his voice, in acknowledgment of the fact that Lucilius had, for some reason, decided to cross the line between idle gossip and character assassination, and that his every utterance in this new, uncharted territory was both irrevocable and chargeable against him.

"You know, I think you're right, Anicius. I do feel quite bitterly about him. I'm not sure I even realized it until just now."

"The bitterness of a friendship betrayed?" Martialis suggested. Lucilius nodded thoughtfully before responding.

"In a sense. That is, he never said a word against me, as far as I know, or acted in the least way against my interests. In that sense, he was utterly loyal—as was only wise, seeing as I was one of the few who stuck by him in his exile. What he betrayed, I think, was the tenor of our friendship. It began in mentorship, but he never really allowed it to outgrow that. He always had to be the sage, always had to teach. Even when I was at the height of my profession and he had been laid low by his own conniving, it was always a one-sided arrangement with him—he lectured, I listened. Even with all his hypocrisies laid bare before the world—his fawning and flattering, his cupidity, his status-consciousness, all the rest—he never once dropped the act before me, never once acknowledged me as someone who might be of help. It was always 'See the great Stoic in adversity! You, too, Lucilius, could learn to bear your misfortunes as well as I if you followed my example.' Somehow, though, now that our situations were reversed, my successes were symbols of worldliness, my service to the state an unworthy distraction from the study of philosophy, my acquaintance with powerful men a sure sign of unbridled ambition. Everything was grist for his mill. It was all he had left, his so-called integrity, and he clung to it even when it was nothing but a tattered old rag, and shoved it in my face at every opportunity. You could hardly call it a friendship at the end."

"And yet you allowed him to think himself your friend to the end?" Martialis offered.

"I *was* his friend—it was he who was not mine."

"That can't be right. There cannot be one friend only, any more than a bird can fly with one wing. If he is not your friend, you cannot be his. It is impossible."

"You may be right, Martialis. Perhaps it was not friendship by then. You know, Seneca once wrote that one should consider oneself alone in the presence of a friend. What he intended, of course, was that one should feel free to say anything in the presence of a friend, as if one were alone with one's own thoughts. But what he really meant without realizing it was that one should feel free, as he did, to talk and talk in the presence of a friend as if there were no one else in the room. His only concept of friendship—and especially toward the end, when his wits were frayed with worry and despair—was in the abstract, as a philosophical conundrum. I had this idea that I would set myself up before him, right in his very face, and provide an alternate example, the very model of a loyal, silent companion who was always available, always present, never critical or judgmental. I wanted to show him how a real friend acts, and yet never have to tell him. If I'd had to say 'See what I am doing, Lucius. This is how a real friend behaves,' it would have defeated the whole purpose. I wanted him to figure it out for himself."

"He never did, I suppose?"

"No, never."

Martialis spoke softly, venomously. "As you'd always known he wouldn't, or couldn't. Wasn't it all finally just a form of cruel, subtle revenge, Lucilius? You may claim you were simply trying to be a moral exemplar of friendship, but you never really expected him to take the bait at all, did you? You knew he was constitutionally incapable of such a change. Instead, you could make a fool of him by showing him up as the hollow shell he always was, and then the whole world would see who the real wise man in the relationship was. This so-called loyalty you boast of, it was nothing more than an elaborate ruse to stake out the moral high ground. Perhaps you're hoping they'll call the book *Lucilius: The Rise and Fall of Seneca* instead of *Seneca: Letters to Lucilius?*"

Petronius could see quite clearly that Lucilius's feelings had not been hurt by Martialis's attack, as Martialis had surely intended them to be and as anyone else's might well have been. But Lucilius was a seasoned lawyer, long immunized against oblique, *ad hominem* arguments, a solid Roman political man whose only vulnerabilities were ornamental, worn or left at home as the occasion demanded. Instead, Lucilius was struggling with the appropriate response. His instinct, Petronius knew, was to seize the offensive immediately with a cool, calculated violence of rhetoric, as he would in court. Moreover, in some uncertain way his honor had been impugned and must be defended. But he was a guest tonight, and a guest is bound by certain obligations to the host, one of which is to respect the rules of civility under the host's roof. Martialis's failure to do so did not exempt Lucilius from that duty. And tonight of all nights, of course, Lucilius would be especially sensitive to the need to keep the peace. As for Martialis, he seemed determined to take the opposite tack and pick every fight that came his way. Ultimately, Petronius knew, Lucilius was too clever to be baited so clumsily.

Lucilius sighed sadly and allowed his head to slump between his shoulders, like a man forced to concede that he has been bested in argument. "Perhaps you're right there, too, young Martialis. We learn as Stoics that we know nothing until we know ourselves. I'm happy to admit I know nothing. You have done me the favor of revealing a weakness in my self-knowledge as well, for which I thank you."

"And you can all go to hell, for all I care," Martialis grunted, turning his attention to a grape.

A natural lull descended upon the diners as the slaves moved in to fill wine glasses and clear away the remaining platters in preparation for the next course. Petronius watched as each of his friends drifted into a temporary cubicle of solitary thought, as if they'd each wandered off for a moment into separate rooms to gather their wits. He thought perhaps that some were sad— sad for him? Sad for the dying season? Sad for the harsh words spoken?—and it grieved him that he was powerless to redirect the evening. Anything he could say now would be taken as an artificial attempt to revive their spirits, and thus as an awkward reminder of the purpose of their gathering, and he thought perhaps it would be best to leave them to their own devices for the moment. It was, after all, too soon to call for more poetry and music.

He turned to find Melissa's familiar smile upon him. Had she been gazing upon him all along, or had she only just now focused on him as he turned? It was a look—part question, part mirth—that he had grown accustomed to from their very earliest days together, but its implied condescension, which once had endeared her to him as no sincere solicitude could ever hope to do, he now found irritating. She raised her hand to his face and stroked his cheek with her knuckles. Petronius ducked his head and gazed out across the terrace to the sea, where a gay argosy of pleasure boats, their lanterns blazing, was converging on the dock at Vatia's villa.

"I wonder why Seneca is so much in our thoughts tonight?" Pollia, sounding just like a young girl. "I never even met him, and yet I find the idea of him disturbing me. Do you believe in ghosts, Petronius?"

"Of course."

"Might his ghost be haunting us here tonight?"

"I don't see why it should. Apart from Lucilius, none of us was especially close to him. This house meant next to nothing to him."

"I'm thinking maybe it's the occasion that's brought him."

"Pollia!" Fabius chided.

"No, that's all right. Go on, Pollia."

"Well, as you know, Petronius, Fabius and I live small lives, on the periphery of power and politics, but even we have heard the rumors about Seneca's suicide. They say he botched several attempts and that he wavered in his resolve. They say that Paulina decided at the last minute not to go through with it— that is, she decided not to die alongside her husband, although she'd said she would—just so she could stay behind and engineer a false, heroic account of his final hour, because she understood that his entire life's work would be held up to scorn and ridicule if it was known how he had died. Actually, I have no idea if it is true . . ."

"It is, substantially," Anicius murmured.

"But if it is, I was thinking that perhaps he was here tonight as a kind of presiding spirit to ensure that what happened to him did not happen to someone he admired. Could that be, do you think?"

The entire company burst into merry laughter. Petronius, as he laughed, observed Pollia's confusion and shame with deep affection, and found himself aroused once again by the girlishness that occasionally urged itself through the barrier of her womanliness.

"My dear, sweet Pollia," Anicius chuckled, wiping a greasy tear from a crease in his flabby cheek. "First of all, Seneca's death did not 'happen' to him. He'd rehearsed it over and over again, as we all have, and it was his responsibility and his alone to ensure that it went well. Nothing Seneca could possibly do or say from beyond the grave can help Petronius prepare for what he has to do tonight. A man can talk great words, as Seneca did, but dignity and poise cannot be summoned at will like a chaise. Petronius is solely responsible tonight for his actions. He is alone, he knows he is alone, and no one and nothing can touch him, beyond what we are doing now: making his final hours happy ones, to tide him on his journey and to leave a favorable impression with those whose duty it will be tomorrow to bear witness to the nobility, wisdom, and courage of his final act. Besides which, Seneca despised Petronius."

"Did he? Whatever for? How could he possibly?" Pollia asked.

"Petronius was Nero's right-hand man at the time Seneca fell from grace. Seneca always thought Petronius was to blame."

Pollia and Fabius were ashen, speechless, as they turned aghast to their host. Petronius returned their stares calmly. His smile sought to convey an avuncular compassion for the young couple, to make them feel the weight of their own ignorance and see that he had nothing to hide and was not afraid of their questions, but of course he was. To discuss such matters would be a grave mistake, perhaps fatal to the prospects for the evening's success. There was no time now for opening that sort of discourse—he was no Socrates, with days at his disposal to amble through the corridors of his life with these innocents. And suddenly he felt dizzy and disoriented, as the hours ahead, which only a few moments ago had seemed to yawn with promise, abruptly shrank within themselves, like a snail into its shell. He closed his eyes, but even as he did so he pictured how Pollia and Fabius would take it as a shame-ridden inability to meet their gaze, and he opened them again.

"I had nothing to do with Seneca's downfall, but it's true I was the emperor's impresario."

"But that was only a few years ago."

"As governor of Bithynia," Petronius began carefully, "one of my responsibilities was to plunder the province of its classical antiquities to stock a new palace being planned for the Palatine. I sent these back to Rome with long, eloquent letters describing their provenance and value, and I suppose as a result the emperor came to see me as the very embodiment of refinement and erudition. Later, when he summoned me back to Rome, I foolishly allowed myself to be drawn into his inner circle, from which there is no safe or simple way to extricate oneself. I can't say exactly how it happened—some might call it a death wish, one that is only now bearing fruit. In any case, I was thoroughly ensnared. I made myself indispensable, Nero's exclusive adviser on all matters aesthetic. He called me his 'Arbiter of Elegance.' When it came to the finer things in life, he did nothing without my say-so. At least for a short while."

"No, no, no," Fabius protested, sounding very much like a thwarted toddler. "That can't be. He is everything you are not. He is your enemy. He is your murderer."

"He was always my enemy and my murderer. I knew it even then. But he was nonetheless my patron, and I advised him to the best of my ability."

Pollia spoke almost in a whisper. "I don't understand, Petronius. How could you have allowed such a thing to happen? How could you?"

"Let's just say I lost my moral bearings. It was a dark time in my life. But here is the fish. Let us talk about all this later."

As the slaves descended upon the diners, bearing great bronze platters and crucibles, Petronius took the opportunity of the general distraction to watch Fabius and Pollia, who, with all attention focused on the arriving food, imagined themselves unobserved. Lying upon their stomachs, they were engaged in a furious, silent conversation with their eyes. Fabius's face was concealed from Petronius's view by a flop of hair, but Pollia was clearly pleading with him to moderate his emotion and remember his place in the party. Both, naturally, were deeply chastened by the revelation—information that was news to them alone—and further humiliated by Petronius's abrupt interruption of their inquiries. Now he had three angry guests to contend with.

Had it been a mistake to invite them? It was true, they were not of his innermost circle of friends, although for Pollia's sake they certainly would have come to be if circumstances had allowed. And it was also true, now more evidently than ever, that their youth and relative inexperience set them apart from everyone else present, not only in what they could and could not take for granted, but also in their bookish sense of honor and integrity. In that, Pollia was precisely the opposite of Melissa, whose only sense of right and good came from her heart, whereas Pollia was young and sheltered, her encounters with moral complexity and compromise limited to her genteel readings in history and philosophy. Petronius was sure that Pollia would learn from the experiences awaiting her, and probably even mature into the kind of woman Melissa could admire, but in the meantime they were—as Socrates might say—unlike and unlike, and Petronius could feel the older woman grow tense at his side every time the younger prepared to open her mouth.

Petronius had only wanted to balance the party between old and new, the tired and the vigorous, the past and the future, and perhaps, too, to provide Martialis with companions closer to his age, to sweeten what he had known would be a bitter draught to swallow. That, of course, had been a forlorn hope, and all the more misguided in that Fabius's tutored morality was alien to everything that Martialis respected. It had been foreordained that they would have nothing to say to one another, and Petronius ought to have anticipated that. And now Fabius and Pollia were feeling excluded and foolish, and that was Petronius's fault, too. In hospitality, as in poetry, every tension that arises must ultimately be resolved, and Petronius sighed wearily, knowing that he would have to revisit this whole sorry mess before the evening was out. A host can never relax, of course, but he would have wished tonight to be spared this duty along with all his others.

A silver charger was placed before him, burdened with fish: delicate fillets of sturgeon and red mullet, gleaming in their sauce of parsley and green peppercorns; a dome of Baian casserole; a disc of fried lamprey, dripping with black vinegar. Petronius glanced at it all disdainfully.

"Nereus, what are you doing?" Melissa said, quietly yet with severe matronly authority. "Petronius does not take his eel with sauce."

Nereus bowed and moved to remove the charger. "Forgive me, madam," he whispered.

"No, leave it, Nereus. Maybe something new tonight." Melissa's outrage was yet one more expression of ill-feeling that Petronius felt he could not endure, and he made show of pinching off a flake of the yellowish flesh and slipping it between his lips. The acid stung his gums, as if they had been chafed raw; but, vinegar or no, he had no hunger left at all. He sadly acknowledged its absence. He had somehow imagined, for reasons he could no longer fathom, that his appetites would be enlivened by the catalyst of their imminent extinction, as the colors of the sky are intensified by the setting of the sun. He recalled the hawk's speech to the nightingale, learned by rote from his tutor some forty years earlier: "Miserable thing, why do you cry out? One far stronger than you now holds you fast, and you must go wherever I take you, songstress that you are." Petronius must not cry out, nor even struggle in the raptor's grip, but rather flutter his wings as prettily as he might until his neck was broken.

"What is this dish, Anicius?" Pollia asked. "I've never seen it before. It's delightful."

"That is Baian casserole, my dear. A local delicacy."

"What's in it, do you know?"

"Well, you'd have to ask Lucullo for the full list, but the main ingredients are minced oysters, mussels, and sea urchins, fresh from Orata's ponds, or what's left of them since they built the shipyards."

Cornelia raised herself regally onto her left elbow. "If I'm not mistaken," she said confidingly, "you'll find it contains toasted pine kernels, celery, and rue."

"Pepper, coriander . . ."

"Cumin, raisin wine, dates . . ."

"But they must be *caryota* dates . . ."

"The best Spanish *garum*."

"And most important of all, olive oil from Venafrum. And only from Venafrum. Anything else would spoil the balance."

"A hint of Corycian saffron?"

"I think not."

A raw belch of a laugh cut off further conjecture, and they all turned as one to see Martialis, red in the face, mopping Falernian from his beard, chortling evilly and shaking his locks in exasperation. "You people," was all he managed to squeeze out.

"How have we offended this time, O Master?" Petronius asked.

"Forget it."

"No, tell us, do. So that we may avoid giving offense in the future."

"Avoid it? You *live* it."

"Marcus, if you insist on being insufferable, the least you could do is let us in on the joke."

Martialis sat up, all Iberian fury and hair. "Me insufferable? If you could only hear yourselves! Saffron this and Venafrum that, as if you're the cleverest fucking people in the world! What is it about patricians that allows them to believe that a taste for refined food and a facility with interiors give them nobility of soul? When the rest of us are lucky enough to eat something tasty, we feel sated and grateful. But for the idle rich, you *patrons of the arts*, eating well makes you feel virtuous, as if you'd done a good deed. You've done the world a favor by conferring your seal of approval on its bounty. You're so pleased with yourselves, with the art you've made of living, the gods *must* be smiling on you. As if an expert eye for a fine Greek marble, or the ability to distinguish top-rate *garum* from *muria*, has opened every gate of heaven for you! Welcome, you *discerners*, you cream of the crop, the first race of men. Hesiod must have been thinking of you. 'And they lived like gods without sorrow of heart, remote and free from toil and grief: miserable age rested not on them; but with legs and arms never failing they made merry with feasting beyond the reach of all evils.' Oh, but what's the point? Even in the lamplight I can see your smug, indulgent smiles. 'There he goes again, the fiery Spaniard. He doesn't feel alive unless he's fucking or fuming. It doesn't really *mean* anything.'"

"Now, let me see if I've got this right, Martialis. You are attacking us because we appreciate the beautiful things this world has to offer?"

"No, Lucilius, because you do *not* appreciate them. You use them the way a whore uses a mirror. You peer into them and they make you look beautiful to yourself."

"Those are harsh words, coming from a poet. Will you tell me that your poetry doesn't make you feel superior?"

"The difference is that I make the poetry, I don't consume it."

"How about making some poetry for us now, poet?"

"No."

"Don't sulk."

"I'm not sulking. I'm just not up to it tonight, that's all."

Melissa leaned across the couch to whisper in Martialis's ear, lightly touching the back of his neck with her fingertips, as a patient mother might do to an obstinate child. Petronius watched the anger and hurt release their hold on his features, and felt a momentary stab of jealousy, followed immediately by one of shame. Who, if not Martialis, should be the beneficiary of Melissa's motherly instincts? He had far greater need and had shown far greater appreciation of them than Petronius ever had.

After a moment, Martialis glanced up, met Petronius's gaze for the briefest instant, then lowered his eyes and nodded his head.

"Hooray!"

"Something young and risqué!"

"Something very rude, please."

"'Away let us fly to the renowned cities of Asia.'"

Martialis eased himself off the back of the couch and loped

self-consciously around the side to face his audience at the head of the water table. Out of the shelter of the screens, his long hair and tunic, smeared with grease, sauce, and wine, snapped and fluttered wildly in the breeze, framed by the black silhouette of Mount Gaurus and the stars about it. His eyes were in deep shadow, his hands clasped demurely before him. He began to recite immediately, without introduction, his Spanish accent suddenly thick and unctuous, as if it were a separate, complementary instrument to the well-worn poem. After declaiming the first couple of lines, he raised his eyes and addressed himself exclusively to Petronius.

> The Syrian barmaid, her hair swept back in a Greek headband,
>   expertly sways her sweet backside to the castanet,
> dances tipsy, luscious, in the smoke-filled tavern,
>   tapping the noisy tambourine against her elbow.

> "Why stay out in the heat and dust
> when you're so tired? How much better
> to lie back on a couch and take a drink!
> We have booths here, a gazebo, goblets, roses,
> pipes, lyres, and a summer-house
> cool under its awning of reeds.
> Just listen to the country pipes play a shepherd's tune
> as gently as in any dale of Maenalia.
> We have house wine freshly decanted from its pitch-sealed jug,
> and a brook running by with a raucous gurgle.
> We have garlands of violet-blossom and yellow flowers,
> melilot twined with crimson rose, and lilies
> gathered in willow baskets by a nymph
> from beside a virgin stream. We have little cheeses
> dried on rush mats, waxy autumn plums, chestnuts and
> sweet red apples; we serve bread, and love, and wine.

Look here, we have blood-red mulberries,
thickly clustered grapes, green cucumber still hanging
from its stalk. There's the Guardian of the orchard,
armed with his willow sickle—
no need to fear his massive tool!

"Come, traveler, your weary donkey is bathed in sweat,
let him rest! Vesta loves a little donkey.
The song of the cicadas is bursting through the treetops,
the lizard's cooling in his rocky nook.
If you're wise you'll come lie down
and drink straight from the summer jug,
or call for crystal flutes if that's your fancy.
Come now and rest in the shade of the vine,
wind a wreath of roses around your nodding head,
and taste the lips of a fresh young girl.
To hell with your prudish scowl—
what good are fragrant garlands to a heap of ashes?
Are you saving your wreath for your tombstone?
Bring on the wine and the dice, and damn anyone
who worries about tomorrow!
Death is plucking at your ear: 'Get on and live,'
he says, 'I'm coming.'"

There was a brief pause, then a smattering of hollow-handed applause as Martialis continued to hold Petronius's gaze. He knew perfectly well that it was one of Petronius's favorites—that was why he had chosen it, among far more obvious and appropriate recitals for the occasion—and Petronius struggled to maintain the apposite balance of gratitude and cool poise. There would be no weakening of resolve here, certainly no tears or moist eyes (as there might be on a less fraught occasion), in response to the provocation. Now was the moment to hammer home that fact for the boy once and for all, to persuade him to abandon the role of spoiler for the rest of the evening. Petronius had no difficulty winning the staring match, and Martialis lowered his eyes submissively.

"Sublime!" Anicius whispered.

"They call it a minor work," Cornelia said breathlessly, "but to me *The Syrian Barmaid* is Virgil at his best."

"It's not Virgil," said Lucilius.

"What do you mean it's not Virgil? Of course it's Virgil. Isn't it Virgil, Anicius?"

"No one knows for certain who wrote it, Cornelia, but it is now thought not to be Virgil."

"Oh dear. What I don't know. You have a Surisca, don't you, Petronius? A lovely young thing like the barmaid, I seem to recall. What's to become of her?"

"I haven't quite decided yet. As things stand, she goes to my brother, but I'd hate for him to have her. I may well alter my will before the evening is out. I'd offer her as a gift to Martialis, but he'd only spoil her. I think he ought to be made to pay for her, so that he can learn to appreciate the value of property and the responsibilities of a propertied man, but of course he can't possibly afford her."

"I'd be pleased to lend it to him," Anicius said. "What's she worth to you?"

"She's worth nothing to me now. On the market, she'd fetch at least thirty-thousand sesterces, I should think."

"You said twenty-thousand earlier," Martialis protested.

"That was the insider's price, dolt. You'd have known that if you'd put your mind to business once in a while instead of pussy. You could have leveraged the purchase and turned it around tomorrow. You'd have a hundred gold pieces in your purse instead of breadcrumbs. I may set her free instead."

"What a waste!"

"She has a boyfriend in the village, it seems. A baker. They want to leave Cumae and set up in Rome. I could leave her the money to pay her taxes and start up a small business, but it's a recipe for disaster, I'm sure of it. That country boy would be fleeced raw after five minutes in the Subura. The truth is, I don't know what to do about her. I'm quite fond of her, and I don't want to see her ruined."

"Now, if she were only a boy, I'd take her off your hands this minute."

"I'm sure of it, Anicius."

"What about Lucullo? Where's he going?"

"He's already got his freedom. He's more than earned it, don't you think?"

"Oh, Petronius, how could you? Now he'll go into the catering business and we'll have to pay through the nose for meals we used to get for free."

"Yes, you'll have a hard row to hoe, that's for certain. Now, please polish off all this fish while I attend to a little unfinished business. I'll be back shortly."

"I can't believe it's not Virgil. I always thought it was Virgil. That line about the little cheeses . . ."

Petronius slid off the mattress and sat at the edge of the couch, taking care to rise slowly, but the headache and dizziness had subsided and he was able to stand almost effortlessly, without wobbling. Aware of the eyes and the subtle lull in conversation behind him, he strode purposefully toward the house, trying to keep his shoulders back and to look straight ahead, not down at his uncertain feet. Commagenus was waiting for him at the foot of the stairs, his arm outstretched for support, but Petronius ignored him and took the steps unaided, even skipping up the last two.

"Is the vineyard company here?" he asked over his shoulder.

"Yes, sir."

"Have they had their supper?"

"Yes, sir."

"Good. Meet me in the little room in five minutes."

At the far end of the dining room, Petronius paused by the Hagesander bronze as Commagenus went on ahead to make his preparations. It was an essentially perfect work, priceless, Diana in full hunting regalia, posed in rest, leaning with one shoulder against her lance, left hand curled around the shaft just below the spearhead, cold eyes focused on some prey in the middle distance. Of course, she was magnificently youthful and vigorous, yet by depicting her at a moment of contemplation the sculptor had provided her with an immortal maturity, with none of the restless muscularity of the avid hunter in her prime. She would always be in her prime, so it meant nothing to her, less than nothing, not even the inchoate truth lying dormant in the bones and sinews of the heedless youth who thinks she will live forever, or doesn't think about it all. Hagesander had understood precisely how such ignorance would affect her stance and the architecture of her body. She was untouchable, unmoved and unmovable, both more and less than human. Strange that he had ever found her lovely. Even in her rare, fleeting moments of officious disapproval, Melissa was infinitely more desirable and touching. The Diana had once been a prized possession; now she was nothing to Petronius—in fact, he felt rather sorry for her. Tomorrow, Petronius knew, Nero would claim possession of her and anything else that took his fancy. Perhaps it was better that way—better, in any case, than that it should all fall to Turpilianus. At least with Nero the statue would end up on public display in the vast new imperial palace going up on the flanks of the Palatine, instead of being salted away in that gloomy tomb of a villa Turpilianus had recently purchased up north. Petronius stroked Diana's cheek with the knuckles of his left hand. Funny, he seemed to have more empathy for his statuary today than for his heirs and protégés. He moved on through the inner courtyard and into the kitchen.

The kitchen staff had all but finished their cleanup. The room smelled of burnt honey and sawdust. The dishes had been washed and stowed already, and two slave girls were sluicing down the tiled floor with buckets of water. Platters of fruit, pastries, and cheese sat ready on the table to be taken out to the guests at Vellia's command. Vellia perched on her stool in the corner, mumbling to herself as she pared a sorb apple, a crock of mulberry wine at her feet. Lucullo was nowhere to be seen. The members of the vineyard team, some dozen men of all ages, sat in sullen silence on the floor, barefoot and clad in their filthy work cloaks, enduring a harangue from their foreman, Marsius. They rose, slowly and wearily, upon Petronius's entrance, but none would meet his gaze as he surveyed them from the doorway.

Unlike his household staff, he barely knew these slaves, and not one by name, save Marsius. His vineyards were far up the slope, beyond the road to the bay, and on his rare inspections Petronius tended to reserve his communications for the foreman. In a sense, these men were more Marsius's slaves than his own, and he suspected that Marsius was neither lenient nor generous with them. By now, they would have been apprised of the situation, but Petronius had no illusions that their grim silence somehow reflected sympathy for their master. Tomorrow, they knew, they would have a new owner, almost certainly someone equally remote and careless of their welfare, and little would change for them. More likely, they were fearful and superstitious in the presence of a walking dead man, eager to be away as fate closed in upon him and anxious to escape its mysterious net. His death meant nothing to them—some, perhaps, were glad of it—but the stench of it made them uncomfortable, as it does to cattle and all creatures whose life, howsoever circumscribed and brutish, is their sole possession. Perhaps, too, they gloated inwardly at his downfall as an instance of divine justice. They would endure a while longer in their misery while the lofty were cut down in their prime and pride, and Petronius stood coolly puzzled that this thought could be of any comfort to them.

Marsius stepped up and made his obeisance. Petronius nodded and turned from him so as to include the entire company in his statement.

"Men, I'm sure you know by now that tomorrow you will have a new master. Perhaps it will be my brother, Petronius Turpilianus, or perhaps the emperor. That will be at the pleasure of Nero Caesar. Either way, you will serve him loyally as you have me. Each of you will have five silver denarii from my estate. Marsius, you will have leasehold of your cottage and its kitchen garden, to revert to the estate upon your death, plus one gold denarius. Now you are all free for the evening. Enjoy the festivities."

"Io Saturnalia!" the men responded gloomily, already shuffling toward the back door.

"Hail, Petronius!" Marsius tried halfheartedly to rally them to one expression of respect, but the muttered response was more curse than farewell, and Marsius was left to shrug sheepishly as he followed them out. In the end, even he owed nothing more to Petronius than this.

Petronius stood in the center of the room, quite at a loss about what to do or think. This feeling of dismay was new to him, and disturbing in its own right. Of course, in the army his men's high opinion of him had been of great concern, but that had been for practical reasons of effective leadership; and, besides, the admiration had been largely mutual. He had never, for the most part, extended that concern to his own slaves. This was the second time today that he had felt himself disappointed by a slave's lack of interest in his welfare, and he found it curious that his heart should choose to indulge this particular foible in its waning hours.

Petronius was put in mind of a story he had once heard Seneca tell. It concerned a vulgar, wealthy freedman, one Calvisius Sabinus, who had paid 100,000 sesterces apiece for slaves who had committed the entire life's work of various poets to memory. One slave knew all of Homer, another Hesiod, and so on through each of the nine lyric poets. Sabinus had done this, Seneca insisted, because he believed that whatever any of his slaves knew, he himself also knew. It was not only their bodies and their labor, but their minds and everything therein that Sabinus claimed to own. Petronius remembered the moral that Seneca drew from the story—"No man is able to borrow or buy a sound mind, but depraved minds are bought and sold every day"—but Petronius had seen it differently. Sabinus had most surely not been motivated by generosity, but he had given these slaves a purpose in life. Each was trained to do only one thing, and to do it superlatively; had they been given any other task than the one their master assigned them, their gifts would have been squandered, their destiny thwarted. As it was, however, they were given the opportunity to fulfill that destiny—an opportunity afforded to so few on this earth, free or otherwise.

Petronius had no such gift for his slaves, and in consequence was never quite certain what it was he expected from them in return. Their labor, their loyalty, their cooperation, assuredly. And beyond that?

How foolish it would be to expect love from one's slave! Petronius knew this as well as anyone, having been raised, educated, fed, clothed, and cosseted by them his entire life. The nature of the relationship between master and chattel was, ultimately, one of brute force, or at least its implicit threat. And yet even this affiliation was not entirely free of fuzzy, porous borders. After all,

Plato and every other philosopher agreed that men love what is good, and Petronius liked to think of himself as a good man, or perhaps as a man aspiring to goodness. Was love between master and slave theoretically possible, then? What of Demetrius, who knew his intimate thoughts, in whom he had confided and to whom, in moments of doubt, he had even turned for advice and solace? What of Lucullo, who permitted himself liberties of address with his master that not even Martialis would entertain? What of Surisca, upon whom he had lavished expensive gifts, and whose pleasure in bed he catered to as assiduously as he did the most high-born of his lovers? He was genuinely fond of these people; he was protective and solicitous—more, surely, than what was merely required by the defining behavior of a "good master"? Could a master permit himself transgressions of intimacy that a slave must never reciprocate? If a master could be fond, could a slave also? Petronius doubted this, having seen so little evidence of it in his own life and that of society, so why now, of all times, did he feel it as an absence and a reproach that his slaves could not love him, nor even summon the energy to bid him a fond farewell? He recalled Demetrius's face earlier in the evening, how he had misread the scribe's fear as affection, and felt like a man who has left his home with something terribly important, yet something he is unable to identify, undone.

"Master?" It was Vellia, still in her corner.

"What is it?"

"I only wish to say, sir, that you have been a good master to us, and we all know it."

"Thank you, Vellia."

"And we'll all be very happy for you when you die like a man tonight."

"Thank you, Vellia."

Petronius turned and left the room.

The granite slabs of the dark hallway were cold against his bare feet and silent, absorbing all sound like a tomb. Petronius thought of his own tomb, dark and ungiving like this, wherein he would be laid tomorrow. He felt, impatiently with himself, as if he were already his own ghost, wandering the subterranean halls that connected his vault to the rest of the necropolis, the temple of Apollo, the acropolis, and ultimately to the cave of the Sibyl and its hidden entrance to the underworld. How long would he wander, padding silently like this, searching for the way out? Months, years? Having crossed the threshold, would he even remember what it was he was supposed to be looking for, or who he was or had been? He paused, and allowed the chill to seep up into the bones of his feet. There would be no ache like this, of that he was reasonably certain, and possibly no sensation of any kind, no sense of pressure, weight, temperature, humidity, breath entering and leaving the body, light pushing against the ragged edges of shadow. The very walls and archways, perhaps, would seem as insubstantial as mist, translucent and shifting, their layout arbitrary and mystifying. What purpose could they serve to a spirit who can walk in a straight line through mountains and seas, through the center of the earth? And yet he was quite convinced that he would be wandering them dutifully this time tomorrow, that even in the daze of the newly dead he would somehow recognize the patterns they traced, their dim echo of some immutable law of nature, as a newborn bird somehow knows to open its beak skyward to receive its first meal. Yes, surely the dead have instincts to guide them through their new world, and quite probably they heed those instincts the way animals in this world heed theirs, with unthinking trust, instead of ignoring and despising them the way living men do. But do they have memories?

Petronius passed along the corridor to the little room where

Commagenus awaited him in the lamplight. The brass krater and the gold-hilted dagger had been washed and polished. There was a clean roll of bandages on the table beside them.

"Let's go," he said, stepping forward through the doorway. He held his wrist out and Commagenus began to unroll the bandage. The first few layers of cotton were white and loose and came away readily, but then it began to turn brown—in patches first, finally solid—stiff and recalcitrant; nearer the skin, it became hopelessly glued, both to itself and to the wound. Any attempt to force it, both men saw, would result in a messy, uncontrolled opening of the gash, blood everywhere. It must be done cautiously, with dignity and an eye to posterity, even with no one but a slave as witness.

"I'll fetch some warm water," Commagenus muttered, and slipped from the room. Petronius propped his damaged wrist in the palm of his right hand, as if it were a dying child, though he felt no sympathy for it, and looked vacantly about the spare chamber. There was nothing to catch his eye but a small round window, high up on the outer wall, that framed a few bright, indeterminate stars. Had he followed a more traditional career path, Petronius would have studied for some priesthood or other, he would have learned to identify the constellations in their multitudes, and they would not be such strangers to him as they were tonight. Was it possible, after all, that they held a message for him? Or that, on some other night—one spent, perhaps, lying on one's back at the side of a sleeping lover, wondering how to draw blood from a stone—they had been speaking to him of alternate ways and he had been deaf to their advice? How unlikely it all seemed, yet even if it were true he doubted there was any consolation to be found there, or in the flights of wild birds, the steaming entrails of sacrificial beasts, the omens that served as currency to the augurers. The omens were always bad. You didn't need to be a priest to know that.

Commagenus returned with a bowl of water and some hand towels draped across his forearm. Petronius sat on the edge of the bed and the slave knelt at his feet. Moistening a towel, Commagenus began dabbing delicately at the encrusted wound, and shortly the soiled bandage fell away into the bowl, immediately turning the water a sickly pink. The exposed gash, some two inches long, was raw and pulsing, almost a living thing in its own right, and clearly ready to reopen at the slightest pressure. Commagenus continued to swab it lightly.

"Get on with it," Petronius snapped, although he was rather touched by the slave's solicitude. "It doesn't need to be clean. Get the krater."

Commagenus lowered the bowl to the floor and replaced it with the brass krater beneath Petronius's wrist. He held it by the stem in both hands, his fingers splayed along the underside as if he were a priest receiving a libation. With his right hand, Petronius grasped his own left forearm, pressing his thumb into the soft flesh above the wound. He pulled the thumb back toward the elbow, and the scab gave way with only the mildest sensation of tearing. The blood immediately poured forth as it had earlier, splashing raucously into the hollow of the krater. Petronius felt a bubble of nausea rise in his belly and subside. He willed himself to focus on the matter at hand and to closely monitor the flow of blood, lest he spill too much and incapacitate himself for the rest of the dinner.

It was only as the krater began slowly to fill that he noticed that it had been assiduously washed and polished since the first bloodletting. Had Commagenus done it himself, or had he delegated the distasteful chore to a lower-ranking member of the household staff? What had happened to the blood? Had it been poured down the courtyard drain, to be sluiced away into the sea? Petronius was abruptly struck by the odd image of its being carried to the kitchen, where Lucullo might set it aside to allow the fat to separate and congeal, later to be incorporated into his justly famous black pudding, or as a thickening agent for one of his rich wine-and-honey-based sauces. Alternately, it might be fed to the pigs on the farm, who would surely be grateful and perhaps, like the vineyard slaves, enjoy some short-lived thrill of vindication.

Petronius had tasted human blood before—both his own and that of friend and foe, whipped into his face and open mouth in the frenzy of hand-to-hand combat—and it evoked little fascination or revulsion in him. But was blood sacrificially spilled different somehow? Was there something hallowed about it, or accursed? He searched his mind for some forgotten instruction or ritual exaction. Oh, let the pigs have it, then! Or maybe Martialis would want it, should he ever return to Spain, where certain ancient Celtic practices were said to still be practiced. Perhaps it could be used to summon his spirit from the underworld? It was only when the absurdity of this last thought struck him that Petronius realized that his mind had been wandering, and that he had already drained the requisite pint, and a little surplus.

"That'll do," he said curtly, and even in these brief words heard the slurring in his voice.

Again, Commagenus pressed a thick wad of cotton on the wound and wrapped it tightly in linen. Again, the dressing held. Petronius dismissed the slave with a flick of the wrist, and continued to sit with his head slumped between his shoulders. The nausea had returned, his face felt hot and prickly, his sandals as heavy as lead slabs. Two more pints would kill him off. Two more pints, two more pints. It sounded like a marching song, and for a moment he thought himself on horseback at the head of a column riding to Volandum in Armenia, where great things awaited him if only he could rid himself of these damned locusts chirping in his ears. It was a brutally hot summer's day on the high plateau, his cheeks burned, but water was short and it would hurt morale if he were seen to be abusing the rations. His mouth was parched and evil-tasting; he rode with his head bowed to maximize the shade upon his neck and chest. Two more pints, two more pints, the men sang. He tried to harness his attention to the marching rhythm.

Melissa stood at the door with a bowl of wine in her hands. He could hardly place her at first, but then the room and the night snapped into focus, and he knew that he would be all right.

"Is this a place for you, Melissa?" Petronius said coldly, turning his back to her. "Is it right that our guests should be left unattended?"

There was a light rustle of fabric, and then he felt her hand on his shoulder. It was not the first time she had touched him all evening, and it still felt wrong, ill-balanced.

"Would this be a good time to talk?"

"You pick your moments."

"There aren't many left."

She held the wine to his lips, and he drank. It was cold, and sweetened, and tasted good.

"You are angry with me tonight, Titus. Why is that?"

"I am not angry with you, Melissa Silia."

Melissa considered him pensively. "We expect a great deal of you tonight, Titus, as much as you expect of yourself," she said. "And as for all this silly, secretive bloodletting, I don't think you should go through with it."

"I'm surprised at you, Melissa. You know better than that. Of course I have to do it. I *want* to do it."

"No, Titus . . ."

"There is no life without honor, no honor without . . . Are you really going to force me to preach to you at this late hour? Please go back."

"You misunderstand me, Titus. Of course you must act as

honor requires. I simply mean you need not do it now, while the others are here. It can wait until supper is over and the guests have gone. If you lose any more blood tonight, you're not going to be able to see to your guests. You were almost delirious earlier. What if you were to pass out in the middle of the symposium? Where's the dignity in that?"

Petronius stared down at the bandage on his wrist, already spotted with blood. Certainly there was nothing beautiful about it, nothing seductive. It looked like the sheath of skin discarded by a diseased, elderly snake.

"If that's what you came to say, you've said it now."

"Actually, I came to tell you that the captain of the guard has stopped by to pay his respects. You ought to go out to him."

"What's his name?"

"Sextus Gnipho."

"I know him. Does he not know me?"

"Of course he knows you. You know he knows you."

"But you said earlier . . ."

"He did not mention your acquaintance when we were making our arrangements."

"Perhaps he was being discreet, thinking you are my wife."

"Discretion was hardly the hallmark of his behavior."

"Well, go along. I'll be out shortly."

"Shall I wait with you?"

"Go along."

Petronius was tired, light-headed, nauseated, and anxious, but he had recognized the wisdom of her suggestion the moment she'd made it. It made little sense to carry through with his original plan. Nero was unlikely, at this time of night, to dispatch his thugs to finish the job. Far better—more dignified, yes—to do it in one final act in the early hours, when all had gone. He could have a quiet word with Martialis, persuade him to tweak the account of his death to reflect his dramatic intentions, just as Paulina had done for Seneca. It would only be a minor fabrication, not a wholesale reinvention. Biographers operated on hearsay all the time.

But he had been very rude to Melissa. He was angry, it was true. In fact, he recognized that he had been irrationally resentful of her all night, and now, perhaps, he understood why. It was not, of course, about what she had done with Gnipho that afternoon in return for the liberties they were all enjoying this evening. She had done it for him, Petronius, and with evident distaste and reluctance—an act of heroic, matronly martyrdom straight out of Republican myth. It can't have been pleasant, allowing herself to be pawed and poked by that grizzled, hairy Gaul. Of course, ever thorough and courteous, she would have feigned pleasure, climax even, to ensure Gnipho's complacency, make him feel he'd got the best of the deal. Maybe she'd even enjoyed it, though he doubted it—she liked smooth men with sophisticated technique. Where had they done it? Up against a tree by the roadside, within earshot of the guardsmen? No, Gnipho would have been too respectful for that. They'd have gone to the tradesmen's cemetery up the hill, and he'd have had her sprawl over a moss-covered sarcophagus, her synthesis hitched above her waist, and taken her from behind. No danger of seeing her opinion of him reflected in her unruffled gaze. He'd have grunted like a hog, given her a moment or two to compose herself, then resumed his martial demeanor, stood to attention before his superior, and she'd have smiled at him gently, not forgiving, but open and cool, like a hostess greeting a guest she had never met before, to let him know that as of that instant they had no history together of any kind. Of course, Gnipho would never have had a woman like Melissa before, and would immediately feel abashed, a thief and a liar. Petronius had seen legionaries lustily, hilariously cut down little children in the fever of a broken siege, then later weep to themselves in shame in some darkened corner where they thought they could not be seen. Gnipho would feel like that after fucking Melissa. He would not be the first upon whom she'd had that effect.

But none of this was the cause of Petronius's displeasure with her tonight. She was free to do as she pleased; Petronius could make no claim of exclusivity upon her. It was, rather, her unwonted actorship in his drama that bothered him, the fact that she had come to play an adult role, the role of an equal, in a performance he had written for himself as sole protagonist, director and impresario. Had she not always before been to him precisely what he had asked her to be, especially when she had understood better than he did what that was? Two years earlier, when he had sent her away—or at least encouraged her to explore her independence—had she not gone in precisely the right, forward-looking spirit, without a word of recrimination? And last week, when she'd offered to remain with him to the end—to today—it had all seemed so natural that she alone should be the companion of his last days. He had seen her as a silent spectator, or at best a prompter, whispering his cues when he lost them; instead, in the course of the week, she had become a principal player in the production, hiring the supporting cast, arranging their blocking, stepping into his character when he fell short. She had made him feel inadequate at precisely the moment when he most needed to feel invincible, just as she had surely done to Gnipho. It was not her fault, of course; he had pushed her into it with his own insufficiency, and she, naturally, had proved her unflappable competence at every step along the way, as she had always done. That competence, of course, had been their undoing. It was despicable, but he wanted her grateful and worshipful, and even though he knew perfectly well that she could be none of these, he wanted to punish her for it. Oddly, there seemed to be no way to do right by her, precisely because she made it so easy for him. She'd come to him, and he'd sent her away—again. How childish, and typical! Well, perhaps there was still time to set it right. Yet he had to admit to himself that even this prospect of atonement was self-serving and polluted with self-regard. He hung his heavy head. Had it always been this way between them? He closed his eyes and allowed the past to overtake him.

ருருருருருரு

WHEN HE RECEIVED confirmation that the ninth cohort had marched for the eastern frontier, Petronius dispatched his own lictors to Prusa with a letter and orders to escort Melissa to Nicomedia. In the letter, he excitedly described the tasteful little townhouse he'd purchased for her in a quiet residential district near the palace; the domestic slaves he would place at her disposal; the generous allowance she would enjoy to decorate her new home and clothe herself presentably; the privacy and freedom that would soon be theirs for the first time. He also sought to anticipate her objections. "Please understand," he'd written, "I am trying neither to buy your loyalty nor to entice you into a gilded cage. The deed to the house is in your name and will remain so regardless of your decision."

Petronius was not terribly surprised when the lictors returned from Prusa with nothing but a written response. "Governor," it read, "I wish you had consulted me before going to such great effort and expense on my behalf. Now please understand me: It is precisely because I have been entrapped and unhappy for so long that I am in no hurry to exchange one situation of dependency for another. I know you think it unfair of me to compare you, patriarch of the Petronii and Proconsul of Bithynia, to a lowly centurion, but I have spent half my adult life regretting one decision and have no intention of spending the other half regretting another."

119

As he galloped that afternoon for Prusa, Petronius was forced to ask himself a question he had hitherto managed to evade: Could she be playing him for a fool? Was it possible that she—about whom, after all, he knew so very little—was simply raising the stakes to a point at which Petronius would offer her anything, even her own independent fortune, to secure her commitment? He considered it highly unlikely, though not impossible, yet decided that it made no difference to him whatsoever. So long as he could have her, and keep her, and not have to share her, he was prepared to go to any lengths necessary. If that was what she wanted, that was what she should have. Yet, as he approached the city gates, his confidence began to waver as he recalled that he really had no idea what she wanted from him, and never had, and perhaps never could, because he was so obtuse and ridiculous, and because she refused to explain herself. It was not a question of throwing offers at her, any one of which was likely to offend her, but of throwing himself upon her mercy, and promising to do whatever it was she wanted him to do, if only she would condescend once and for all simply to tell him how to please her.

The camp was all but deserted, with the exception of a few officers' wives and a handful of sentries too old or feeble to make the march eastward. Petronius was carelessly, perhaps foolhardily indifferent to the stares he attracted as he tracked her down to the barracks washhouse, where he found her rinsing white sheets at a trough of cold flowing water. She did not seem in the least put out to see him, but simply offered her cheek and went on with her washing. Still, when Petronius found himself incapable of opening his mouth, painfully conscious of his almost limitless potential for aggravating the situation with a single word, she was kind enough to launch the negotiations.

"What have you come to say to me, Governor?" she asked, keeping her back to him.

"I've decided to do whatever you tell me to do."

Her shoulders heaved once or twice in silent laughter. "You know I can't do that," she said at last.

"Why not? What's wrong with telling someone, directly and frankly, what you expect of him?"

"I've told you before. Unless you already understand it, no words can ever explain it, and once you've understood it, no words will be necessary to explain it. Just keep trying. It will come to you eventually."

"What will come to me? Why must it be so impossible for you to tell me how to love you?"

She snorted through her nose. "And that is precisely what you must learn for yourself. I've waited twelve years for my husband to learn it, and I'll tell you something—I don't hold out much hope for him, but if he were to learn it tomorrow, I'd turn you away and never give you another thought. I won't go to Nicomedia or anywhere else with you until you can prove to me that you are not exactly like him."

She went on with her washing. Petronius considered the possibility that all she really wanted was to be made to obey, that somehow, miraculously, if he were to stride across the room, bend her over the trough, raise the hem of her dress, and take her forcibly, he would actually be giving her exactly what she wanted. It seemed improbable, but what did he know? It was as likely as anything else, he supposed; as likely as her extorting him for money, or wanting no money at all, or suing her husband for divorce, or remaining with him for the rest of her days, or learning to be docile and compliant, or sending Petronius away forever without an explanation. He advanced upon her in anger and lust, but stopped after only two steps.

"Wait," he said. "What if I ask nothing of you at all? No promises, no declarations until the day you say you love me?"

She stopped washing and raised her chin. "You don't have it

in you, Governor," she said thoughtfully. "I know you—you won't be able to help yourself."

"You can leave any time I fail." Another silence.

"You promise never to say you love me until I give you leave to do so?"

"Never."

"Never to ask me to say I love you?"

"Never."

"Never to talk of our future together, or of all that you will give me, or of how happy you'll make me?"

"Never."

She sighed, dropped her shoulders, and cocked her hips. The sheet floated to the far end of the trough, where it bunched up against the drain. A few moments later, the water began to overflow the entire length of the trough, splattering her dress and crawling in a steady sheet toward Petronius. Barefoot, she seemed not to notice, to have lost herself in thought as she did after sex, but then she straightened her back, leaned across for the sheet, unplugged the drain, and resumed her scrubbing.

"Go back to Nicomedia," she said. "I'll make my decision by morning."

He awaited her in the interior courtyard of her new house, standing beside the *kouros*. She was wearing the synthesis of cream-colored Indian silk that he had personally selected for her in anticipation of this moment, along with strands of Arabian pearls that she had woven into her hair. His eyes filled with tears when he saw her, and he fell to his knees and pressed his face into her belly when she joined him in the garden. Her hands gently stroked the back of his head.

"Now, now," she said gently.

The next few months were the most joyful of his life. At last he let fall all pretense of attending to his duties, and devoted almost every waking hour to Melissa. There was no question of her living with him in the palace, but there was nothing unusual or scandalous about an unmarried official keeping a mistress, so he was able to come and go from her house as he pleased—a most gratifying change from the secrecy and paranoia of their trysts in Prusa. She, on the other hand, remained a married woman, and there was always the slim but real chance that she would be recognized in the streets by one of her husband's comrades in arms or his spouse. To protect her reputation and his own, her forays into the city, either in Petronius's litter or strolling on his arm, her face veiled, were limited to the early morning or midafternoon, when most shops were closed and citizens at their midday meals and rest. Occasionally, to escape the increasing oppressiveness of the summer heat, they would arrange to meet outside the city walls and take long walks in the hills or along the seashore, admiring the cargo ships, laden with Bithynian pine, boxwood, sour cherries, and saffron, as they plied their way through the gulf to the Marmara, the Hellespont, and the wider Aegean beyond. Finally, when July grew murderously hot, he took a modest villa for her on the shore of Lake Sophon, just a few well-paved miles east of the city, where they would meet uninterrupted for days on end. What his deputies and the citizenry thought of these absences, he never discovered and didn't care.

She awaited him in bed each morning, confident that he would arrive long before breakfast, and he always did. With the harsh, particulate light and the noise of awakening commerce filtered by curtains of the lightest undyed cotton sheeting, he would shed his tunic at the door and join her on the linen bedclothes without so much as a greeting. She might conceal herself beneath the blanket, or he might find her naked on her stomach, the top sheet thrown back, her legs spread, a bolster wedged under her midriff. At such times, foreplay was entirely superfluous. With her cool buttocks pressing into his abdomen, she would turn her face to the side and look off into the middle distance; should he attempt to meet her gaze, she would turn her head in the opposite direction. And always, that contented yet ungiving smile played on her lips, as if she were contemplating her next move in a game of robbers and soldiers against an over-matched opponent. Never a moan, never a term of endearment, never an abandoned exclamation of release. The closest she ever came to demonstrating unmediated passion was when she had her little Numidian maid warm a cruet of honey and saffron, which she would slowly pour over him and even more slowly lick off. He tried this trick on her once or twice, but found that he far preferred her natural taste, which was sweeter to him than any honey.

He tried always to be mindful of the rules, but so delightful were their hours together that he occasionally lost himself in a stupor of contentment. Mealtimes, often following upon long, timeless sessions of lovemaking, found him at his weakest and most forgetful. They sometimes ate at the palace, secluded be-hind billowing muslin curtains on the great terrace overlooking the harbor; more often than not, they took their meals in the townhouse garden—cool, shaded, and scented with verbena and rosemary—because they both preferred the cooking of her Persian chef, purchased at enormous expense in the slave market of Ephesus, to that of the proconsular kitchen.

It was the Persian who introduced her to the miracle of saf-fron, the taste of which would forever recall Petronius to those early months of first love. Lingering in comfortable silence over great platters of rice steamed with raisins and mint; cold salads of parsley, cracked wheat, olive oil, and citron; chilled oysters and urchins scooped raw from the shell with warm scraps of fragrant flatbread; grilled cubes of spring lamb marinated in cumin and allspice; and green Lebanese wine iced with shavings from the Taurus mountains, Petronius was at his most vulnerable to his unspoken yearnings.

"Do you know?" he said one day, in what he took to be a clever circumvention, "I believe I could go on like this forever. Couldn't you?"

She hesitated a moment, then spoke in a noncommittal monotone. "I could certainly go on like this for the rest of the afternoon."

"Why not for the rest of our . . . of your life?"

"The afternoon is good enough for me."

"Must you always be so casual about everything?"

She closed her eyes and sighed with resignation, then sat up on her couch and leaned across the table to grasp his free hand in both of hers. She stared him intently in the eyes as she spoke.

"I am truly sorry if you think I'm being casual. That is your mistake, Governor. I am anything but, I assure you. I am weighing everything in the balance, everything. And that is why it is so important that you learn to respect my wishes. Can you please do that for me?"

Throughout that hot summer they fucked in the house, on the waterfront shingle, on the lakeside veranda. It was always the same from their very first encounter: she cool and detached, he desperate to penetrate deeper than it was physically possible to penetrate. What kind of a man is excited by his lover's indifference, he asked himself? Every time they fucked, it was an opportunity to pose the question in a slightly different way, but the answer lay always just beyond his reach. In someone else's hands, would this be a difficult riddle to solve? Would it be a riddle at all? For Petronius, it was as unfathomable as the Eleusinian mysteries, and just as foreign.

Somehow, he came to see, it was himself that he was seeking to penetrate, down to the roots of his need, to where humiliation and shame became the catalysts of pleasure and self-knowledge, but the unbearably intense sensual gratification he derived from feeling perfectly superfluous to his partner became an insuperable barrier to its own understanding, like a fortress made entirely of ramparts but no keep. The arousal was so strong that it made all intellectual effort invalid, distracting, and coarse, and when it was spent its memory was furred with languid regret. Climax was the least rewarding phase of love-making for Petronius, because it brought to an end the blissful oblivion wherein her strength and presence reduced him to the state of nothingness that he had come to crave beyond all things. Did she want him for his money, his power, his name, his learning, his conversation, his devotion? When, in rare moments of lucid solitude, he reasoned with himself that she must want him for *something*, he found that he didn't care to consider what it might be, lest the knowledge shatter the delicious illusion that she wanted him for nothing at all.

He understood quite clearly what he wasn't to say or ask, but there were peripheral subjects that might be safely broached. He was curious about her husband, a man whose very existence baffled him and about whom she always spoke with a kind of generous resignation, as if he were a troublesome but fondly tolerated pet dog.

"He's the kind of man who will stick his face right up into yours and spend the next hour talking about fishing tackle or the best way to polish bronze. He gets so close you can't even turn your face to breathe. And yet he always means well."

"He has never abused you, then?"

"The only wrong he has ever done me is to marry me. After twenty years of marriage, he still can't believe his luck. His gratitude is a tomb."

"You might have divorced him at any time."

She sighed and turned away. It was one of the very few times he had ever seen her give in to sorrow. "It would kill him. And anyway, where would I go, what would I do?"

"I suppose I'd take you in."

She shook her head without turning around.

But there were moments, many of them, when the urge to speak out, and to test the limits of her proscriptions, was almost too strong to bear. Had she perhaps forgotten what she had made him promise? Had the good life, and the prospect of so much more to come, not weakened her resolve? And did she not recall, as he did with a terrible sense of foreboding, that his term as proconsul would lapse in the early autumn, and with it all this blithe, careless pretense?

One blistering afternoon of early August, they sat naked on the steps of the boat landing at their country villa, chest-deep in the cold, viridescent water of Lake Sophron, each in a broad-brimmed straw hat against the hazy white sun. They watched a family of swans ease its way along a thicket of bulrushes. Of all the world's creatures, the swans seemed to be the only ones awake.

"Have you heard from Junius?" he asked absently.

"My friend forwarded me a letter from the barracks last week. The ninth is on maneuvers on the Armenian border. Minor skirmishes, he tells me. Nothing dangerous."

"He may be there for years, you know."

"He retires in a year."

Petronius allowed a minute or two to go by in silence, as if the subject had entirely faded from his thoughts. Then he spoke again, in what he hoped was a convincing quintessence of nonchalance.

"I'll be leaving Bithynia in a month or two myself, you know."

"Mmm."

"Have you given any thought, you know, to . . . to what you might do?"

"About what?"

"About coming with me?"

"No."

"Don't you think you ought?"

"Careful, Governor."

"Why should I be careful? I'm not exacting any promises."

"You've done so well up to now. I know what an effort it's been. I'm genuinely proud of you."

"You can't honestly tell me you haven't given it any thought."

She slid beneath the waters, and there was silence on the hot surface of the lake. She reemerged some six cubits out, her lovely flaxen hair plastered to her head, one onyx earring flashing. She was just close enough to be able to speak without raising her voice, just far enough for her voice to be oddly amplified by the water's agency.

"Anything I might say now, you would misconstrue. You're not yet ready to hear me speak. Please be patient, Titus. There's time yet for all to come out right."

"You called me Titus."

"There, do you see now?" And this time, when she submerged herself, she resurfaced beyond earshot.

෬෬෬෬෬

PETRONIUS WAS FEELING stronger now. The buzzing in his ears had subsided; his face no longer burned. He pushed himself to his feet, where he remained for several moments, unsteady but relatively clear-headed. Melissa had left the wine bowl on the side table, but he did not yet trust himself to reach for it. He closed his eyes and took several deep breaths, tried one step, then another, and found that he could manage well enough. His left hand was quite numb, but otherwise he seemed to be in working order still. With his arms braced against either wall, he guided himself toward the center of the house, revived by the feel of cool, smooth plaster against his palms. In the inner atrium, he paused to splash his cheeks with water from the fountain, and presently found himself sufficiently fortified to consider returning to his guests.

Drying his face against the fragrant yellow wool of his tunic as he crossed the reception hall, Petronius stopped at the top of the stairs that led down to the terrace. The night had turned positively chilly; in setting below Gaurus, the moon had stolen away with any vestige of warmth left behind by the long-departed day, and the stars now glistened in the bed of the night like ice at the bottom of a mixing bowl. The braziers blazed, bright wasps of flame and spark rising on the wind, and a second counterpane of dully gleaming red silk had been overlaid upon that of purple, yet the guests huddled beneath them seemed drained of their party spirit by the labor of feigning to ignore their discomfort. Of course, they would not have presumed to adjourn to the dining room in the absence of their host, but they were clearly ready to move indoors. Well, it wouldn't hurt them to wait a while longer.

They were being entertained by a soldier in a hooded military cloak buckled at his right shoulder, revealing the short leather arm-straps of his cuirass and the bronze greaves strapped to his shins. His Praetorian helmet was tucked beneath his left armpit, and the bulge of a short sword was evident at his right hip beneath the fabric of his cloak. Gnipho was dressed for battle, entirely unnecessarily in this posting, yet a touching token of respect for his former commander. He stood at ease on the far side of the water table, his back to the house. Martialis and Pollia had noticed Petronius loitering at the top of the steps, but the others were listening raptly to Gnipho, who was no doubt retailing grossly exaggerated tales of his exploits in Asia. Indeed, so thoroughly absorbed was he in his storytelling, and enthralled in his novel role as center of attraction to an audience of the high and mighty, that he failed in a very unsoldierly manner to register Petronius's approach. Petronius briefly considered disarming him from behind, a prank that would be much appreciated among the ranks but that would certainly be deeply humiliating to the centurion in present company, and instead cleared his throat at several paces' distance. Gnipho snapped to attention with barely a glance over his shoulder, and Petronius slapped him on the back.

"At ease, centurion."

"Hail, General."

"It's good to see you, Gnipho. How long have you been back in Italy?"

"Almost two years now, general."

"Left the Third, have you?"

"Once we took care of Tiridates, there didn't seem much point in sticking around Armenia. Too much loot and not enough to spend it on."

"So you bought yourself a commission in the Praetorians. Splendid."

"Wasn't cheap, but worth every penny, sir."

"Captain Gnipho was just regaling us with your exploits in the war, Petronius," Cornelia said.

"Was he, now? Did he tell you about the time he saved my life outside Artaxata?"

"Thrilling!"

"All lies. It was I who saved him. He'd impaled himself on a broken ox-cart trace, trying to make off with his booty."

"The general was the best legate ever served under Corbulo, ma'am, and it was an honor to save him from drowning like a kitten in the frozen Araxes."

"Two years the Third Gallic spent under canvas. Murderous heat in the summer, winters so cold men snapped their own fingers off like icicles, up and down the Armenian plateau, the enemy always just over the next hill. Never enough food, never enough water. A grand time was had by all."

"All that lived, and some that didn't. You were sorely missed after your transfer to Bithynia, sir."

"How are your men set up at the gate? Have everything they need?"

"They thank you for the feast, sir, and for the blankets. It's a cushy posting for them."

"It's the least we could do, seeing as they're missing out on the festivities."

"Soldier's life. Still, I've pulled the pickets off the beach. Saw no need to make them suffer in the wind."

"You're getting soft in your old age, Gnipho."

"As you say, General. I'll be getting back to my post, if you have no further use for me here."

"I'm happy to see you've done well for yourself. Good luck for the future. Dismissed."

The centurion offered a regulation salute to his commander and a half bow to the general company, and slipped away through the orchard. Petronius watched him fade into the night. He could not resent Gnipho for accepting Melissa's favors that afternoon; a soldier's life is a lonely one, the only women he ever sees are whores and bedraggled, terrorized refugees. It was not, after all, a betrayal in any real sense of the word, since Gnipho was actually doing him a genuine service at some risk to his own career. And it was impressive that Gnipho had been able to address his former commander with such a lack of self-consciousness. Petronius wondered if he himself would have been so at ease in the centurion's position. Probably, that was the difference between a truly great soldier, like Gnipho, and a merely competent one. In any case, Melissa would not have offered herself if she hadn't been sure of being accepted.

Petronius turned back to his guests. Dessert had been served in his absence—apples, pears, apricots, and peaches on balsawood boats floating on the water table, along with a wide platter of beaten brass laden with Melissa's favorite saffron honey cakes, golden and glistening in the lantern light. Smaller bowls of almonds, filberts, hazelnuts, pistachios, and walnuts, and rush mats of fresh Trebula cheese—the same cheese described in *The Syrian Barmaid*—had been laid out along the rim, untouched. Petronius could sense the tension in the air—Gnipho's slip of the tongue had escaped no one. Who would speak first—one who could not bear to let the revelation go unremarked, or one who would seek to drown it in a torrent of banalities? An owl called from a distant cypress, the wind moaned in the empty sky, and the windbreaks thumped against their burden. They all waited.

"Nice fellow, that centurion," Anicius ventured hesitantly.

"There are no pickets on the beach, Petronius," Martialis said quietly, almost as if he were offering a threat. "He was sending you a message. He was presenting you with a gift."

Petronius sighed and lowered himself gingerly onto the edge of the water table. "There are no pickets, Martialis, because the tide has gone out and my yacht is beached until dawn. There was no message."

"Must you treat me like an idiot? The tide is high and you are free to sail. Why don't you escape, for god's sake? For the sake of those who love you?"

"I have always been free to sail, Martialis. And it's for the sake of those who love me that I . . . oh, somebody else explain it to him. I'm tired of it."

"Don't bother. I'm leaving." But no sooner had the young man begun to push himself up and back toward the rear of the couch than Melissa stopped him with a gently murmured "tut."

"Petronius is about to make his offerings, Marcus. You can't leave now without offending our household gods."

"If they're not offended by now, nothing can offend 'em." But he grudgingly resumed his place, glaring impotently at his host. Nereus and Persis circled the water table with pitchers, and the guests held out their hands to be washed in anticipation of the blessing.

A small bronze tray bearing the necessary accessories had been placed before him, although Petronius had had no intention of saying any prayers to anyone tonight, and could scarcely muster the strength to stand. He saw now, however, that it would be easier and quicker to go through with it than to protest and make a scene, as this was what Melissa wanted. He could barely even remember the names of the tribal and family hearth gods, let alone their functions and order of precedence, but he rose to his feet and began to run through the ritual, muttering obscurely enough to mask his incompetence and indifference. Mechanically, repeating the standard liturgy that was drummed into every Roman from infancy, he pinched a few strands of saffron between his fingers and dropped them onto a mound of embers glowing in a gold dish, where its crackling and sparkle were to be taken as a good omen. He repeated the ritual with a dash of salt, a cube of raw lamb, and a palmful of wheat berries, dedicated respectively to Mercury, god of commerce; Pales, the shepherd god; and Ceres, patron of the harvest. A splash of wine on the soil went to Liber, god of fertility and the vine, and the superstitions were satisfied. At that very moment, as if triggered by the offerings, a distant roar of voices and a confused clanging of bells arose from the direction of the village. Exhausted, Petronius took a seat, then stretched out tentatively beside Melissa.

"Midnight," Lucilius muttered. "Festival's begun."

Petronius turned to Martialis.

"You can go now, boy."

"I've thought better of it, father Petronius," Martialis responded, gazing up from his reclined position with mock ingenuousness, or disingenuous mockery. "You've promised your guests a story, and I'd like to stick around to hear it."

"What story did I promise?"

"You promised young Brutus here and his dame the tale of how you came to be the emperor's pimp."

"For shame."

"No, that's all right, Cornelia. He can say whatever he likes tonight. Besides, he's not that far off. I never was Nero's pimp, but I could have been if I'd chosen to. He badgered me often enough, that's for certain. I found it distasteful, and so I declined. Tigellinus doesn't scruple that way, and he thrived as I fell from favor."

"Your scruples didn't stretch that far, but they were awfully elastic, weren't they, Petronius?"

"They were, Martialis, they were. But this evening is about celebration, not retrospection. I made a vow not to make any speeches tonight."

"No speeches?" Martialis boomed grandiloquently, appealing to the others with arms outstretched. "Who ever heard of a grand public suicide without a valedictory?"

"Best leave it, Martialis."

"I will not leave it, Anicius! What are we here for, if not to be witnesses to history? Who is this Petronius to deprive us of our rights? We are all here in expectation of a speech. You said so yourself, Melissa."

For the first time in all their years of acquaintance, Petronius saw Melissa blush. She dropped her face into the sleeve of her synthesis, and shook her head helplessly; when she returned Petronius's gaze a moment later, she had recovered her composure, but Petronius resolved to spare her any further discomfiture.

"I said nothing about a speech, Martialis," she began, her

tone restrained but unsteady. Petronius raised his arm to interrupt, and she fell silent. He knew what he would have to do. To balk now would seem churlish, and cast a pall over the rest of evening. He had set a trap for himself and walked right into it. Perhaps he had done it on purpose. There was so much that remained unclear to him, his own motives and impulses above all, and nothing that had yet transpired this evening—no fortuitous exchange, no pointed witticism, no unspoken communication—had justified his foolish hope in a moment of redemptive transcendence. Only now did he see that that was what he had been waiting for all night—for something to come along and knock him off his feet, to put all this turmoil into perspective—and that it wasn't going to happen of its own accord. Whatever insight was going to come out of all this, if any, could only be the fruit of his own labors. Nobody was going to do it for him. A speech, then.

"Well, what about it, Fabius, Pollia? You were indiscreet enough to be shocked by my sordid past. Are you genuinely curious enough to hear the rest of it? Will it ruin your dessert?"

Fabius turned away, supine on his dignity and refusing to be drawn into the discussion. But Pollia, delicious Pollia, refused to be abashed, despite blushing so furiously that her slim neck glowed carnelian in the lamplight reflected off the water table. For the third time that night, Petronius found himself aroused by her precocious discipline. Their eyes were locked, and along the viaduct that now connected them he sent her an army of couriers, each bearing an image of the life they would lead together in the alternate universe in which he survived the dawn. And in the opposite direction, she sent but one lone priestess to meet him with a Delphic ruling: If you had been with me, and not with her, you would not kill yourself tonight.

"Well, Petronius, will you begin?" she offered with a sympathetic smile.

"I don't quite know where to begin."

"Come help yourself to a honey cake and a cup of this excellent Falernian, and I'm sure a beginning will suggest itself to you."

The wind picked up a little more, whistling now over the sulfurous comb of Mount Gaurus; the flames roared in the braziers, the sea beat against the granite escarpments, and there were eight of them in the night, spokes on a half-wheel, lying under two heavy blankets on a broad, deep couch, their faces almost touching. Petronius looked long into the depths of his cup, seeing nothing. He took a breath, pushed himself to his feet, and opened his mouth.

There was a pebble pressing painfully into the back of his head. He reached round to remove it, and opened his eyes. It was not a pebble, but a square glass tile, much like the one he had found earlier, only turquoise. Perhaps it was time to call Cethegus the tiler in, have him refurbish the entire terrace while he was at it. Petronius made a mental note to have Antiochus see to it in the morning. There was a group of people gathered around him, peering anxiously into his face, and one of them—it was Martialis!—was blubbering like a baby. Petronius realized that he was lying on his back, and that they were all hovering above him, looking down.

"What's going on?" he asked.

"You fainted," someone said.

"Did I really?"

"Good thing Fabius was there to catch you. Could have been very nasty."

"Thank you, Fabius. I'm feeling much better now. Somebody help me up. No, stand back."

Petronius rolled over onto his elbow and vomited up his entire supper, splashing a widening pool of reddish slop across a trio of prancing naiads. Melissa remained crouched beside him, her hand flat against his back, until he was fully drained. He felt quite lucid, quick-minded even, but his elbow trembled beneath him like an old man's.

"Where's Persis?" Melissa called. "Oh never mind, they're all gone. Marcus, bring Titus some water, will you?"

"I'll have the mulsum, rather."

"I'll get this mess cleaned up. Where do you keep the buckets, Melissa?"

"How should I know? Just use one of those wine bowls, will you?

"Stay down there, Petronius. Don't try to get up just yet."

"Don't worry about me. Thank you, Marcus."

The wine was sweet and cold as well water, diluted by melted ice shavings. Petronius took a few sips and paused to see if it would stay down. When it did, he drained half the goblet in one draught, smacking his lips for effect and wiping his mouth with the back of his hand like an old campaigner. Martialis was still hovering, his arm poised in midreach as if Petronius might drop the goblet at any moment, and his face was still wet.

"You're still crying, Marcus?"

"You're still dying, Titus?"

The others, reassured that the crisis had passed, had moved off to allow the patient to recover in dignity, but Pollia remained, kneeling at his side on both knees like a seamstress. Her head tilted to one side like a puppy's, she stared into his face with a look of stricken febrility while her palm rested absently on Petronius's upper thigh. He suddenly realized that he was hard, very conspicuously so through the thin fabric of his tunic. Melissa, behind him, would be unable to see it, but Pollia had only to look down. Her hand was inches from his erection. What would she do, he wondered, if he contrived to move his thigh just so? Would she startle and pull her hand away, blush and stammer and scurry off? Or would her eyes widen and her fingers close around him, ever so slowly so as not to attract Melissa's attention? Petronius recognized the fantasy as the memory of a long-forgotten episode, an afternoon spent in the emperor's box at the hippodrome, and the recollection made him harder still, almost painfully so. What kind of new perversion was this? Was it his imagination's conflation of the two women that had brought it on, or the thrill of public shame? More likely, he supposed, it was the same process as that which causes plants in the extremity of drought to flower prematurely before they die.

"Hand me that cape and help me up, will you, Marcus?"

"I don't think you need my help getting up."

"Just help him to his feet, will you, Marcus?" Melissa said.

Carefully positioning himself between Petronius and Melissa, Martialis first draped the cape over Petronius's shoulders, allowing it to fall appositely across his hips, then hoisted him to his feet. Petronius imagined that Martialis would have to drag him across the terrace, but in fact his legs were in full working order and he had no trouble guiding them to the balustrade overlooking the south cove.

"Wait with me here while I get my bearings."

They leaned over the parapet just as they had done at sunset, and in almost precisely the same spot, but now, of course, everything had changed. What had that been—six hours earlier? More than half a lifetime, and Petronius only had half a life left in his veins in any case. He was abruptly struck by an abject sense of futility. When it comes down to it, he thought, isn't all civilization just an exercise in measuring time, in pacing off the foundations on which to build a model of the universe of oneself? But what's the point when one can have no confidence in the constancy of what one is measuring? When forty years can go by faster than four hours, or a generation can be swallowed up in a matter of moments? What bearings can there possibly be in such a world? Petronius stared down into the black, restless waters of the cove, and realized that he did not especially care to live out the next few hours, the last ones given to him, and that he would have to find a justification for himself without much further delay.

"She's very attractive, your Pollia," Martialis said noncommittally.

"Very."

"Not my type. I like them slutty."

"Really?"

"And foul-mouthed. But still."

"Not easy to find a slutty, foul-mouthed patrician virgin in your price range."

"She's out there, I assure you. It's just a matter of time. And patience. And money. And charm. And tact."

"I'd been thinking about bedding her. Pollia."

"Better get a move on."

"Too late now."

"What would Melissa say?"

"Melissa? What's she got to do with it?"

"Titus? I was wondering."

"Yes?"

"Do you think it would be all right if . . . After you're gone . . . If Melissa and I . . ."

"You must be joking."

"Well . . ."

"First of all, she'd never have you."

"You don't think? I fuck like a lion."

"So do lots of men. Many of them endowed with patience,

money, charm, and tact, all of which you lack. And besides, she thinks of you as a son."

"It's just that I thought, if the two of us could somehow get together . . . afterwards . . . it would be keeping something intact. Perpetuating this . . . whatever it is we have, the three of us. Almost like building you a shrine."

"That's very sweet of you, Marcus. Why don't you just build me a real shrine, and the two of you can make me chaste offerings whenever you like."

"It was just a thought."

Martialis would always, and forever, be able to make people laugh, even, or perhaps especially, against their own better instincts. Petronius was grateful to him now, and grateful to have known him, however briefly, and pleased, despite all the anger, with all he had brought to the evening. He was fairly confident now that it would all work out for the best, that Martialis would prove himself a faithful and good-faith biographer, and a steady comfort to Melissa, at least in the short term. Still, he worried about the boy, about his ability and willingness to keep his impulses in check—the sarcasm, the surfeit of emotion, the puritan honesty. Did he genuinely not understand how to get along in Roman society? Of all people, a poet at the mercy of patrons had to understand how to work the system; and yet, in spite of all his vaunted ambition, he made no effort to sweeten those who needed sweetening, to flatter those who needed flattering, or to cultivate a successor to Petronius, despite Petronius's utter and abject failure to promote his career. And what would he do tomorrow?

"Marcus, why do you cry all the time?"

"I don't cry all the time. I cry when I'm sad."

"And why do that?"

"That's how we do it in Spain. We cry when we're sad, laugh when we're happy, shout when we're angry. It's a relatively easy concept to grasp, even for a Roman. You should have met my uncle. He was a champion crier. He could turn it on and turn it off like . . ."

"What I mean is, why don't you try harder not to? It does you no credit, and will not endear you to potential sponsors."

"Endear me to potential sponsors? I've been accused of many things in my short and disreputable life, but no one has ever had the gall to call me 'endearing' to my face."

"Oh, stop. It's not a game."

"You are so right. It is not a game. If it were a game, I should have no qualms about playing a role, counterfeiting my sincerity, making nice to those I despise. But it is my dignity, my integrity that we are talking about, the wide-open, unguarded corridors that connect my imagination to my pen. Those I will not compromise at any price."

"Oh, listen to you, a man without a denarius to his name. Can't you see there's no one else out there like me?"

Martialis burst into tears and buried his face in Petronius's shoulder, heaving and shaking.

"But there is!" he snorted wetly.

"There isn't! I know my own peers far better than you do."

Martialis pushed away angrily. "And there's something you will never know, Titus. There *is* another you out there somewhere, and he's waiting for me, he's waiting to give me his money and his friends and his prestige. He knows what I look like, and if I go about dolled up like a pimp and a clown he won't recognize me. I'll walk right past him and lose him forever if I take your advice. It's bad advice, understand? It's *bad* advice. And I need a drink. Why am I always so thirsty around you?"

Martialis stalked off, leaving Petronius to marvel at the consistency with which every conversation with the boy ended in absurdity and recrimination. One might imagine that, on a night like this, their exchanges would be mellower, conciliatory—reflective, even. But that would hardly be in character, for either of them. Maybe it was better this way—after all, wasn't the entire conceit of the evening that all should proceed as if nothing unusual were unfolding? Of all of them, Petronius included, Martialis seemed most determined to observe the edict, to play the petulant contrarian to the bitter end. Petronius shook his head. No, not bitter.

Petronius shut his eyes and allowed the rhythmic sighing of the tide to envelop him. After a few moments, it felt as though the sea had invaded him, that he had become its container, that its ebb and flow were gently rocking him back and forth from within. He knew the feeling was just a side effect of the blood loss, but he permitted himself to indulge the pretense, that this was how his spirit would be absorbed into the natural world when he was dead. It was a lovely feeling, soothing and benumbing, but he could also sense resistance. His mind, or his soul, or whatever, was not ready for that release and would not plunge absolutely into that dissolution. It still had work to do, and it pulled him elsewhere, away.

ᘒᘒᘒᘒᘒᘒ

SHE DID NOT take the news of her husband's death with the equanimity Petronius could have wished for. He would have hoped that she could share in his joy, but she was positively mournful. She did not weep or make sacrifices, but she remained thoughtful and quiet for several days, as one might upon hearing of the death of a long-lost companion of one's youth, and she forbade him to touch her.

He allowed as to how she had certain ambivalent feelings for the late Junius—an all-but-illiterate, clumsy brute, as far as Petronius could make out—of which Petronius had but the dimmest grasp. In the circumstances, he thought it perhaps best not to be overly demonstrative in his newfound optimism, and to allow some time to pass before raising the subject of altered circumstances.

Finally, one evening in mid-September, with the crushing heat of the day just beginning to release its grip on the city, and the first hint of breeze for days stirring the muslin hangings on the palace terrace, as they sat on a vast daybed sipping at chilled pomegranate juice, Petronius felt he could hold off no longer.

"Melissa," he began tentatively. "I'm sorry, but I don't think we can put off this conversation any longer."

"I agree," she said softly. He turned to her in surprise, and found that she was smiling, perhaps somewhat sardonically, in his direction.

"You don't even know what I was going to say."

"Of course I do. You were going to ask me to come to Rome with you. And I will, Governor."

Petronius was so flabbergasted, and so at a loss for words, and must have been wearing such a ridiculous, clownish expression on his face, that Melissa burst into laughter. It was not happy laughter, nor yet even loving laughter, but Petronius reveled in it nonetheless. Rolling across the daybed, he took her in his arms, and although, consciously or not, she had crossed both her own arms over her chest, he allowed himself to bask in what he took to be a triumphant, threshold moment.

"You don't know how happy this makes me."

"I have an idea."

"What made you change your mind?"

"I haven't changed my mind. I'm a widow now, and my hand has been forced. I can't very well return to my father in Cremona."

"I understand," he said, burying his face in her neck to distract himself from the very brutal fact that he did not understand anything, and that it made not the slightest difference to him.

In the following weeks, he tiptoed around the issue of their future plans. It was odd that, now she had finally made an unequivocal commitment to their life together, he felt the slightest strain, or constraint, in their relations, as if they were in an arranged marriage. Having dreamt of this moment for months, he now found himself almost embarrassed to be asking her about her preferences and desires, as if he barely knew her. He'd been summoned back to Italy without receiving an immediate new posting, and he assumed, for instance, that she would want to avoid living in Rome, preferring the quiet life of a rural estate in Campania or Tuscany. Yet when he began painting a delightful picture of their life in such a place, a life of letters, philosophy, and simple pleasures such as Horace himself would have approved, she interrupted him forthwith.

"Won't we live in Rome, then?"

"I didn't think you'd be interested. I have so many social responsibilities in Rome, too many business and tribal connections. It would be a whirlwind, and Nero's court is a viper's nest."

"No. I've spent my entire life in the provinces. I won't finally return to Italy, only to be isolated in some backwater yet again. We'll take our chances in Rome."

Petronius had misgivings about this course of action, and about the wisdom of exposing Melissa to the snobbish and gossip-riddled Roman aristocracy, but he suppressed them in his eagerness to accommodate her in any way he could. His heart, however, was heavy with foreboding.

It was in this solemn and far-from-satisfactory atmosphere that they prepared for their journey westward. There was remarkably little to do, as Petronius insisted that everything she chose to leave behind could be replaced with more and better in Rome, and she was pleased to acquiesce, packing just a modest trunk of clothing for the sea voyage. He deeded their lakeside villa to the Fourth Scythian as a house of recuperation and recreation for wounded soldiers. As for himself, aside from his several ceremonial togas, he chose to return home with only his gold-hilted dagger, the myrrhine ladle, and the Prusa *kouros*.

In late September, word came from Rome of the election of his successor, who arrived shortly thereafter. He told Petronius that his star was on the rise in Rome, and that his letters to Nero were often read aloud at imperial dinners and literary gatherings. The emperor, it was said, had lofty ambitions for Petronius upon his return. Petronius spent two days briefing the new governor on his duties—the very least he could get away with without an unseemly appearance of impatience—but even that minimal nod to duty was too much for his successor, whose attention often wandered to the drapes and furniture, which apparently were not to his taste. In the end, he was kind enough to lend the couple the proconsular yacht, equipped with a luxurious stateroom, for the homeward journey. They left Nicomedia in early October, calling at Smyrna, Athens, Knossos, and Syracusa.

At first, the sea air and new prospects appeared to agree with her. She spent several hours a day alone at the railing on the prow of the ship, her face uplifted into the sun and wind. At meals, for the first time since they'd met, she seemed genuinely curious about Petronius's life and occupations in the capital, peppering him with questions about domestic arrangements on the Esquiline and how she might expect to be received. She appeared to be genuinely eager to prepare herself for all the personal adaptations and accommodations she would need to make. Yet as the coast of Sicily hove into view and the yacht eased its way throught the Straits of Messina, the weight of the unknown began to sap her of her vitality, and she fell silent. She seemed to be living in a state of suspension, neither in one world nor in the other, like a fish hibernating beneath the ice. He thought that perhaps she was in shock, not yet fully able to grasp the immensity of the gift that fortune had bestowed upon her, and so he gave her some space to grow into understanding. The subject of her husband's death, and most particularly of Petronius's hand in precipitating it, did not arise. For his part, Petronius had not a single thought to spare to the luckless Aulus Junius or his sacrifice to their happiness.

It would have been much faster to bypass the city center on their way to his house, but she had never been to Rome before. If she was awestruck by her first sight of it, she kept her impressions well concealed. As their litter negotiated the crowds on the Ostia road, passing through the old cattle market, with the racetrack to the right, the ancient temples to the left, the imperial palaces looming above, and the great central forum directly ahead, she nodded serenely at each, as if she were running down a mental checklist or, better yet, as if she were an empress passing through a crowd of well-wishers. "Look!" Petronius would say, as they trundled down New Street, "There's the rostrum" or "It's the Temple of Apollo," and she'd say "Yes, there it is." It was like watching someone talk in her sleep, in response to some unseen questioner in a dream. As for Petronius, it had been three years since he'd last seen the city of his birth, and he was giddy enough for the both of them. Beyond the forum, the road began to rise, and they soon found themselves on the hushed, immaculate streets of the Esquiline, with their walled gardens and discreet mansions.

She took the grand tour of the Esquiline villa in dumbstruck rapture. Seeing it through her eyes, he understood just how intimidating it might be. "You call it a villa," she said, almost in a whisper, "but it's twice the size of the governor's palace in Nicomedia." Through the vast foyers, vestibules, reception galleries, and dining halls, each with its own coffered ceiling leafed in silver or gold, its gleaming columns of exotic stone, each floor a masterpiece of mosaic or marbling; the endless suites of bedchambers, salons, fitting rooms, and secluded offices; hot baths, cold baths, swimming pool and steam room, the private theater, the sprawling kitchen, each of its three hearths larger than her bedroom in Prusa; the army of attendants, clerks, managers, servants, and slaves, each with a name and a function to be mastered and remembered—they spent several hours on the first pass alone, until at last she could take no more and, with a sigh as much of resignation as of contentment, she collapsed in the shadow of a swaying cypress at the margins of the sculpture garden, under the sober gaze of Mars and a war party of Amazons. Petronius thought that perhaps he had asked too much of her on her first arrival, and that he ought to have introduced her more gradually to the overwhelming reality of her new home.

"It is all too much," she said hoarsely.

"Does it not please you?" he asked hopefully. "My country estates are more modest."

"No, it's all quite spectacular." She sighed again, this time less ambiguously. "It shall come to me in time. As you did, Titus."

In the days that followed, Petronius worked feverishly to put the household in order, examined the books and accounts, received his various agents and managers, and generally reacquainted himself with his business affairs, all ably and honestly managed by his Syrian freedman Antiochus in his absence. He hardly saw the new mistress of the house, but on those occasions when their paths crossed it was clear that she had taken to her new role with quiet zeal and determination. Her job, of course, was not to manage the enormous household staff—they had freedmen aplenty for that—but to set the tone, and because she had ample experience as an army wife in the discipline of decorum, she had an instinctive feel for dealing with the slaves, addressing the freedmen with respectful dominance, and dressing and acting the part of matron. She was swept up in the constant procession of dressmakers, cobblers, and jewelers called in to provide her with a suitable wardrobe. The choices she made showed both restraint, conditioned by a frank acknowledgment of her limited grasp of metropolitan fashions, and a joyous flexing of muscles she'd previously had little use for and barely realized she possessed. She seemed to grow larger and more powerful with every passing moment. And yet the consummate dignity with which she oversaw the household was precisely the same as that with which he'd seen her bargain for cabbage in the market at Prusa.

As word of Petronius's return spread through the circles of his former society, they were besieged by well-wishers, distant cousins, debtors, and would-be parasites, all duly welcoming and deferential to them both. He introduced her under a plausibly northern pseudonym. No one, he thought, can have been taken in by the ruse, as she could scarcely pass for the patrician that her alias suggested she was. At the same time, given his name and reputation as a new favorite of the emperor's, few would have ventured to offer her the least hint of disrespect, even had the truth of her origins become known.

He marveled at her confidence. "Will they not consider me inferior?" she asked him casually one evening at supper, a now-rare moment of intimacy and repose.

"Some might. None would say so to your face. Does it worry you?"

"Not especially. We had our share of snobbery even in the barracks. Let them think what they like. But I would be sorry to be a burden on your prospects."

"I don't think you need to be concerned about my prospects, darling."

Petronius had sent word to the Quirinal immediately upon his arrival, but at that particular moment the emperor was preparing to inaugurate the first of the four-year games dedicated in his own name, and sent a brief note begging his patience. The games were to be modeled on the Greek festivals, with contests in music, poetry, gymnastics, and equestrian skills. Petronius himself attended several, and was present when Lucan introduced his *In Praise of Nero,* a dismal screed of shameless flattery that nonetheless won him fame and fortune—much good it did him. It was as the games were winding to their end that a messenger arrived informing Petronius that the emperor was ready to receive him.

"I think I'd better attend to him on my own this first time," he told her. "He was just a little boy the last time I saw him. I'm not quite sure how much they say of him is true, and it might be best to keep you out of harm's way for the time being."

To his surprise, she was not in the least put out at being left behind. "Please do," she yawned. "None of my dresses are ready in any case. I wouldn't know what to wear."

Petronius knew, even before he entered the palace, that it was not a place he would care to spend much time in. The outer courtyard was milling with thuggish young men, knights in their teens and early twenties who swaggered and jostled and spat and swore, and who grudgingly made way for him as he pushed his way through the throng. These were the "Augustans" he had heard so much about, Nero's preferred companions on his nightly rounds of bullying and mayhem through the darkened streets of the city. Petronius had long been aware, of course, of the emperor's aversion to philosophers and intellectuals—after all, his mother had entrusted his education to a dancer and a barber—but he had attributed the rumors to exaggeration and patrician resentment. Now he saw with his own eyes, as his praetorian escort guided him to the reception hall, that it was all true. The corridors swarmed with the low-born and the venal, moneylenders and syndicalists and horse traders, and Petronius recognized hardly a single face. It was difficult to imagine how he would make a place for himself in this world—not that he would want to. He had never considered himself a snob—after all, he had spent much of the last three years entrusting his life to brave and honorable knights and commoners in the ranks—but merely being in the presence of these courtiers brought out a sense of superiority and disdain in him that would be hard to conceal. Just as a man who works in the sewers or the pig sties longs to feel himself clean at the end of the day, Petronius found himself from those very first moments at the court wishing to distinguish himself from this mob of cutthroats and boors. He drew some comfort from the fact that the hallways were lined with the sublime works that he had sent home from Bithynia, even if the louts paid them not the least attention or leaned against them as if they were hitching posts.

The crowd in the reception hall was somewhat more refined. A number of senators lingered in a desultory way at the margins of the room, gathering in small, defensive clusters against the hordes of delegations that had come to congratulate the emperor on the successful completion of the games. Several of Petronius's peers recognized him and tried to wave him over, but he bowed and pressed on toward the dais at the back of the hall, where Nero and his coterie were receiving their encomiums. As Petronius approached, he saw his escort whisper to one turbaned courtier lounging near the edge of the dais, who immediately rose to his feet and crossed to another who sat directly beside the emperor. This second courtier, a chubby, rosy-cheeked man several years older than the rest, scanned the room with the eyes of a choleric hog and fixed him with a look of languid malice. Then he turned to the emperor, spoke in his ear, and pointed at Petronius. Nero's countenance lit up in apparently genuine delight, and he waved him to the dais with a broad grin. A hush fell upon the room and all eyes turned to Petronius, a wide path suddenly opening up down the center of the hall to let him through.

He studied the emperor's face as he approached. He was still the same wicked boy Petronius had met eight years ago, only now a young man in his early twenties: broad head tapering to a narrow jaw; bulbous nose and jutting, ill-proportioned ears; under a forceful brow, wide arrogant eyes the color of a fish pond; full lips curled in a perpetual sneer, even when smiling in pleasure; straight, glossy black hair, now graced with wispy sideburns. His cheeks were already beginning to fill out with the evidence of sloth and self-indulgence. Around him, a pride of young barbarians in various poses of torpor stared at Petronius with the impassive curiosity of juvenile predators. Nero rose from his chair and strode to the edge of the dais. He wore a victor's laurels at his temples.

"So what do you think, Petronius? I have just been awarded first prize by these Greeks." His voice was a pure, aristocratic baritone, most out of consonance with his cruel features. He was speaking to Petronius, but his words were directed at the entire assembly.

"Forgive me, Sire. I did not know you were a contestant."

"I wasn't!" He laughed absurdly. "I am recognized in my role as presiding deity."

"When all are equally inspired, it is the muse who must take credit."

"I'm the muse, am I? Lucan said much the same in his poem, didn't you?" He gestured toward a young Spaniard couched uncomfortably at the back of the dais, apart from the others. "Did you hear it? It's a gem. He'll recite it for us one evening soon."

"I look forward to it, Sire."

"So, you're back in Rome. I need you here most desperately. What did you bring us from Bithynia?"

"A rare *kouros*, in perfect condition, a time traveler from the dark ages."

"You can keep the *kouros*, Petronius. You know I don't go in for such rubbish. And a woman, yes? A northerner?" He said it without guile—gods, of course, expect no one to be surprised by their omniscience.

"A mistress. A keepsake, Sire."

"You'll bring her to meet us. Octavia could use some decent company. Tigellinus here"—he waved toward the rosy-cheeked man—"will organize a banquet in your honor. Come then, both of you. But now I have these tiresome delegations to attend to. We'll talk more."

They bowed to one another, and the audience was at an end. Petronius decided to walk home, leaving with a stronger determination than ever to avoid being sucked into the inner circles of the court. His first instinct had been spot-on. For someone like him—an aristocrat, a power broker by default, a gentleman steeped in the ancient republican virtues, philosophy, and ethics—cultivating Nero's friendship would be a thankless endeavor fraught with danger and the need for constant, enervating vigilance. Only twenty minutes in that festering cesspool had reminded him—in a way that years in the senate and on the battlefield had not—of all that he had once sought to be: a good man living a good life, making every decision on the basis of an immutable set of beliefs and standards of behavior and honor. It had made him feel old, and wise, and virtuous, none of which he was except, perhaps, in contrast to Nero and his courtiers. Some ambitious men had gravitated into Nero's orbit by necessity, being independent neither of means, birth, nor mind. Their connections were all they had, intrigue their sole exchangeable currency, ruthlessness their only motor of ascent. None of that applied to Petronius. He had the wealth, the detachment, and the motivation to break free. It would mean, of course, abandoning all political ambition and civic duty while Nero remained enthroned—which, given his age and strapping good health, would probably mean the rest of Petronius's life—but he knew beyond any doubt that it was a price he would be pleased to pay, and that ultimately it would bring him to greater wisdom and peace of mind than a life devoted to navigating the treacherous maze of imperial politics.

He would have to go about this disengagement very cautiously. One does not simply say "no" when a man like Nero invites one into his inner sanctum. Petronius's letters and dispatches from Bithynia had convinced the emperor, according to several reports, that Petronius was the very paragon of discernment, the embodiment of all that was tasteful and refined; it would not be safe to disappoint him or to be in the least offhanded in declining to embrace his friendship. Nero had made his point most eloquently by reminding Petronius that even his closest companions were under perpetual scrutiny, and that his informers had, in the space of only a few days, penetrated into the very heart of Petronius's domestic arrangements. If Nero wanted him as his friend, or his adviser, or in whatever capacity he had in mind, that's just what he would be until such time as he could extricate himself gracefully. There were surely others who had been in his predicament and successfully resolved it; it wouldn't take long to sniff them out and learn how they had managed.

As for Melissa, there was no doubting now, if ever there had been, that coming to Rome had been like a second birth for her. Whereas most people, newly come into wealth and status, might overcompensate through vulgar displays of extravagance, Melissa maintained exquisite poise and restraint. If anything, she moved more slowly, spoke more deliberately and modestly, like one who has nothing to prove to anyone. In short, she behaved as if she had come home to a beloved safe haven. It was not what Petronius had expected, nor, if he were honest with himself, quite what he had hoped for. It was not that she had changed; on the contrary, she took the very same competence and candor that had buoyed her through the bleakest years of barracks life and applied them with consummate ease to her new circumstances, thereby seeming to change the entire world around her just by her presence in it, the way a flock of geese gains in dignity and grace when a swan appears among them.

From a secluded corner of his study, Petronius sat one day contemplating Melissa through an open doorway as she read in the garden. A kitchen slave came to her with some query or complaint. Melissa unobtrusively allowed the scroll to drop to her feet, as if she were too courteous to acknowledge that she had been interrupted, and listened with solemn concentration. She responded briefly, and the slave bowed and departed, only to return a few moments later with three other slaves in tow. Melissa stood to speak to them at their level. This was clearly a conversation with genuine give and take, and Melissa accorded each her full attention. When it was over, the issue having evidently been settled to everyone's satisfaction, Melissa returned to her reading. As they retreated, the slaves conferred among themselves with obvious pride. With no experience in managing a large household, and despite all the little uncertainties of her own status, Melissa had already mastered an extremely fraught and complex relationship.

Although she was clearly ready, she neither expressed nor demonstrated any particular desire to be introduced to society. Nor was Petronius, who still clung to the forlorn hope that she would fail among his peers and be compelled to retreat to a quiet life in the country, especially eager to put his theory to the test. Instead, he limited their social contacts to intimate dinners with his few real friends. They dined frequently with Lucilius, his lawyer and childhood schoolmate, who lived directly next door— that is, they shared a common garden wall three-hundred cubits in length—and his wife Cornelia. The two women were not an obvious match, yet Melissa had had Cornelia domesticated in a matter of moments.

"Tell me, my dear," Cornelia had asked her, with mischievous if not malicious intent, on their first evening together. "Do you miss Bithynia at all?"

"Do I miss Bithynia?" Melissa pretended to give the matter due consideration. "You could never have asked me that question if you'd ever had the pleasure of living in a garrison, Cornelia. The wide open space of the parade grounds; the solid, unpretentious architecture of the barracks; the simple, wholesome gruel of the mess tent; the scintillating company of your fellow officers' wives; the honest joy of serving a grateful nation. I miss it terribly!"

Cornelia had turned to Petronius with a wink of approbation, while Lucilius had gaped with carnivorous admiration.

Petronius had no better luck with his father's old friend Anicius, who was immediately charmed by Melissa's lack of pretension and preceded to regale her with all sorts of off-color anecdotes of Petronius's childhood and youth. Although Anicius was a scholar and a classicist, and Melissa had no education to speak of, they each found a kindred spirit in the other, to the extent that Petronius often felt superfluous in their company. Anicius straight away offered himself as Melissa's tutor of Greek and republican literature, and she became a devout and dedicated pupil.

After they had been in Rome a month or so, Petronius was informed that the banquet that Tigellinus had been ordered to arrange in his honor had been scheduled. Melissa took the announcement with typical equanimity, and Petronius had to struggle mightily to keep his own trepidation at bay. This was her coming-out, so to speak, and much was at stake, though he took care not to stress that to her. He had no fear of her making a success of it. He told himself that his desire for her to fail was based on his conviction that life in Rome was ultimately impossible for one of her sobriety and integrity, and that it was in her best interest to be removed from its temptations and pollutions. He could scarcely acknowledge that he wanted her only to himself, and took no pleasure in seeing her admired and distracted by others, and feared above all things that his tenuous hold on her affections would be fatally compromised by her exposure to others, men especially, whose qualities might overshadow his own.

At the same time, as he sat on a stool in the corner of her dressing room and watched her spend hours directing her new, very expensive Athenian chambermaid at her hairdressing in anticipation of Nero's banquet, he had to admit that he would be hard-pressed to maintain his vision of her as the demure mistress of a country estate, however well appointed. It was becoming increasingly clear that the sort of genteel retirement that he had foreseen would not be to her tastes or harmonize with her new social ambitions. He had to ask himself how well he really knew her—and acknowledge that, until recently, he hadn't been especially motivated to know her better, so long as she continued to enthrall him—but one thing was now coming rapidly into focus: she belonged in Rome. It was all too easy to forget, as he observed her astonishing metamorphosis into a Roman society dame, that only six months earlier she had been the wife of a lowly, brutish centurion in a dismal provincial outpost, with no prospect before her but endless days of drudgery and privation. She had taken all her strength of character, all the coiled energy hoarded through a lifetime of powerlessness, and dedicated it to the quiet glory of her apotheosis.

"Well?" She stood before him on the night of the banquet in all her reborn splendor. A synthesis of palest azure and amethyst-hued Indian silk, encrusted with rubies, emeralds, and purple nacre, hung from her shoulders in elegant, weightless pleats.

Bands of red, white, and yellow gold climbed up her forearms like wild vines. The soles of her sandals were sewn with diamonds, her hair was a glade of gold and ivory combs, woven with strands of tiny, bluish pearls from the seas beyond India, at the very edge of the world. A light dusting of white powder on her cheeks, brow, and chin set off the red of her lipstick and the kohl lining her eyes.

Petronius did not know what to say to her. That she was beautiful? Elegant? Unsurpassed? It was disturbing, frightening even, to look at her. She seemed scarcely human at all, at once too dazzling and too fragile, a rare Nilotic dragonfly or the fulminating deity of some beleaguered cult. She looked, above all, unlike herself, and yet precisely as she was always meant to be. It was as if he had known her only as a lovely block of marble, and a master sculptor had come along and hewn out the perfect form that had lain dormant within. Petronius didn't much care for it.

"You are every inch a Roman," he stammered at last. She gave him a sharp look.

"Are you feeling all right, Titus? You're positively ashen."

"Just a little nervous, that's all. Big night for us both."

"Well, I promise you needn't worry about me."

Petronius was given the place of honor on the middle couch of the emperor's dining party, while Melissa was similarly honored at the Empress Octavia's table. Evidently, Petronius had taken Tigellinus's place at Nero's side, and he glowered with his piggy eye throughout the evening from his exile on the outer couch, never deigning to address a single word to Petronius. It seemed that Tigellinus was a horse breeder by training, which surprised Petronius not in the least. The other members of their party included one horror named Vatinius, a clubfooted shoemaker grown fabulously rich as the major vendor of footware to the army; Menecrates, the emperor's pet lyre player; and a gaggle of inoffensive, semi-anonymous senators, including Nero's fellow consul Cornelius Lentulus. The emperor's voice coach stood nearby at the alert, and on several occasions was compelled to admonish his master for endangering his voice by speaking too loudly or immoderately, but he did not join them for supper. Petronius had expected to find Seneca there, but thought it perhaps unwise to ask after him, given the reportedly tempestuous nature of his relationship with his former pupil.

They discussed the topics of the day: the financial crisis and the recent depreciation of the coinage; the rising of the Iceni tribe in Britain under its Amazon-like queen, Boudicca; the appearance of a comet in the northern sky that had caused great alarm. When Menecrates, who had recently received an estate in Umbria as a gift from Nero, complained about the difficulty and expense of furnishing it, Petronius offered to advise him on selecting statuary and other artworks, and this gave the emperor his opening. He began by praising Petronius lavishly for the refinement and subtlety of his taste, declaring that he would have no one else to direct and guide him when he built his new palace. Petronius responded with self-deprecation, but the conversation in general took a learned, aesthetic turn that effectively excluded everyone but Nero and himself. They spoke at some length, as if they were the only two present, not only about Greek and Roman sculpture, but about verse and music, musical instruments, murals and mosaics, the various materials appropriate for furniture-making. Nero surprised him by the breadth of his knowledge, given his youth and other pursuits, and so long as they kept to such topics their conversation was quite natural, informal and reciprocal. Not that it made Petronius eager to rethink his resolve to shun the court, but at least he would have someone interesting to talk to while he was bound to it.

At some point in the evening, Nero turned to Petronius and

spoke to him in a low, conspiratorial tone, his hand on his shoulder.

"I must have you here at court with me, Petronius."

"Me, Sire? Of what possible use could I be to you?"

"I need your eye. I'm surrounded by boors and vulgarians, you know. I need an adviser of taste and sophistication. Someone who *understands* me."

"Your majesty flatters me. I'm a simple soldier, more suited to canvas and gruel than to marble and silk."

"Indeed I doubt it."

"Even as we speak, arrangements are under way for my retirement to my estates, where I hope to tromp grapes and press cheese for the rest of my natural days."

Nero ran his tongue along his lower lip and eyed Petronius suspiciously. "Very well," he said slowly. "But should you find that your plans have changed, I'll expect you to come to me first."

Octavia's party was set up on the dais in a parallel grouping beside the men's. Like Nero, she was of the most distinguished patrician stock, but her company, unlike her husband's, reflected the nobility of her lineage. Melissa was the sole plebeian. Like Petronius, she enjoyed the place of honor at Octavia's left, and whenever possible he cast a glance in her direction. She seemed to be holding her own with casual aplomb—indeed, to be monopolizing the conversation and thoroughly charming all within earshot. Of course, so long as Nero remained at his place, Petronius was not free to mingle at his own pleasure, but on the several occasions when the emperor rose to make his rounds of greetings, Petronius was able to pay brief visits to the ladies' group. On one such foray, he found Melissa deep into the relation of a complicated story involving her Mauritanian maidservant, a swineherd, and a purse of silver denarii found under a mulberry bush. He stood behind her chair and listened, his hand

lightly draped over her shoulder. She told the story with a delicate balance of reserve and bawdy wit, perfectly modulated for
her high-born audience. It was as if she had been training for this
night her entire life. When she was done, the ladies all laughed
and clapped their hands with genuine delight and begged for
more. She glanced up at Petronius for the briefest instant, and in
her eyes he read gratitude, joy, and love. It was like a slap in the
face, that look. Perhaps he staggered; in any case, he made his
excuses, bowed, and returned to the emperor's party.

He did not remember much of the rest of that banquet. On
the way home in their litter, Melissa was uncharacteristically
jovial and forgiving about her evening and her social prospects.
She did not act like one who has triumphed over adversity or
concluded a business transaction greatly to her advantage. She
acted instead like one who has been restored to the good graces
of a dear friend with whom she had quarreled.

"Of course, they're mostly a bunch of breathless hens. Take
away their jewels and hairdressers and they're no better or clev-
erer than any wife you'd meet in the barracks. Easily led, you
know, easy to please."

"But it all seems like such a waste of time and energy. Why
bother making the effort to cultivate such people, when they
have nothing to offer you?"

"Are you jealous, Titus? It's only a bit of fun. I have more than
enough time for serious pursuits; I'm sure I can spare an evening
a month to being frivolous, for once in my life. Why else come to
Rome? I love it. I feel as if I had come home, as if this was where
I were meant to be."

"They'll suck you in, you'll see. You think you're stronger than
they are, and you may be, one on one. But it's seductive and re-
lentless and ultimately irresistible. All this was why I left Rome
in the first place."

"Really? I thought you'd left Rome to meet me."

He allowed her to rhapsodize uninterrupted for the rest of the ride. If she noticed his silences and reserve, she made no comment on them. At home in bed, she made love as if Petronius were an inanimate object. Normally, that was just the way he liked her; that night, he was simply glad to feel that he was alone.

He lay awake long after she had fallen into a deep sleep. It took him some time to identify the source of his upset. At first, he traced it to the look she had given him at supper. She had never looked at him that way before—in a way, it had been more disturbing to be at the receiving end of her gratitude and girlish elation than if she had expressed undying hatred for him. It came as a shock to him to find that he did not actually want her pliant, female, and dependent. He wanted her aloof and condescending, as she had been to him in the beginning, when she had first opened his eyes to his own true nature. That was the woman he had fallen in love with, not this . . . matron. If he wanted a social appendage or a congenial equal—howsoever beautiful, accomplished, or obliging—there were a thousand such in Rome to choose from. He wanted his cruel mistress. What if she were gone for good? Who was this female Proteus, changing her shape at will? Who had she been ten minutes, one minute before he had met her? How had it come about that she, an uneducated commoner, had found herself at home in this exalted circle, whereas he, born and bred to it, found himself alienated and disconsolate? As he lay in bed that night, he was desperate enough to consider the possibility that, were he to tear her from Rome and return her to provincial squalor, keep her entombed in some sleepy outpost with only goats and tax inspectors' wives for company, she might revert to form. Evidently, her happiness and fulfillment were not good for either of them.

He was silent at breakfast the next morning, and she could not draw him out.

"What's come over you, Titus? Are you ill?"

"I don't want to talk about it."

"Talk about what?"

"I can't stand it here any longer."

Her tone in response was cautious and measured, as though she were talking to an eccentric stranger who might yet prove to have a dagger concealed about his person. "When you say 'here,' where is it, precisely, that you're referring to?"

"Here in Rome, of course! This terrible place, these awful people."

Again, she considered carefully before answering. "Titus, you spent three weeks on the boat extolling Rome's virtues and raving about how happy we'd be here."

"But that was before *you* were here. I see it all now. A person like you doesn't belong in a place like this. It was a mistake to come."

"Where do you imagine a person like me belongs?"

"Somewhere far away from all this. Somewhere where we can be alone. Somewhere simple and quiet, where we have room to think and breathe and be ourselves. A haven, a hideaway."

This time her delay was even longer, and when finally she spoke her voice was subdued. "But I've just come from a place like that," she said.

Something rotten came over him. In the following weeks, he watched her as she went about her business, and he watched himself watching her. In Bithynia, it had been just the two of them together; their love had been something supremely remote, otherworldly. That was how he had come to understand the very definition of love: two people on a raft in the middle of a cold, inhospitable sea, clinging to one another for safety and solace. It had been a beautiful, comforting vision. He had imagined, too, that their life in Italy would pursue the same course, that she would never have to show him any other face than that which she showed him when they were alone together. All he needed to survive was her; what else could she need but him? That was not how things had befallen—he continued to cling desperately to her, but now her eyes were fixed on the approaching shore, and he couldn't bear it. He had never considered what would happen when they made landfall; he had wanted to be alone with her forever.

She had rejoiced with her first step on dry land; he had despaired. She was walking away from him, embracing her salvation; he had imagined himself to be that salvation. How could she do this to him? The more confident and ebullient she was, the more peevish and resentful Petronius grew. He could feel it happening; he was changing—*something* was changing, or had changed. In his more lucid moments, he recognized that he was acting like a child denied a privilege that it felt was its due. He hated what he felt himself becoming—a fearful, grasping, panicked man, barely a Roman at all. He had a knot in his stomach from morning to night, and at times imagined that his breath had gone sour from whatever was putrefying inside him. She could not have been unaware of the transformation that had taken place in him, but she chose not to confront it. If she had, she would have been compelled to admit that her every apprehension concerning Petronius had been well founded, and that it had been a mistake to trust in his assurances. Acknowledge it or not, he felt himself turning into her worst nightmare, and helpless, like her, to reverse the slide.

And then one night, Petronius had a dream, or perhaps it was a visitation. He dreamed that the centurion Aulus Junius came to see him in his tent on campaign in Armenia. Petronius was sitting at his desk with a large map of the eastern empire spread out before him. Aulus stood to attention on the other side of the desk and told him that he had been killed in battle and wished to discuss the terms of his discharge. Petronius responded that he seemed in good health and demanded some proof that he was indeed dead. Aulus raised his tunic to reveal his penis, which he placed on the desktop between them. It was enormous, heavy and inert, at least a cubit in length, and black and shiny like an eel. Indeed, even as Petronius watched, it came to life and began to writhe and squirm like some hideous snake. Petronius looked to Aulus for some explanation, but he merely smiled sadly, then turned his attention back to the penis. Petronius could see now that it was inching across the map in a westerly direction. Having begun its journey in the Euxine Sea, it had traversed Anatolia and had almost reached the Aegean. Petronius realized with a start of horror that it was making for Italy, and that when it reached Rome something tremendous, cataclysmic, would occur. He woke up, bathed in sweat, heart pounding, his own penis painfully erect and pressed up against Melissa's buttocks. Without thinking, he took her there and then, from behind; it must have woken her up, but she did not stir.

The meaning of the dream was as clear as day, as if it had been interpreted by a priest. His guilt in the death of Aulus Junius had followed him home and finally caught up with him, just at the moment when his spirit was in turmoil and vulnerable to its message. That he was experiencing a crisis of conscience there was no doubt, but he had gone through those before without feeling that his entire world had been turned upside down. This was of an altogether different order. He had become Phineas tormented by the harpies, Odysseus pursued by the wrath of Poseidon. It had been sheer hubris on his part to imagine that he could escape with impunity the consequences of his own crime.

He lay awake all that night, consumed by panic and despair. At the darkest hour, he felt even that he was on the edge of madness, and laughed pitilessly at himself. It was not his part in Junius's death that ate at him; after all, every soldier takes his chances on the battlefield, and no officer could ever lead were he to assume personal responsibility for the death of every man under his command. Rather, it was the dream's revelation, or reminder, that Petronius had staked the entirety of his future happiness, and that of Melissa as well, on a shameful, cowardly deceit. He might have sought to win her through patience and constancy; instead, he had abused his power and authority to dispatch an ill-matched rival. What was more, he had no doubt that Melissa would never have recognized her husband's death as an acceptable price for her own liberation. It was not enough that Petronius had betrayed every moral and ethical principle on which the actions of a Roman patrician, soldier, and man of honor must stand, the very foundation of his understanding of what it means to be a man; he had also made Melissa an unwitting accomplice in the betrayal. And he knew now with utmost certainty that no good, or serenity, or happiness could ever come of it. Confident in her right, Melissa had already embarked on a path down which he could not follow. Either he must bring her up short with a confession of the truth, and risk destroying everything, or he must allow her to continue on her way alone.

Shortly before dawn, he nudged her awake.

"Do you never feel sorry for what we've done?" he asked her. She was instantly alert to the tone of his question.

"What is it you think we've done?" she answered tentatively.

"You know what I mean."

"I don't."

"All this. All we have. Your husband died so we could have it."

"The Parthians killed my husband. He was a professional soldier. He died honorably in the line of duty. It was his destiny, and nothing we did or could have done would have saved him. Why do you torment yourself?"

Now was the time to tell her, and yet Petronius could not

even bring himself to look her in the eye. He sank back upon the mattress. There would be no point in pursuing this line of thought. She would have to be as raw and defenseless as he was if it were to be at all fruitful, and very obviously she was not. Why should she be? There was no "we" in this matter to begin with. It was Petronius who had ordered Aulus Junius to the front, not she. She had asked for nothing, not even a divorce. She still did not know what he had done—or pretended not to know—and Petronius did not have the courage to tell her.

జజజజజజ

PETRONIUS TURNED AND slowly crossed the terrace, unsteady on his feet. Aware that he was being observed, and uncertain as to how long he had absented himself, he tried to approach with measured dignity. It was a pathetic exercise in futility—his entire body was trembling, and everyone could see it. Melissa made room for him on the couch, and he slipped under the covers beside her. No one was talking now.

The fires still roared in the braziers, but the wind had spent itself, and the tide was at full flood, drowning the rattle of shale and the sucking of the tidal pools. The silence made Petronius dizzy. A lightness of body, an almost nauseating sense of incorporeality, made him feel as if he might float off the couch, lifting the heavy counterpane with him through the garlanded pergola and into the bed of stars above. The moon was long gone and the stars were unmoored, waving to and fro like anemones in a gentle current. He stared at them, uncomprehending; they were pinholes, but instead of allowing light to flow in from the outer spheres, they drained it from the inner, and the night now pressing in was the product of that centrifuge, a void at the center of a spinning orb of which he himself was the axis. And here, to add to his confusion and disorientation, he felt a return of the painful sensory acuity that had overwhelmed him earlier. From the village up the hill he suddenly perceived the din of frenzied revelry, laughter, and song, as piercing and mirthless and imminent as the clash of metals on the battlefield. The upper slope and the acropolis were bathed in the ghostly red of bonfires, and Petronius fancied he could detect the smell of old vine stumps and burning garbage. A lone lamp hung from the stern of a darkened yacht anchored offshore, and he caught a hint of the hushed conversation of its occupants, sleepy and dissatisfied after a night of sparring. He found his left hand trailing in the water table, and the caress of the water on his fingertips made him feel as if his entire body were naked and immersed. His perceptions were birds, emerging from their shelter when the storm has spent itself. Or not birds, but bees—each scent, each fleeting shadow, each sound far and near an angry bee, circling his head, attacking and distracting, protecting the queen hidden at the core of their swarming multitude. He lifted his head and smelled the dawn rising in Asia Minor.

Someone was talking to him. There was a hand on his shoulder.

"Are you all right, Petronius?"

"Where am I?"

Silence. The fire crackling.

Anicius clapped his hands and slid out from beneath the blanket. "Time for some light-hearted verse, I think."

"Oh, yes!"

Anicius positioned himself before the company, at the far side of the water table. He anchored his feet firmly in declaiming position, coughed into his fist, placed his left palm flat against his chest, raised his right arm, and began to recite.

The day being humid and my head
heavy, I stretched out on a bed.
The open window to the right

reflected woodland-watery light,
a keyed-up silence as of dawn
Or dusk, the vibrant and uncertain
hour when a brave girl might undress
and caper naked on the grass.
You entered in a muslin gown,
bare-footed, your fine braids undone,
a fabled goddess with an air
as if in heat yet debonair.
Aroused, I grabbed and roughly tore
until your gown squirmed on the floor.
Oh, you resisted, but like one
Who knows resistance is in vain;
and, when you stood revealed, my eyes
feasted on shoulders, breasts and thighs.
I held you hard and down you slid
beside me, as we knew you would.
Oh, come to me again as then you did!

They all applauded and laughed rather more hysterically than
was strictly called for. Petronius knew that his unsteadiness and
silences were making them uncomfortable, and he regretted it
deeply. He could hardly blame them for giving way to false hilarity, but he chided himself for losing control of the evening.
There was very little time left, and perhaps he should be making
a greater effort to steer the mood away from thoughts of death.

"That was rich, coming from you, Anicius," he said.

"You're right, Petronius. Yet somehow it speaks to me, that
poem."

"What's in it for you? When's the last time *your* eyes feasted
on breasts?"

"It's all in how you look at it. There's less difference between a girl's breasts and a boy's buttocks than you might think. Anyway, my tastes have served me well over the past sixty years, and buggery is a good deal safer, politically, than running around with other men's wives."

"Was that intended for me, Anicius?" Petronius asked.

"No, for me, I think," Martialis said.

"For Cornelia, perhaps."

"Honestly, will I never live that down?"

"The pot finds its own herbs."

"Can't you find anyone else to quote but Catullus, Martialis?"

Despite the prevailing tension, the poem had left a lingering perfume in the air that seemed to have touched everyone with languor and wistfulness.

"You know," Fabius began dreamily, "when I was a boy, I never could understand that bit about the vibrant and uncertain hour. What could it mean? The poet didn't know if it was sunrise or sunset?"

"And now that you're a man, what do you make of it?" Martialis asked, but his sarcasm was lost on Fabius.

"I'm still not sure I catch his meaning, to be honest."

"It's about love, surely?" Pollia ventured.

"You mean, how the person you love is always there just when you need her?"

"No, I mean how we create the person we love from our own imagination. We don't see the person standing before us, but the image we impose upon him, like a mask. Ovid imagines a beautiful girl dancing naked on the lawn, and his lover becomes that girl. That's why he can't get her back—she's a figment, a chimera."

"A Platonic ideal?"

"Not necessarily an ideal, Cornelia. It can work both ways, I suppose. You can imagine unpleasant traits that aren't there, too."

"I hate to drag your pretty little ideas through the mud," Martialis said. "Ovid has a heavy lunch, he's a little worse for the retsina, lies down to take a nap, falls asleep thinking about pussy, has a wet dream. *That's* why he can't get her back. End of story."

"Marcus Valerius Martialis," Cornelia scolded. "Must you always be so coarse and cynical? Pollia was trying to elevate the conversation."

"There's only one elevation that matters in love."

"Don't you believe in love, then?"

"Oh, I believe in love. I believe in love just as I believe in empire. They're both transactions between partners of unequal strength, dressed up in heroic rhetoric. When I used to get into fights in the school yard, I'd squat on my opponent's chest and spit into his face until he said the magic words. Either he could say 'Marcus is the best!' or he could say 'I love you!' I didn't care which, but I wouldn't let him up until he said one or the other. That's much my view of love."

"You're a horrible person. Lucilius, won't you defend a lady's honor?"

"I'm a lawyer, Cornelia, not a necromancer."

"Petronius?"

"If you'll excuse me, I have to piss."

Petronius felt painfully self-conscious as he sought to extricate himself from the counterpane and make his exit with dignity. All eyes were upon him; no one now pretended light-heartedness or diversion—the night was too late for that—as he tottered to his feet and stumbled off into the darkness. Seemingly from out of nowhere, Commagenus stepped forward to offer his arm, but Petronius waved him off and faltered on, his mind a sodden bale of straw and sawdust. The house was dark now, a single torch burning at the door to the dining room. Had the other slaves abandoned the household for the festivities, or simply gone off to bed? Perhaps they had run away. No matter; there was wine left in the bowl, and Martialis to sniff out more if they should run short. It was still a beautiful night, and some conversation perhaps left to drain from its lees.

He heard the crunch of shells. Looking round, he found that he had wandered into the kitchen garden; the oyster-shell path-way should have been sharp and abrasive against the soles of his bare feet, but he felt nothing. He lifted his tunic and stared off into the dark orchard, where not a branch now stirred, as if the very night had tired of itself (or of him and his protracted drama) and gone to sleep. Even his heavy stream of urine made only a drowsy drumming as it thudded into the dry soil of an empty vegetable bed. Petronius shook himself off and turned to leave. But here was a sound—a whimper and a cry—and he turned back. It came from the darkest part of the garden, a cor-ner where the outer walls of the kitchen and the larder met, a spot so sunless even at the height of summer that nothing would grow there. Now, as his eyes adjusted to the layered dark, he found that just the dimmest light from the dying embers of the oven room, glowing through the kitchen window, picked out the quivering form of a tiny animal at the foot of the wall. It was the same brown puppy he had seen tethered to the gardener boy's ankle that afternoon, now tethered to the hinge of the kitchen door. The creature was clearly both terrified and elated by this nocturnal apparition; it cowered, averting its head in submission, yet its tail thumped vigorously in the dirt. Petronius considered the dog. This dismal patch was no place to leave a lonely and frightened animal, alone in the world and in the night. How could it ever know or hope that dawn would bring release? That was not something you could teach or explain to a dog. It would think that the night lasts forever, and come the day it would forget the night and worship the sun. And if, in the midst of the eternal night, someone should come to rescue it, or if at the height of the blazing day someone should beat it and lock it away in a dark room for some unknown infraction, well—that is what life is. For a dog. If it is a trained dog, it is pleased to obey orders; if it is a neglected dog, it skulks and flees and will not be made to work. But either way, it is always a dog and cannot ever be compelled to understand its own limitations. It is a self that creates the world and fills it entirely, and yet remains at the mercy of its own creation. Look at this poor, pathetic creature at his feet, not twelve weeks on this earth and it knows already to fear the night and solitude, and to praise the day and companionship. What else could it possibly need to know? Yet who would stoop to call that wisdom?

"Come with me, little one."

Petronius untethered the puppy. It groveled and shrank from his grasp, then buried its head gratefully in his armpit as he clasped it to his chest and inhaled its oily, sour-milk scent. Somehow, the smell revived him instantly, as if it were a potent tonic or drug, and he returned to the party with a lighter step. Yet, as he approached the group, he became aware of an ominous silence, and almost at the same time he caught sight of a dark, motionless figure watching them from the shelter of the colonnade. The others had seen it too. Nero had sent his men after all, then, and it was time to call an end to the party and make his hasty good-byes. Petronius sighed and got to his feet, and the executioner stepped forward. Petronius knew him immediately.

"Are you still alive then, Arbiter?" Turpilianus called out, extending a hand that Petronius ignored as they closed in on one another.

"I always feel alive in your presence, brother, whether I am or not. Is it really you he's sent? That's resourceful."

The other guests had risen, too, automatically, assuming that the time had come, and loitered uncertainly some paces away. The newcomer did not appear to be armed—was clothed, indeed, in the finest red toga, as if he had come directly from a triumph—but there was surely a contingent of soldiers waiting just out of sight in the event of trouble. Petronius imagined that, even in the dim light, the family resemblance must have been striking to them, and disconcerting. Titus Petronius Niger and Publius Petronius Turpilianus were of the same height, the same build, the same bearing, the same black hair flecked with gray and worn unfashionably long by both. In this gloom, of course, they would be unable to see the cruelty in Turpilianus's eyes, or the corruption of his heart. Perhaps there was nothing to distinguish the brothers in the dead of night.

Turpilianus lowered his voice. "Don't worry, you've got a few hours left. They've only just now wrapped up your trial."

"How did it go?"

"You lost."

"My sentence?"

"You need to ask?"

"So what have you come for?"

"I've come to say good-bye, Arbiter. Hope you acquit yourself nobly."

"Well, good-bye then. I've got guests, you see."

"Yes, I see. The emperor will be gratified to know that there are still Romans who value loyalty above their own personal safety. They'd do well to clear out before dawn."

"Thank you, I'll see to it."

"Is there anything you'd like to give me? For safekeeping, I mean. Deeds, wills, that sort of thing?"

"I don't think so. Good night, Turpilianus."

"Good-bye, then, Arbiter."

Just as he had appeared, Petronius's brother melted into the shadows and was swallowed up by the night. Petronius stood his ground, just to make sure there were no further unpleasant surprises. When he was convinced that he had seen the last of his brother, he sighed and turned back to the guests, who sat in a row on the edge of the couch, glum and ill at ease, like petitioners outside a magistrate's office. Petronius put a little bounce into his step, clapped his hands, and rubbed his palms together.

"That was pleasant," Martialis said.

"You will all do me the favor of returning to your places and filling your glasses. We must not give my brother the satisfaction of imagining that he's ruined our evening."

"What is the matter with that man?" Lucilius demanded furiously. "Has he no decency whatsoever?"

"He has the face of a man swimming underwater."

"How could two such different men spring from the same loins?"

"What makes you think we are so unlike? Anyway, he is only my half-brother."

"Just look at him, prancing about in his triumphal regalia in the middle of the night. And for what? He disgraced himself utterly in Britain."

"His triumphs cannot mitigate his lack of human qualities."

"No," Petronius said quietly. "But Nero certainly will, as he did mine. Now can we please change the subject?" He took his place on the couch, and the others moved to follow suit, with the exception of Melissa and Pollia, who hung back to pursue their private conversation.

Silence settled heavily upon the diners on the couch, each seeming, or pretending, to be lost in thought. In normal circumstances, such a pause would have been most worrisome to Petronius, the surest alarum of faltering conviviality, and as host he would have taken urgent, if subtle, steps to revive the party or to end it. Now he did not care to act. Let them reflect, if they wanted to; they'd certainly earned that right tonight. He wondered what each one was thinking. Was there one among them who was considering how best to cut the evening short and make his excuses without giving offense or appearing anxious to leave? He doubted it. It was more likely that each was scheming how to contrive to be the last to go; this was, after all, a historical event in its way, and, even without the considerations of friendship and tact, well worth seeing through to the bitter end. Who, after all, would want to say "Yes, I was invited to Petronius's notorious suicide banquet, but I left early"? Petronius instantly chided himself for his cynicism; and yet, if these were indeed his dearest friends, why did he need to keep reminding himself of that fact? It was, he understood, because he was so utterly alone in what he would have to do after they'd left, and in his mind and in his heart he had already said his good-byes. And suddenly, with blinding conviction, he knew what each of them was thinking. Each was asking himself at that very moment what it must feel like to be in Petronius's shoes, and to know that it was now a matter of a few meager hours before he would be dead. Dead forever. They would try to wrap their minds around the notion of the absolute, irrefutable inevitability of their own imminent dissolution—"Dead, dead, dead! I will be *nothing*!"—but Petronius knew with equal conviction that they must fail. Ultimately they must come to that fork in the road so familiar to every soldier in the field when he finds himself thinking: "It will happen to him but not to me." That was natural, and perfectly reasonable, as he himself knew from personal experience. But he was already well embarked on the other tangent, the one never taken until now, and so he had left them behind. In a way, it was not he but they who were the living ghosts, already fading from view in the mist at his back. The little world was as nothing, its panoramas and inhabitants but feeble, flickering, translucent shadows, when set against the great unknown universe yawning before him. In a strange way, he realized, he felt almost proud of himself—he could now say that he knew something, understood something known and understood by no one else. Achilles, too, had sailed wittingly to his preordained fate, and that knowledge had been the source of the greatest measure of his courage; but not even Achilles had known precisely, to the place and the hour, where it would happen. Was this grateful resignation courage? Petronius was doubtful; he had attended too many dissections of courage over the years to believe that it could ever be truly understood by those who seek it, wield it, or forsake it. He only knew, as Achilles knew, that courage was for lesser things. He had no need of it now.

"It's gone cold, hasn't it?" Lucilius asked.

"Would you like to go inside?"

"No. I like it."

"We could build up the fires, but they've all gone off to the Saturnalia. I don't know where we keep the firewood."

"Never mind. There are plenty of blankets."

At some point, Pollia and Melissa had wandered off together to the far side of the terrace. Now they reappeared, arms wrapped about one another's waists, Pollia resting her head on Melissa's shoulder. When they reached the couch, they separated with a kiss. Melissa climbed in beneath the counterpane beside Petronius and laid her hand across his chest. Pollia perched herself on the edge at Fabius's feet. Fabius gave her a quizzical look and beckoned her to join him, but she shook her head and hugged her shoulders.

"What have you two been plotting?" Cornelia asked, a conceit of jealousy in her voice.

"We have been discussing second chances."

"Second chances?"

"What we would do if we had the chance to do something over again."

"And?"

"That would be telling, wouldn't it?"

"Oh, come on!" Cornelia snorted rather coarsely. "It's a game, isn't it?"

"Pollia?" All eyes turned to Pollia, but she shrank into herself and shook her head again.

"Sorry."

"Be a spoilsport if you like. I for one know exactly what I would do. I would never have married Dolabella, my first husband, the impotent lout. I'd have held out for Lucilius from the start, and by now we'd have lots of lovely children. Perhaps even a grandchild or two."

"How very sweet of you, darling. The problem is, if I could do it all again, I should have chosen to stay in Sicily after my term as procurator, instead of seeking my fortune in Rome. And then I'd never have met you, and even if I had, I'd be poor and you wouldn't have me."

"Beast! How could you?"

"Sicily's a delightful place. Quiet, good wine. Nothing more complicated to adjudicate than a few vendettas and the occasional act of piracy."

"I think I'd have taken my studies of Greek rhetoric more seriously."

"Ah, how noble of you, Fabius. What about you, Anicius?"

"That's easy. I'd have had more sex when I was young enough to enjoy it. A lot more sex."

"An entire generation of grammar-school boys thanks you for that omission."

"Yes, and I should have been kinder. I wish I had been a kinder person."

"Rubbish!" Cornelia exclaimed. "How could you possibly be kinder than you are?"

"I was not so kind as a young man. There are many who are not with us today to whom I should like the chance to apologize."

"And you, Petronius?"

Petronius thought long and hard. He knew perfectly well that there was only one answer he could give; the question was whether he should give it. He couldn't be sure of saying it correctly, and saying it wrong would be worse than not saying it at all. Everything had to be simple now, pared down to its essence.

"I have never apologized to Melissa for a wrong I once did her."

"That's it?" Cornelia shrilled. "Do you mean to say that if you offered her this apology, there is nothing else in your entire life you would regret?"

"That's right."

"Do it, then, Petronius. Do it now!"

He held on to Melissa's smile, which, without changing, grew stronger, pulled him in closer to her.

"I may well yet," he said.

The silence that followed was broken only by a vine stump popping in the brazier, and by Pollia's muffled sobbing. Melissa enwrapped her in her shawl to hide her face, while Fabius merely lay staring into the embers, his face a blank cipher. If he had felt stronger, Petronius would have given that stupid boy a good crack across the face.

Cornelia cleared her throat and ran a bloodred fingernail across her right eyebrow. "I suppose you win the game, Petronius," she said sheepishly. "Unless Melissa can top you."

"Petronius," Melissa said, "I believe Pollia and Fabius are ready to say their good-nights."

Petronius sat up in alarm, suddenly feeling light-headed and nauseated again. "No, no. It's too early," he said, aware of the whine of panic rising in his throat, and ashamed, yet unable to suppress it. "I won't hear of it. Come, another glass."

"It is not early," Melissa insisted. "The dawn will be here in two hours or less, and you still have business to transact."

"Are you evicting our guests, Melissa? What kind of send-off is that?"

But the others were already beginning to stir, shifting their weight and leaning over in the poor, flickering light to locate their sandals at the foot of the couch. Petronius felt the atmosphere dissipating as rapidly as a breath of steam on a winter's day, and he had reached this juncture of the evening too many times to pretend to himself that it could be salvaged. The party was over; the guests were ready to call it a night; and to insist that they linger, even for five superfluous minutes, would be to color their memories of the entire endeavor with a pallid wash of regret. Like a man's life, a dinner is best quitted while it still has a warm soul to see it on its way. Nevertheless, he gave it one last try.

"Lucilius, you'll stay, won't you?"

Lucilius had already pinned his tunic around his shoulders, and was helping Cornelia on with her shawl. "Petronius, I would stay to the bitter end if you asked me to, and hold your hand all the way. But it is not my place, and you know it."

"Titus, my dear," Cornelia said. "It is time for us to say good-bye."

"Anicius?"

"Kiss me, Titus. I will be going."

"Marcus may stay, Petronius," Melissa said with quiet authority. "The others will take their gifts now."

"Gifts! Of course, how could I forget? Marcus, hand me the ladle in that wine bowl, will you? Gather round, the rest of you."

The six guests drew together in a small circle around their host as he accepted the ladle from Martialis, while Melissa waited to one side. It was, of course, the priceless myrrhine ladle from Arrabona that her late husband had once given her in his ignorance, and that she had later given to Petronius in her pride. And now it was Petronius who must try to pass it on in all humility. It was a task, one of his very last, that he dearly wanted to get just right, but the ladle itself would make that difficult, for it was one of the least humble objects he had ever encountered. Even now, in this dismal, volcanic glow, it shone with an arrogant light, as if it had an inner spine of eternal liquor, the colorless blood of the gods flowing in its translucent veins, responsive to envy and fear and grasping and anger. When Petronius held it out at chest height, it absorbed the yellow of his tunic and discharged it again as bile.

"Look carefully at this ladle," Petronius said. "You will almost certainly never see such exquisite craftsmanship again in your lifetime. It is the very embodiment of perfection, you will agree. It is said to be invaluable, but it most definitely has a value. In fact, it has been appraised at 300,000 sesterces, enough to pay a legionary's salary for a thousand years. Whoever owns it is a wealthy man indeed. And yet, strangely, it has meant very little to any of its recent owners. It clearly had little value to the merchant who sold it for a pittance to Aulus Junius in Arrabona. Aulus Junius, in turn, passed it on to Melissa to serve cheap wine at his drinking parties. Melissa gave it to me, simply because she could find no other way of expressing herself. And now I, its last owner—well, perhaps I am able to appreciate something of its beauty, but I hold its perfection cheap. Perhaps it would mean something to a god, but it means nothing to me.

"Nero has seen it, and he covets it. In a few hours, when he sends his henchmen to pillage my house, the ladle will be at the top of their list. I am determined that he shall not have it. I cannot give it to any of you, because its mere possession will put its possessor at great risk. I cannot return it to Melissa, obviously. So Melissa and I have come up with a plan that will both keep it out of Nero's hands and restore it to its true value."

Petronius held the ladle out at arm's length and allowed it to drop to the granite pavement. The sound as it shattered was like the cracking of ice on an Alpine lake in the spring thaw. The guests, rather than gasp in dismay, felt its destruction as a communal release of tension, and sighed each to themselves, as if they had only been waiting for this moment. They stared down in calm silence at the dozen or so lumps of crystal that were all that remained of the ladle. Then Petronius stooped and gathered the pieces into a fold of his tunic.

"Each of you will take a fragment home with you, as a memento of me and our time together. The shards are quite valuable in their own right—the emperor himself owns several precious myrrhine specimens—but that is hardly the point. In the daylight, you will see that each fragment emits the same light as the whole. Each pulses with the same inner life. It is my hope that these fragments, the living heart of the crystal, will seem even more beautiful than the body from which they came. And perhaps, if I am very, very lucky, that is how my friends will remember me."

He held out a piece of crystal to Anicius, who took it and enfolded Petronius in his embrace. "You are a *good* man," he whispered. "The world will know of this night. Your glory is assured." And then he was gone.

Next came Lucilius. They clasped forearms, and Petronius could feel Lucilius tremble and almost falter. "You are a *brave* man," he said, choking.

Cornelia, eyes red-rimmed but resolutely dry, grasped Petronius's face between her palms and planted a long, lingering kiss on his lips. "You *poor man*." Then, as an afterthought, she gave him another, longer kiss, and hurried on to her waiting husband. And they were gone.

Fabius stepped up, his arms by his side, eyes downcast, like a boy awaiting instructions from his father. Petronius took him by the shoulders, at arm's length, but could think of nothing to say. How like him to feel awkward and shy at this juncture! But as he fumbled with his gift of crystal, Fabius found his tongue. "I wish you safe passage to the underworld. You are a great, a *great* Roman," he muttered, and executed a clumsy salute.

Pollia threw herself into Petronius's arms, pressing her face into his chest and sobbing inconsolably. And just as he had responded inappropriately to Fabius's hapless formality, Petronius found himself ferociously excited by the heat of her body and the dampness of her tears soaking through the cloth of his tunic. As he struggled to understand what she was saying, her voice muffled by proximity and emotion, he was only dimly aware of the vision, flitting and fleeing like a thrush through the empty hallways of his mind, of himself on top of her, pinning her arms to the ground, her thighs wrapped around his hips, her sobs of ecstasy and gratitude ringing in his ears. And then, the fantasy exhausting itself at the same moment that it had sprung to life, he grasped what Pollia was saying.

"I love you, Petronius, I love you," over and over again, until he had to push her into Fabius's waiting arms, and they stepped away.

Petronius turned toward the house to watch them go, but time must have been playing tricks on him, for they had already vanished. The only figure that remained was the Hagesander Diana at the far end of the dining room, and she had never been of much comfort to him. He tried to think back—had he been daydreaming? Somehow his memory of the past few seconds had become all muddled. Perhaps he had not entertained his fantasy of making love to Pollia until after she had gone, until after he had heard her say she loved him? But if that were the case, what had he been thinking about when she was in his arms? He tried to remember; it had only been moments earlier, but it felt as if it had all occurred a thousand years ago in a distant land. Suddenly it seemed enormously important to him to retrieve the memory of the past minute precisely as it had unfolded. These thoughts and visions were of great moment; he had a strange feeling that he would need them with him in the afterworld, that one carried one's last memories like currency down there, and the more precise they were, the more valuable; or perhaps they were armor down there, and the more specific they were, the more protective; or perhaps they were travel documents, and only those who could recite them faithfully would be allowed to pass; or they were genealogical testaments, and those with the most impressive memories enjoyed the most prestige among the dead. Petronius had no idea why these thoughts were occurring to him, rushing upon him with such irresistible impetus. He knew objectively that they were foolish and meaningless, and that he was wasting precious time indulging them, but he felt as one does in a dream in which there are multiple time schemes, and enemies can leap and fly while one's own legs can barely move through the viscous, clinging seconds. And then, with a start of recognition so pure and true that it made his heart race, as if he had just inhaled the entire universe in one gasp, he realized that this whole thing—his fantasy with Pollia, and his confession, and the dinner party, and the death sentence, and his years at Nero's court, and his return to Rome—was all just a dream—of course, it had all occurred in the blink of an eye, he could see that now!—and that when he turned around again to Melissa and Martialis, the whole fabric of reality that he had known for the

183

past eight years would be stripped away, and he would open his eyes and find himself in his bed in the villa at Lake Sophon, and the sun would just be rising on a quiet summer's morning, the cranes tiptoeing silently through the rushes, and Melissa would be at his side, naked, pressing herself against him. He swung about, his arms open wide to his salvation, and his legs gave way beneath him. When he came to, he found himself crumpled on the ground, his face drenched in hot tears, his head cradled in Melissa's lap as if he were the aged father who had just taken that fatal fall, and he felt a shame deeper than he could ever imagine possible.

"I must get up," he said.

"Rest a moment," Melissa whispered.

"No, I must."

"Shh." The very slight pressure of her palms against his cheeks was enough to hold him down, and the coolness of her hands on his wet skin made him understand that the tears were not hers, but his own. He closed his eyes.

"I don't want to die," he said, feeling that somehow it was safe to say with his eyes closed, and at the same time knowing how childish the feeling really was.

"Of course you don't."

"There's time still. I'll live if you tell me to live."

"Shh."

He lay there a few minutes as she rocked his head gently, like a baby in a cradle, and felt his tears dry in a cold, almost imperceptible breeze—it was the sun, rising five hundred miles away over Greece and pushing the night air before it. Calm gradually settled upon him, until after a minute he realized with mild surprise that the moment had come, without thought or premeditation, the moment of serene acceptance that he had trained for his entire life and sought in vain this entire long day and night.

It was here; it had stolen upon him like a long-absent lover—or no, like the mother who died long ago from a withering disease, whom one no longer remembers except as a shattered husk, but who returns in dreams clad in shining light and health, bringing her enveloping love to the dreamer who had never thought to feel its like again. He could hardly believe it; it was too good to be true, precisely as he had hoped it would be—this feeling of strength, joy, fearlessness—but never quite believed himself capable of mastering. Now he saw that it was not a moment that one mastered but that one submitted to, and that was its mystery for those who sought it. It was odd, interesting, he thought, that in just the past minute he had felt both like an old man and like an infant. The infant he had been, once, but recalled nothing at all thereof; the old man he would never be. Still, a lifetime in the interim. More than enough. One could live forever, and not have this moment of peace that he was having now. Why ruin it with stupid, vulgar thoughts of escape? How could surviving a thousand more years improve on what he had found right here, right now? He took Melissa's hands in his own and kissed each one.

"Well?" He looked up into her face. She stared back at him, her eyes sparkling with amusement and affection, and stroked his cheek with the back of her hand. There was no hypersensitivity now—the whole world was contained in that touch, the rest of his body numb. He grasped her hand and held it to his skin.

"Well?"

She laughed and looked away. "I'm not going to immolate myself at your side, if that's what you're thinking."

"You know what I mean."

"Oh, Titus—or should I call you 'Governor'? Can you really be as dim as that, after all these years? Of course I knew what you'd done. I knew it right away. Who else could have given him his marching orders but you?"

"And yet you've never said anything about it. You pretended to know nothing."

"I understand the way men think. You'd have found a way to blame me if I had."

"And now?'

"And now what?"

"Have you forgiven me?"

"There's nothing to forgive. You did the best you could with what you had."

"You don't really believe that."

"Of course I do. Anyway, why ask me? You'll be dead in an hour or so. Take it up with Junius when you run into him. He's the one you should be asking for forgiveness."

Petronius sighed contentedly and closed his eyes. He'd forgotten how perfect it was, lying with his head in her lap. Perhaps he should kiss her, make love to her right now, a touching communion, a fitting remembrance? But no, everything was right the way it was; the time for such intimacies had passed. They seemed too encumbered now, too earthbound. Besides, who would get to be on top? Petronius laughed quietly, and sighed again. Then he remembered what he'd wanted to ask.

"Melissa, what did you say?"

"What do you mean?"

"When you and Pollia were talking about second chances. I can imagine what she said."

"She said she was in love with you, and she asked for my forgiveness. She said she wished she'd never married Fabius."

"Naturally. But what did you say?"

"Are you sure you want to ask me that question, Titus?"

"Of course I am."

"I said nothing."

"Nothing?"

"I said there was nothing I would wish to change. There is no decision that I have ever made that I would wish to undo."

"What about all the pain I caused you?"

"That was your decision, not mine. The only way I could have avoided that pain would have been to decide not to be with you, and that I could never have done."

"Why not?"

"I had a mission to make you a wiser man. And to bring us to this moment. Isn't that enough?"

She was right, of course. It was more than enough, this moment. It was the moment for which one waits an entire lifetime, and Petronius had. But what of Melissa? Tomorrow, in just an hour or two, the world would change for her forever, and what would it mean for her then, who must find a way to preserve it? Petronius thought of the *kouros*. Born eight hundred years earlier, in a world so different from his own, it might very well endure another eight hundred, or more, into a world that would be even more different still. It was only a rock; it did not retain or remember the world through which it had passed, and yet it served as a reminder of all who saw and touched it, not just at the moment of its creation and of the living, breathing man who put his chisel to the stone, but also of every age it had seen, of every generation that had preserved it, or neglected it, and passed it on intact. And it occurred to Petronius that this love of his, this moment, did not actually belong to him at all, or to Melissa, or to the next man on whom she might bestow it, should there be one. Perhaps this love was a *kouros*, created in ancient times, and passed from keeper to keeper, through him and Melissa and on into the unknown future. And though, like the statue, it would not remember either of them, still, to some lover a thousand years hence who had never heard their names or known their deeds, it would serve as a reminder of all the lovers who had received it, cosseted it, and passed it on. Its very existence would be a testament to their care of it, and maybe, just maybe, in a moment similar to this one, those impossibly distant lovers will think back in gratitude on all those who had held it and saved it on their behalf.

As if she were reading his thoughts, Melissa leaned over, held his cheeks between her palms, and kissed him full and long on the lips. After that, they were quiet, listening to the breath of the sea. And then Martialis sneezed somewhere off along the terrace.

"I have one more thing I have to do," Petronius said, and rolled off her lap to pick himself up off the ground. Martialis was over by the balustrade, staring morosely out over the black water.

"I'll only be a moment, Marcus. Wait for me, and we'll take a walk." He strode off into the house.

The rooms and corridors were dark and quiet, as was normal for this time of night, yet they seemed especially lifeless now. Petronius suspected that there was not a slave in the house, with the possible exception of Commagenus and Demetrius, who were not much given to revelry and, ever diligent, were probably in their quarters preparing themselves for their new life as freed-men. Petronius considered rousing Demetrius for the task at hand, but decided that, having already said their good-byes, it would be uncomfortable for both of them to have to reprise them. Besides which, given the possibility that members of his household might still be tortured for any further information that could be of use to the state—and a scribe was certainly the most obvious potential guardian of such information—Petronius wished to spare him the possession of any incriminating secrets. This last job was something he could do himself.

As per standing orders, the lamps were still lit in his study, though the oil had been allowed to deplete itself tonight and would run out momentarily. He sat at his desk, retrieved a fresh sheet of his finest letter papyrus, dipped his pen, and began to write.

Titus Petronius Niger to Nero Claudius Caesar Augustus Germanicus, greetings—

◙◙◙◙◙◙

PETRONIUS HAD LEARNED a simple truth: It is not possible to love another when you despise yourself. Did everyone but him already know it? One thing was certain: Melissa knew it. He taught it to her every day in their growing estrangement; in his anger and in his despair; in the brutality of his lovemaking and then in his inability to make love to her at all; in his indifference to her happiness and to his own; in his peevish response to minor irritations and in his atrophied moral judgment; in his apathy toward her social trajectory and in the carelessness with which he steered his own. Dark times indeed. He had lost Melissa, and gained an empire.

Where else was he to take himself, where else on Earth was more suited to a man like him than Nero's court? Giving in to the emperor's blandishments and launching himself into court society had not been difficult decisions to make. They were barely decisions at all; more like slipping into a warm, perfumed bath. Now that the veil had been stripped from his eyes, and he saw himself for who he truly was, it came to seem his only natural home, and his Tartarus.

For two years he stood at the emperor's right hand, whispering in his ear, advising and cajoling him. He was not, it was true, a political counselor, and he avoided inserting himself into lethal enmities, but that was a spurious distinction. In a tyrant's court, culture and politics are indissoluble, and Petronius knew exactly what he was doing, even as he staggered along in a sort of heedless, drunken haze. He made light of Nero's excesses and couched his sins in apposite classical justifications. Petronius's intellect, eloquence, and refinement flattered the emperor's vision of himself as an aesthete of the highest rank, in a way that the brutal vulgarians of the inner circle—who complemented the butcher and the thug in him—could never hope to compete with. When Nero kicked the pregnant empress Poppaea Sabina to death, it was Petronius who sat with him in private mourning and helped compose her funeral eulogy.

But it was only a waiting game, and Petronius knew it. Compared to Tigellinus and the other ruthless, low-born ministers, he was an amateur in the kind of scheming and backbiting necessary to maintain a career at court. From the moment he had elbowed Tigellinus aside, it was merely a matter of time before revenge was exacted, and allowing himself to be crowned "Arbiter" was just a manner of slow-motion suicide.

The fatal moment arrived with the surprise banquet which Tigellinus organized in Nero's honor on Agrippa's lake. The lakeshore was stocked with exotic birds and beasts, lined with elegant makeshift brothels staffed with willing patrician matrons, and ablaze with a thousand flaming torches. Vibrant song rang out upon the water from choruses cleverly concealed along the embankments. The emperor and his party (including Petronius) were towed upon a raft of gold and ivory and dined with unsurpassed luxury, their every foible and depravity administered to by a crew of professional hedonists. The emperor was presented with a stunning Greek youth who kept him entertained throughout the night. The event was planned and executed perfectly from beginning to end, and everyone involved knew that the Arbiter of Elegance had been made obsolete in a single blow.

When Rome burned not long afterward, Petronius took it as

his cue to bow out. His relationship with Melissa had long since withered into a hollow, misshapen thing; he had fully justified her every fear and misgiving, and she no longer expected anything of him. She let him go without anger or bitterness, but rather in profound sadness for what he had become. He left her to manage the Esquiline villa, retired to Cumae, and waited for his sins to catch up with him.

രുരുരുരുരു

PETRONIUS GLANCED DOWN at the papyrus and reread what he had written:

Titus Petronius Niger to Nero Claudius Caesar Augustus Germanicus, greetings—

Then he continued to write.

Sire, our late friend and colleague, Annaeus Seneca, in one of his more lucid moments, once said to me: "All conversations with autocrats end with expressions of gratitude." At the time, I believed this observation to be a rather sorry commentary on the life he had led in your company. I see now, however, that it was remarkably sagacious—that means "clever," Caesar—as I find myself in the unanticipated position of writing on my deathbed to offer you my undying thanks for all you have done for me. Your own mother, Sire, could not have been more grateful to you than I am when you made it possible for her to retire at the full height of her powers.

Without your guidance, example, and stimulus, I would never have grasped the urgency and reward of being adequately prepared for death. Had I lived to be an old man, I believe that I should never have attained the conclusions and serenity that dire necessity has thrust upon me, and that sustain me now in my final, happy moments. I do not claim to have attained wisdom or understanding; that would be too much to ask. Yet I feel that you have gifted me with an almost equal treasure: a measure of self-awareness that, while modest, has nevertheless cast a splendid new light on the world around me and my place in it. I cannot help but believe that it is a gift afforded to few men, and for that I shall remain eternally in your debt.

One more thing, Caesar. Since it may come to pass that you shall find yourself in similar circumstances in the not-too-distant future, and in pressing need of a medium whereby to record your final thoughts and wishes in haste, may I humbly suggest that you keep about you at all times a quill, an inkhorn, and a sheet of papyrus for that purpose, as I have done for the past several years, living in the shadow of your displeasure. They may prove to be very handy indeed and bring you peace of mind when you are most in need of it, as they have me.

Without pausing to reread a single word of the letter, Petronius sanded, folded, and sealed it with wax, stamping the seal with his signet ring. Next, rummaging through his strongbox, he found the most recent codicil to his will, broke the seal, made some minor amendments, and resealed it. He pocketed a fistful of gold denarii and then, with both documents tucked into a fold of his cape, strode out onto the terrace. He felt full of strength, his every muscle vibrant with energy, like a wineskin filled with new, green wine. He knew it was the vigor of last chances, but it felt very good nonetheless, and he wondered how it might be, and why it cannot be, to feel this way every moment of one's life. He found Melissa and Martialis deep in conversation on a bench beneath the colonnade.

"Quickly now, Marcus, find me a heavy rock."

"A what?"

"Just do it, please."

Martialis threw a perfunctory, sweeping gaze over the pavement and, finding nothing suitable, crossed to the gate set into the wall of the perfume garden. He returned a moment later with a fist-size lump of black basalt, which he handed to Petronius.

"Will this do?"

"No, it won't do. I said heavy. I . . . never mind, I've got it."

Petronius leaned down and plucked the golden statuette of Apollo from its niche. The dead thrush still lay at its feet, a sacrifice disdained. He considered it a moment; earlier, he might have spared a pensive afterthought to the creature's plight, to wondering what it might be like to be twelve hours dead, but now he had no time. He would be a dead thrush himself soon enough, and all such questions would be answered, or not. Instead, he hefted the statuette, considerably heavier than its size would have suggested, and posed it on the balustrade. Then he removed the signet from the ring finger of his right hand and placed it beside the statuette.

"After Lucan killed himself," he said, "Fabius Romanus stole his signet ring and forged the letter that incriminated Annaeus Mela. After my ring is destroyed, I want you to hold on to the pieces and bear witness to the falsehood of any document claimed to have been sealed by me after this moment."

So saying, he raised the statuette with both hands and brought its marble base down onto the onyx signet, which shattered into a thousand fragments, most falling off the far side of the balustrade onto the rocky parapet and into the water, along with the gold ring itself. The three watched the pieces disappear into the darkness.

"Perhaps I overdid it," Petronius said after a moment. He shrugged. "Never mind, you get the idea. Now, on to other business. Here's two documents, sealed. One contains the final amendments to my will, to be delivered into the hands of Gaius Lucilius, and no one else. Understand?"

"But Lucilius left not half an hour ago. Why didn't you just give it to him then?"

"I've made changes since. And anyway, there was a danger of his being detained on his way home. He may be in custody right now, for all I know. But no one's going to arrest you, with your fresh-from-the-brothel mystique. Any more interruptions? Right. The other is a letter addressed to Nero. You give that to Lucilius, too, and he'll find a way of getting it safely to court without endangering the messenger."

"Why not just leave it here for Nero to find in the morning?"

"Idiot! Melissa Silia will still be here, attending to my obsequies."

"Nasty letter, is it? Rancid with accusations of shameful excess?"

"What time do you suppose it is, Melissa?"

"An hour, perhaps an hour and a half to dawn."

"Do Marcus and I have time for our walk, do you think?"

"I shouldn't dawdle too much, if I were you."

"Come on then, Marcus. Melissa, I'll wake you as soon as I get back."

"I'll wait up."

"As you wish."

"And Marcus, will you come by in the morning? I think I shall have need of you."

"Yes, Melissa, I will come. Good night."

In silence, they padded through the orchard, across the canal, and through a small wooden door in the outer wall that gave onto a path through an ancient grove of oaks. Petronius led the way; although it was still too dark to see much farther than the hand before one's face, he had taken this route too often to be waylaid by the night. Shortly, the path and the woods gave way to an olive grove, where visibility improved and the Saturnalia bonfires in the village served as beacons. The slope steepened, and suddenly they reached the road. Petronius stepped confidently onto the flagging, but Martialis hung back warily.

"Don't worry," Petronius whispered. "My gate is half a mile east of here. They'll never know we're gone."

With the dark mountain looming to their right and the gentle vineyards sloping down to the sea on their left, they made for the village gate, keeping a brisk pace. Petronius felt giddy and reckless, like a boy on a caper.

"Let me ask you a question, Marcus."

"Go ahead."

"What is life?"

"You must be joking. You don't expect me to answer that, do you?"

"I have no time left for joking. What is life, to you?"

"People have been asking that question for six-hundred years. Why should I have an answer?"

Petronius said nothing.

"Well, since you insist. Let's see. Life is . . . a series of encounters strung together by flawed memories of previous encounters."

"That's all?"

"What else do you want it to be?"

"A search for meaning?"

"Well, then it's that, too."

"You're very glib."

"It's a stupid question. Petronius, you have, perhaps, an hour or so to live. Have you found your meaning?"

"No."

"And so you must die unhappy?"

"I'm not unhappy. I'm confused. I'd imagined it would all be clear by now. I'd been led to expect it would be."

"Perhaps you've been listening to the wrong people. What are we doing here?"

"That's what I'm asking."

"I mean, what are we doing in this god-forsaken shithole?"

They'd reached the village gate, left open all night for the festivities and guarded by a municipal guildsman, who was passed out on the ground and snoring peaceably in a pool of his own vomit. Stepping around him, they penetrated into the village proper, whose narrow cobbled alleys stank of cheap red wine and burning detritus. Here and there, where the main street opened onto some little square, a bonfire still glowed and sputtered, but the revelry seemed for the most part to have burned itself out. A few stragglers leaned against each other as they stumbled home to their beds, but otherwise the village was quiet. And yet, coming into the central marketplace, they found a young couple sitting on the ledge of the fountain, deep in quiet conversation. Petronius stopped directly in front of them.

"Surisca!"

The girl, startled, leaped to her feet in confusion, then sank to one knee with her head bowed. Petronius noted that her hair was still immaculately braided, twisted, and pinned with his silver brooch. Clearly, she and her baker boy, if this were he, were still in the platonic phase of their love affair. Petronius felt a keen, if transient, pang of regret that this girl, so naturally modest and well-behaved, had been made such a debased plaything at his hands. The boy, a lanky redhead not yet in his first beard, stood slowly and sullenly tried to stare down the interlopers. Petronius reached down and raised Surisca to her feet with a tap on the shoulder.

"Forgive me for disturbing you, my dear," he said. "And for interrupting you."

"Master, I was just on my way back . . ."

"No, no need. That's not why I stopped. I was simply pleased to see you, as I have something I wanted to tell you and didn't think I'd get the chance."

She sat down on the fountain, and pulled her boyfriend, who was still pouting and pointing his chin churlishly, down beside her. Petronius crouched so as to speak to them face to face.

"This evening," Petronius went on, "I made an amendment to my will concerning you. I hope you will be pleased. I have decided to bequeath you as a gift to my client here, Marcus Valerius Martialis."

"You what?" Martialis sputtered. Surisca merely looked bewildered.

"Quiet, please. Now, Surisca, you have known Martialis for some little while. You know he is a kind man, if sometimes ill-mannered. I believe he will be a good master to you, in his way, which is why I wanted him to have you. Accordingly, when you return to the villa this morning, I want you to pack your belongings and go find him in his lodgings in Baiae."

"But Petronius, you know I can't feed a slave!"

"Just a *moment*. Surisca, I have also left you some money. Not a lot, but enough to be useful. It might, for instance, suffice to pay off your manumission tax, should you eventually be freed, with enough left over to start you in a little business." He looked the redheaded boy straight in the eye. "A bakery, perhaps. Now, what do you think of that?"

Surisca seemed not to have understood a single word he'd said, but nodded her head several times and appeared to be on the verge of tears. Petronius patted her demurely on the hand, aware of his own hypocrisy, and stood.

"Very well, then. Good night, Surisca, and good-bye." He turned and continued on his way, Martialis tripping after him and looking back anxiously at the stunned teenagers.

"Tomorrow afternoon," he called. "Look for me at Saufeia's house, down by the port."

By the time he caught up with Petronius, they had already reached the northern gate and passed out onto the road to the acropolis.

"That was a dirty trick. You could have just manumitted her yourself, instead of saddling me with all the hassle."

"She and her boy want to move to Rome. I can't have that. You must give her a stern lecture, scare all that nonsense out of her. Take them to Rome, help them set up their little bakery before you free her. And don't you dare lay a hand on her. She's had more than enough of that already."

"Who are you to tell me what to do with my own slave?"

The road made an uphill, hairpin turn as it climbed to the acropolis, the sanctuary of Apollo gleaming above them on the lower terrace. It seemed to Petronius that the marble columns were glowing, as if picking up some ambient light, but a scan of the horizon showed no sign of incipient dawn just yet. Martialis followed his gaze and put his hand on Petronius's shoulder in a gesture that seemed to seek both to comfort and to speed him up the slope. The sacred road skirted the wall of the terrace, past the ceremonial stairway, and continued on up to the peak of the rise to the temple of Zeus and the crypt, but Petronius stopped just short of the acropolis at a sarcophagus-shaped portal, some fifteen feet high, set into the side of the slope. A tunnel, supported by arches echoing the five sides of the portal, plunged deep into the heart of the mountain. A torch burned somewhere way down the tunnel, but the far end was invisible.

"What is this?"

"The cave of the Sybil."

"Surely you don't mean to go in there?"

"Scared?"

"I'm not scared. It's just . . . I mean, isn't she supposed to write her prophecies on oak leaves and leave them at the entrance? Can't we just scrounge around for some stray communiqués right here?"

"No. We go in. I've brought money."

"What do you need the Sybil for anyway? You're going to be dead in an hour. What sort of future can you possibly have? Can't you find your own way to the underworld?"

"Yesterday you were blubbering like a baby at the thought of my imminent demise. Now you can't wait to get rid of me. What's the matter with you? Anyway, it's not my future we're interested in—it's yours."

"This tragedy is rapidly turning into a farce. Besides, I already know my own future. Find a new patron; eat him out of house and home; kiss some ass, write some poems, fuck some tarts; earn everlasting glory, and die in a bed."

"We're in a hurry. Let's go."

As they entered the tunnel, Martialis took Petronius's hand in his. They walked quickly, ignoring the passages branching off to either side as they made straight for the torch, and their footsteps on the gritty floor rang out ahead of them. One of these side passages, Petronius recalled, led to the necropolis on the other side of the hill; if he knew the way, he could make straight for his own tomb—as he had imagined himself doing only a few hours earlier—and save everyone a lot of trouble. But he was afraid of ghosts and did not have the courage for it. Instead, he pulled the torch from its bracket as they passed, and now they could see that the tunnel ended, about a hundred feet ahead, in a vaulted chamber, empty and unlit. They stopped at the entrance to the chamber and Petronius thrust the torch before him, illuminating a rough stone bench set into an alcove directly before them.

"Sybil!" Petronius's voice was all too loud and assertive for this place, and brought no response. They waited, then entered the chamber. On the floor at the center sat a small iron brazier, cold and ash-filled, and on the bench were a dry lamp and a ragged hemp sack. Petronius nudged at the bag and it flopped over, revealing its contents: a few dry laurel leaves, a half-eaten loaf of flatbread, and a round disk of hard cheese. He sighed.

"That's that, I suppose."

"Not exactly the *Aeneid*, is it? What did you expect? An old witch in a bottle, just waiting up for your millennial appearance?"

"Maybe, yes. I don't know what I expected."

They turned toward the exit. At the far end of the tunnel, a few bright stars were framed in the arches.

"Why are you so worried about me, Petronius?" Martialis asked plaintively. "I'm a grown man. I can take care of myself."

"But you act like a child, as if nothing matters but your own gratification. Look at the fuss you made at the party. That may wash in Spain, but it's no way to get ahead in Roman society. I've been trying to educate you in the ways of the world ever since I became your patron, but sometimes I wonder if you've learned anything at all from me. I wonder, and I worry."

"You needn't. I can take care of myself."

"You've said that, but I do wonder. I've been your father for the past two years, and I've watched over you. I've watched you. You don't know how to behave in company, you don't know how to control your feelings. Those things matter here. Yes, you can be charming and flattering when you want to, but charm and flattery can only take you so far. What you need is to find your solid core, the part of you that won't feel cheapened or weakened when you need to compromise to get ahead."

"I know who I am, Petronius. That's why I never want to pretend to be anything else, the way you all do. I'm sorry if you feel it betrays a lack of character. The fact is, I always thought it was why you loved me."

"It *is*. But I'll be gone, and other people won't love you for it. They'll be offended by you, the way Fabius is. You know I haven't just been acting the part of father to you. I've felt like your father. I love you like a father."

"I know that."

"So I can't simply take you as you are. I can't just be another one of your 'flawed encounters' or whatever it is. I have to *protect* you. Just look at you, blundering around the city half-drunk all the time, dressed in rags, stinking like a pig, insulting senators. Where will you find another patron? Who would put up with you?"

Martialis was silent, apparently pensive and receptive, but Petronius had had these talks with him before and they had changed nothing. He suspected that the boy's repentance was feigned, as always, or perhaps, in this instance, a reflection of his reluctance to talk back at a moment of crisis. The mere fact that Petronius still thought of him, a man in his midtwenties, as "the boy" only reflected the futility of his efforts to change him. The boy had grown up without mother or father, doted upon and worshiped by his extended family, left to run wild in the Spanish hinterlands, never subject to lecture or rebuke. Was it any wonder that he resisted grooming, when being untamed and natural had been the modus operandi of his every childhood triumph? Upon his arrival in Rome, he had been a sore trial to Seneca and Lucan; they hadn't known what to make of him, what to do about him, how to suppress him, who to fob him off on. If Petronius had not taken a liking to him, there's no saying how low the boy would have sunk before money could be scraped together to ship him back to Bilbilis in disgrace. And now, with grief's license and some change in his pocket—Petronius had taken care to leave Martialis just enough to keep him solvent, should he spend moderately, until a new patron could be found;

should he spend immoderately, Petronius's entire fortune would not have sufficed—there was every likelihood of his reverting to character, being carried off by his own profligacy and pride to some irredeemable place. Petronius would not be there to prevent it, and he worried that Martialis's respect for his memory and example would not be strong enough to restrain him. Was it really possible that, twenty years from now, he would represent but the briefest episode in Martialis's life story, an anecdote routinely retailed and tailored for convenience, a twinge of unwelcome regret upon the uncorking of a vintage Falernian—a flawed memory of a previous encounter? If Martialis did not take himself in hand, it would be worse than that—all of Petronius would be reduced to the nagging voice of moneyed respectability that occasionally intruded upon a cruel hangover.

"You know, Marcus," he ventured cautiously, "the first thing a good man says to himself when he knows he is going to die is that everything he has ever done is worthless. This is normal; it is wise, and appropriate. It is also just a beginning, the first step toward something. When he hears himself saying it, he should rejoice—he is about to embark upon a journey. And the first question he must ask himself as he sets out is: Why have I waited so long to say this? I have *always* known that I was going to die."

"Yes, all right."

"Now, listen. I have two reasons for bringing this up. The first is that I don't want to die thinking that my friendship with you has been worthless. If I am your mentor, you ought to have learned something from me. I want to be able to believe that I've helped you in some way. The second is that you have the chance to do what I have not. Don't wait until the last minute to evaluate your accomplishments and your potential. Remember what Epicurus tells us: 'While we are on the road, we must try to make what is before us better than what is past; when we come to the road's end, we feel a smooth contentment.' Do it now. Say to yourself 'Everything I've ever done is worthless, but now I can change that.' So when your last day comes, you won't have any regrets. 'Get on and live,' Death says. 'I'm coming.' "

Martialis was silent for several moments, and it was only now, as they passed back through, out of the village, skirting the port on the Baiae road, that Petronius noticed that they were still holding hands. Finally, Martialis sighed sadly.

"Listen, Petronius. I don't want to fight with you, but what you say is very hurtful to me, and you ought to know it so you can make it right before we part. *First*, as you say, the only thing that matters to me at all in our friendship is the love we bear for one another. That has ennobled me beyond measure; I feel stronger and wiser and braver because I love you, and I would have hoped you would feel the same. The value of a friendship isn't measured in its utility, mutual or otherwise. It's like your ladle there, equally exquisite whole or in pieces, because its beauty is in the warmth it creates, not in what it can be bartered for. I'm surprised, really, that you don't know that yet, at your age. You seem to think you've gone through some conversion today. Maybe you're just expressing yourself poorly, I don't know. In matters of the heart you seem to be just as ignorant as you've always been. And that's said with love, because you still have the chance to change.

"And *secondly*, you tell me to get my priorities straight, to sift my wheat from my chaff, so that when I die I can die proud of myself. Well, that's not living—that's planning. That's *insurance*. Get on and live? I'd rather trade places with you right now than live a hundred years planning for that one moment when, old and smug with a prune for a heart, I'll have finally earned the immortal right to say: 'I've got nothing to be ashamed of!' Well let me tell you right now, Petronius, I don't feel that anything

I've ever done is worthless. I'm proud of all of it! Every minute spent blind drunk in some fleatrap, every skanky whore I've slipped it to, every obsequious epigram that's earned me a cup of watery porridge. And nothing all you *Romans* can throw at me will ever make me feel as worthless as you're feeling right now—as you've felt your entire life. I won't let it, and that will be my life's work. Ever since you were a child, you've tried to be some-one you're not, someone somebody told you you should be, and it's brought you nothing but shame, misery, and self-hatred. Frankly, if all this cheap advice is the best deathbed gift you can think of, you can keep it. Can't you fucking people be honest about anything? I'm sick, sick of it, and I won't take it from you, Petronius. Not now."

They were still holding hands, and Petronius could not help but notice—despite himself, because he wanted dearly to hold on to every word that Martialis threw at him—that they had almost reached the point on the road where they would have to part ways. He slowed his pace, and grasped on to Martialis's hand ever more tightly, and raised his eyes to the sky, which held a few stars less than it had when they had left the village five minutes earlier.

"That's funny," he said. "I thought *I* was the one who was sup-posed to give the great deathbed speech. That's how it's always done in the books."

Martialis snorted a laugh through his tears, and the snot ran down into his beard.

"It's just that I don't see what's so great about certainty. Why does there have to be some great revelation? Why do you need it to be all wrapped up so neatly at the end? Why can't you die in confusion, and shame, and doubt, and anger, and fear, as you have lived? Isn't that the more honest death? Isn't there honor in that, too?"

"I don't know. You could be on to something. I'll have to give it some thought."

"You do that. And get back to me."

They came to a halt. Martialis did not seem to be aware that they had reached the end of their road together.

"Marcus, there's one last thing I need you to do for me. Tomorrow—this morning—a messenger will come for you in your room with a sealed amphora. You must not open it until you are safely back at the Pear Tree in Rome. And even then, I want you to show no one and tell no one about it until Nero is dead and a new emperor has been chosen. Will you promise me that?"

"What the fuck is it?"

"It's a book. A satire, I suppose you could call it. I've been working on it for the past couple of years."

"A book! You? What's it about?"

"It's about you, I think. Well, you and me, in a different world. I've called you Ascyltus."

" 'Untroubled.' I like it. What's it called, this book of yours?"

"I haven't given it a title. You can think of one."

"And is it really so dangerous as all that? I mean, if it's about me, how dangerous can it be?"

"It's not dangerous. It's private. Do you promise?"

"Promise."

"Now say good-night to me."

Martialis started, as if he had been stung by a bee, and the tears sprung immediately, luxuriantly to his eyes, pouring down his face to mingle with the snot in his beard. Petronius clung to him by both forearms, could feel Martialis's knees weaken, as if he would drop to the ground, but would not allow him to fall. Martialis just shook his head back and forth, silently mouthing "no" over and over again. Petronius tried to fix him with the kind of stern, avuncular gaze he had once used to steel the resolve of vacillating legionaries, but it had no more effect on Martialis than it would have had on a two-year-old.

"Come on, man. You'll regret it forever if this is how we say good-bye."

"I told you, I never regret anything," Martialis blubbered, and clung to Petronius just as hard as Petronius clung to him, forcing him to confront his molten mess of a face.

"Look at the sky, Marcus. The day is coming. I've got to go now."

"Keep them waiting. What have they ever done for you, anyway?"

"Marcus, you've got to let me go. *Please*. I want to go."

"What if I don't want you to go?"

"You can come and bear witness to my death, if you like. It won't take long."

As Martialis pondered the offer, Petronius wondered if it had been a mistake to invite him. Melissa would be all serenity, silence, and compassion; Martialis would be likely to weep or, heaven forbid, wail. But it was irrelevant—Petronius knew his answer before he made it.

"No, I'll leave you and Melissa alone. But thanks."

"Then I must be off. Look at the sky. They'll be stirring in Nero's villa as we speak."

That seemed to shake something loose, and Petronius could feel Martialis's grip falter, then weaken. Finally, his arms dropped to his side.

"Forgive me," he said, dragging a swathe of forlorn fabric across his nose. "You're right. The night is over, and it's time to go to sleep."

"No need to get all metaphorical on me."

"I thought that's how you epic types like it. Ripe with portent."

"Give me an epigram, rather."

"Right. Here's one I composed in bed with Chrestina yesterday. 'Charinus is in the pink, and yet he's pale. Charinus drinks sparingly, and yet he's pale. Charinus has a good digestion, and yet he's pale. Charinus goes out in the sun, and yet he's pale. Charinus paints his skin, and yet he's pale. Charinus licks a cunt, and yet he's pale.' Like it? It's yours for ten sesterces."

"I'll owe you. Good night, Marcus."

Martialis hesitated, his sandals kicking up little puffs of dust on the road, sending a few jagged stones over the lip and into the vineyard. His face, when he looked up and into Petronius's eyes, was like a bed of weeds underwater, washed first this way and then that by alternating currents of emotion. But finally it settled into an effigy of grim acceptance, and he reached out to shake Petronius's hand, as if theirs had been a chance encounter in the forum.

"Good night, Arbiter. See you in the morning."

Petronius swiveled on his heel and descended the slope, into the vineyard, shoreward, without looking back. He heard no sound behind him, could not tell whether Martialis had gone on his way or stood where he had left him. As he made his way through the rows of sawn-off vines, pushing through a light, cold, knee-high mist, he tried to clear his head of thought, if only for a moment. What good were thought, understanding to him now, with the stars winking off one by one and the fishermen already repairing to their boats in the port below? He could hear them, even at this distance, as they retrieved their drying nets and hoisted their rigging into the waiting masts, calling out to each other in their archaic Greek. These men had surely been up all night; they were not the type to pass up an opportunity to carouse, and now their night was blending seamlessly with their day. They would not give up a day's work, not even in honor of Saturn. Why should they? Would the fish stop biting, the fishmongers stop buying, the customers stop eating? Even on the shortest day of the year, people must find a way of getting on as usual. Tomorrow, for the first time in six months, there would be a few additional minutes of daylight; the day after, a few more. The Saturnalia would end, but the days would continue to stretch themselves. There was much to be done. A shout rose from the fishermen on the shore. In a moment, their sails would rise, fill with wind, and pull them out into the harbor to begin their day. Petronius passed from the vineyard into the dark of the oak wood, where night still clung to the ankles of the trees, and thence through the postern into his own orchard, where all was quiet. Through the bare branches, he saw a single light burning in a window of the villa—Melissa was waiting. He kicked off his sandals and padded through the orchard, across the perfume garden, and along the colonnade to the west terrace. There were just a few stars left now, hovering on the horizon, far out to sea above Sicily. Petronius knew that if he turned around, he would find the black outline of Mount Gaurus silhouetted against the brightening eastern sky. He leaned against the balustrade and watched the fishing boats push out toward Pithecusa, feeling the last of the night's cold air rushing down the slope at his back.

He felt something warm and soft on his leg, and looked down. It was the puppy, pressing against his ankle in the manner of a cat. It stared out at the sea through a gap between the balusters. He reached down and picked it up, unresisting; he posed it gently on the coping and restrained it with a palm across its chest. The puppy continued to look intently westward, ignoring Petronius, as if it had fixed upon some distant object or were trying to understand some indecipherable puzzle. But there was nothing there, as far as Petronius could tell. What could possibly be of such interest out there to a dog, he wondered, and how long would it take the puppy to realize that he would never come to understand it, no matter how hard he glared at it? Surely the puppy could wait forever before it was graced with such self-awareness, but that would not stop it. On the contrary, it was the puppy's fate to stare forever into the heart of its own ineffable mystery. That was what made it a dog.

Petronius scooped the creature up and replaced it lightly on the flagstone. Then he filled his lungs with air and turned back toward the house.

AUTHOR'S NOTE

Although *The Uncertain Hour* is a work of fiction, several characters are based in historical fact or presumption.

Almost everything we know about Titus (sometimes Gaius) Petronius Niger (born c. 27 A.D.) comes from two paragraphs of Book XVI of Tacitus's *Annals of Imperial Rome*. The events described in this novel are largely consonant with that account. In his *Natural History*, Pliny the Elder recounts the story of Petronius's destruction of the myrrhine ladle to prevent Nero from inheriting it. In addition to a small body of poetry, Petronius is widely believed to have been the author of the *Satyricon*. Although it may originally have been a work of 20 volumes and some 400,000 words, the *Satyricon* was not published in his lifetime, and only fragments of it survive. Petronius committed suicide at Cumae in the year 66.

Marcus Valerius Martialis (40–102 A.D.) was born in Bilbilis (now Calatayud), Spain, and moved to Rome in the year 64. Known in English as Martial, he published twelve volumes of bawdy, satirical epigrams between the year 86 and his death. He enjoyed the patronage of the emperors Titus and Domitian, but fell out of favor and retired to Spain in the year 98.

Melissa Silia is an entirely fictional character, though Tacitus briefly mentions a woman named Silia, "on terms of the closest intimacy with Petronius," who was exiled from Rome following Petronius's suicide for having divulged court secrets.

Gaius Lucilius Junior (birth and death dates unknown) was born in Campania. Starting out as a penniless plebeian, he rose to knighthood and the imperial procuracy of Sicily. He was the recipient of the *Letters to Lucilius* by Seneca the Younger, who called him *"meum opus"*—"my work."

The crimes and excesses of the emperor Nero are, of course, amply documented by the Roman historians Tacitus, Suetonius, and Cassius Dio, among many others.

ACKNOWLEDGMENTS

For their invaluable help, support, and encouragement, I am deeply indebted to my editors Karen Rinaldi and Gillian Blake, and to my agent Gail Hochman.

I also want to thank my dear friends Shelly Sonenberg and Charlott Card for their frank and constructive advice.

I owe a debt of gratitude to Dr. Christopher Stace, who vetted this book for historical inaccuracies. If any remain, it is I, and not he, who is to blame.

Most of all, none of this would have been possible or even imaginable without the patience, forbearance, and wisdom of my wife and first reader, Judy Clain.

REFERENCES

The author acknowledges with gratitude the generous permission of Derek Mahon and The Gallery Press of Loughcrew, Oldcastle, County Meath, Ireland, to reprint the superb translation of Ovid's *Amores I,V* from Mr. Mahon's *Collected Poems* (1999).

Epicurus quotes from *www.epicurus.net*.
Hesiod. *Works and Days*. Translated by Hugh G. Evelyn-White. Cambridge, MA: Harvard University Press, 1998.
Martial. *Epigrams*. I.I.77. Translated by D. R. Shackleton Bailey. Cambridge, MA: Harvard University Press, 1993.

A NOTE ON THE AUTHOR

Jesse Browner is a writer and translator who lives in New York. He is the author of the novels *Turnaway* (1996) and *Conglomeros* (1992), and he has been a contributor to the *New York Times Book Review*, *Gastronomica*, *Nest* magazine, *New York* magazine, and others.